TWO COMPLETE ACTION WESTERNS AT A FRACTION OF THE COST!

GAMBLER'S GUNS: Cardsharp Clag Jamison was on his way to strike it rich in the smoky saloons of a backwater boomtown. But before he could cash in on the gold-drenched yokels and woolhats, he suddenly ran into a spell of bad luck that forced him to give up all he held dear: wine, women and staying the hell out of trouble.

BOOTHILL BRAND: Although he'd sooner eat a plate of dung than look a homesteader in the eye, rancher Greg Mattson had sworn he'd control his temper. But his cattle began to disappear and Mattson knew the source of his trouble—Ric Williams and his gang of low-down no-account sodbusters.

BY THE TWO-TIME SPUR AWARD WINNER

LEE FLOREN

LEE FLOREN

GAMBLER'S GUNS/ BOOTHILL BRAND

LEISURE BOOKS   NEW YORK CITY

A LEISURE BOOK®

June 1991

Published by

Dorchester Publishing Co., Inc.
276 Fifth Avenue
New York, NY 10001

GAMBLER'S GUNS

CHAPTER ONE

THE cloudburst had swept down from the pine-covered mountains. It had smashed rain against the earth, and then a high wind had swept the storm away. Now the sun was bright as Claghorn Jamison rode along a trail that went through the high underbrush. Suddenly he heard three shots—rifle shots—up ahead. Sharp and brittle, they punched holes in the afternoon.

Jamison scowled. He pulled in his bay. He sat his saddle—a slender man of around thirty, his thin face dark with whiskers. Rain dripped off his flat-brimmed hat and fell down on his black oilskin slicker.

And Jamison listened.

But he heard no more shots. The shooting had occurred up ahead—how far ahead he didn't know. Was somebody out deer hunting? Jamison started to turn his horse.

Then he reined in again. He listened once more and he watched the brush. Face bleak, nerves tense, he waited. . . .

He didn't like this set-up. Something was wrong— the three rifle shots out there in the buckbrush. . . . He sensed trouble and he tasted trouble, and he did not like the smell or the taste.

So he waited.

Up ahead something was crashing through the high buckbrush. Jamison thought: Maybe a wounded buck. He waited.

But it wasn't a deer.

A man ran into the clearing. Short and wide, he

wore a brush jumper and levis, and he ran as fast as
he could. He was puffing, panting.

He carried a Winchester rifle.

Then he saw Jamison. He came to a quick, jarring
halt, boots anchored in the mud. He started to raise his
rifle.

Then he saw Jamison's .45.

His rifle hesitated, stopped, stayed down.

'Who in tarnation are you, stranger?'

'You did that shooting, I take it?'

'Who the devil are you?'

'Clag Jamison, and I'm riding through this region
for one reason, and one only.'

'And that reason, Jamison?'

'To get into Saskatchewan, Canada—across the Line.
To get to the town called Wood Mountain, up in
Saskatchewan.'

A dirty thumb had been slowly earing back the rifle's
hammer. Now the thumb let the hammer down into
safety position with a click.

'You don't know me, do you?'

Jamison studied him momentarily. This man had
been up to some mischief. It all added up to one word:
Trouble. Rifle shots in the rain. A rifleman running for
his bronc. Trouble. . . .

'I've never seen you before in my life.'

A cruel smile; a cunning smile. 'And if you ever see
me again you won't know me, will you?'

'I won't know you.'

The smile widened in evil cunningness. 'You're a
smart one, Jamison.'

'You flatter me.'

Jamison's voice was cynical and dry. And the smile
left hurriedly. Beady eyes, animal eyes probed Clag
Jamison.

'I should kill you, Jamison. You've run into a man you should not have met. . . . But you're a fast one with that gun. You had it on me before I saw you.'

Jamison said, 'You won't kill me, fellow.'

It was not a vain, boasting statement, but a simple declaration of fact, nothing more. Confidence was in his words, not vanity.

'Just ride through Mill Iron town,' the man said.

The man looked at Jamison.

Jamison returned his gaze.

The man said, 'Just ride through and you'll be all right.'

Then, without another word, the rifleman wheeled. He ran into the brush again. The brush hid him.

Jamison listened.

He heard a horse leave. Despite the damp earth, Jamison heard the pounding of fast-leaving hoofs. These hoof beats ran out, became lost against space, and Clag Jamison pushed back his flat-brimmed stetson.

What the devil was this, anyway?

He holstered his .45. Then he became aware of one thing—the rain had stopped. The Montana earth was fresh. He smelled its clean goodness. Cottonwoods had been washed by God's tears. Cottonwoods' wide leaves glistened and sparkled.

Still Jamison sat there.

A quiet man, a patient man. A man who had seen lots of life. Some parts of life he loved; others he hated. He sat there, he listened, and he wondered.

Carefully his methodical mind worked. This rifleman, he knew, had shot somebody. Why? Where?

None of your business, Claghorn Jamison. You're just a gambler drifting across this Milk River country heading for Wood Mountain. There's gold in Wood Mountain. Where there's gold, there's gambling.

Big stakes, Jamison.

Jamison smiled at that thought. He didn't need money. He hated money. He gambled because he liked to gamble, not because he won.

Still sitting his bronc, he looked about him.

He was in a clearing. Cottonwoods, boxelders, diamond willows, buckbrush—they hemmed in the clearing. Grass was brown, ripe. Chokecherry trees were black with hanging cherries.

Jamison looked to the south.

Dimly, he could see the trail he had taken into the basin. There the hills were sharp, lifting into a sky now a calm blue. He looked north. He saw a similar row of rimrock ledges, protecting the valley's northern flank.

Finally he said, 'Get along, pony.'

The horse moved. Jamison lifted his head and scented the wind, a wolf. Smoke, somewhere ahead. . . . Rifle shots, then smoke. They tied together, for some reason. The wind moved in, and he lost the scent of smoke.

But within a few minutes he caught the smell again.

He followed the trail through brush and came to another clearing. The cabin, situated in the middle of the clearing, had almost burned down. Jamison looked at the scene. There was no surprise in his eyes.

That burned-down cabin told him much.

Beyond the cabin was a small field of wheat. The rifleman had plainly been a cowpuncher. This cabin, then, belonged to a farmer?

Had the rifleman killed the farmer? Was his body in the ashes?

Clag Jamison rode closer. He thought: Heck of a deal that a stranger has to get involved in a red inferno like this. . . . He rode around the cabin, and then he saw the body. He dismounted.

The man lay on his back, half in the cabin, half out.

His clothing was burned, but the rain had kept the fire back somewhat.

Jamison thought : He must be dead. Three rifle bullets, then the heat, too. But is he dead ?

Jamison moved quickly. Hurriedly he jerked free his saddle. He threw the Amarillo kak to the ground. He had his heavy Navajo saddle blanket in his hands.

A thick, matted blanket, this, woven by the patient dark hands of a Navajo squaw, down in Arizona. Damp with rain and sweat, now—heavier than ever because of the moisture.

Jamison thought : Well, here goes. . . . He went toward the heat, the blanket hanging in front of him. Heat drew sweat on his lean, dark face. He realised he had to dash in, and out.

Blanket shielding him, he ran in toward the man. He grabbed him by both arms, putting the blanket over the man; Jamison dragged him back, boot-heels digging mud. Then they were beyond the perimeter of heat.

Jamison panted.

He knelt beside the man.

His first glance showed that the man was dead. He had seen dead men before, many dead men. But he had never seen a man burned.

A hard hand, swinging in with pendulum sharpness, hit him in the belly. He was almost ill. He caught himself in time.

Three bullet holes were in the man's chest.

Jamison got to his feet. He walked back to his bronc and re-saddled. Nausea was leaving him.

Death, he thought; death. . . .

He did not look at the corpse again. He had figured the man was dead; he had therefore been correct in his surmise. Still, there had been a chance—an outside chance—

And you always play outside chances, Jamison.

He put his boot in stirrup preparatory to lifting his body into the saddle. But he did not mount. He froze there, left boot in oxbow stirrup, body rigid under the loose dark slicker.

Poised, face bland, he was stiff, unyielding. The voice —the harsh, bitter voice—had made him a piece of living statuary.

The voice had come from behind him.

'What the blazes?' the voice repeated. 'What the blazes is going on here?'

CHAPTER TWO

JAMISON thought quickly. He was a stranger on this grass. A man had been shot down, possibly murdered. Maybe killed without being given a chance to fight back. And that man's cabin had been burned.

Jamison dropped his boot slowly. His heel made a small noise as it hit mud. The gambler raised his hands and turned. He was a master at hiding surprise, for his profession demanded he hide his emotions. Yet, for once, surprise touched his high cheekbones, put its mark on his thin face.

He had expected to face a grown man.

The voice had been the hoarse, croaking voice of an adult man. He had expected to turn and look into a rifle, or a six-shooter—held by a man.

But this was no man.

This was a boy of about eight. He was barefooted, he wore torn knee pants, and he had a wide, boyish face. And instead of holding a Winchester or a .45, he held a string of catfish.

And in his other hand he had an old fishing pole. A fishing pole cut from a diamond-willow, a cord and hook on it.

'That's my dad!' The voice was still mannish, mature. 'And he's dead, by gosh. Did you kill him?'

Jamison said, 'No, son, I did not kill him.'

'You're not one of the Heart Bar Nine's killers?'

Jamison said quietly, 'Son, I don't even know where the Heart Bar Nine is located, and I never killed your father.'

11

He saw the boy's lips tremble. He saw the hardness leave the blue eyes; he saw them become boyish, sick.

'I know everybody on this grass,' the boyish voice said, its age-old harshness gone. 'My dad'n me—we knew we was in danger—we made it a habit to know everybody—'

Jamison spoke slowly. 'I was riding through, son.' He told him everything but the fact he had run into the killer. The boy watched him, lips still quivering; the boy's eyes were stunned, but shock had not broken him as yet. Jamison waited for the shock to take effect.

Suddenly the boy broke.

Jamison stood there, feeling the boy's sorrow. The boy lay in the mud, head hidden, and Jamison heard his sharp, harsh weeping. Jamison's face was dark and solid, but grief tugged at him.

Jamison got bits of information: '. . . Just me an' dad. . . . Mom died, in Ohio. . . . The Bateman gunmen . . . they killed him. . . . We took up this homestead. . . .'

Jamison said nothing, waiting. The boy stopped sobbing. He sat up, and Jamison moved over and squatted beside him. Jamison still said nothing. His hand went out and found the boy's face. Jamison put both hands against the boy's face. He felt the tears, he felt the young flesh.

Jamison had his thoughts.

His boy—and Martha's boy—Jim would be about eight, now. Jamison felt a great, terrible longing for his boy. But Martha had taken him in the black of night. Spirited him away. And the world had closed behind her and young Jim. Jamison thought, Jim would be about this age.

Jamison kissed the boy on the forehead.

The boy looked at him. His eyes, tear-filled, were only a few inches away, and he looked at Jamison, and the boy wondered. And the boy said, 'Why did you kiss me, sir?'

'Because I like you,' Jamison said.

The boy stood up. His eyes were still on Jamison—round, puzzled eyes of a child. The boy said, 'My name is Henry. Dad called me Hank. I'm going to kill the man who killed Dad. If it is more than one man, I'll kill him, too.'

Jamison said nothing.

'I'll kill him—or them.'

Jamison nodded. 'We had best go to town, Hank, and tell the sheriff. It is his job to get the man or men who killed your father.'

'I heard the shots.' Hank spoke quickly. 'I was way back in the brush, fishin' below a beaver dam, and I thought Dad had shot a deer—we were low on meat. Then when I saw his body—saw you—'

Jamison said, 'You drew the proper conclusions, Hank. Had I been in your boots, I would have thought the same.'

Hank looked at his father's body. 'He'll get cold, he will. I wish I had a blanket or something—'

Jamison looked at the lean-to barn. 'Something maybe in there, son?'

'A horse blanket.'

The boy ran into the barn. He came out with a yellow, sweat-stained horse blanket. He put this over his father. Jamison watched the boy's face as he laid the blanket over his kin. But this boy, he saw, was made of stern stuff. He did not break; his weeping had been finished; he was all hate. Steely hate.

Jamison asked, 'You have a horse, Hank?'

'Old Flip. In the barn.'

Again, he ran to the barn. He came out bareback, riding an old grey work horse. He did not have a bridle on him. He rode with a rope tied around Flip's lower jaw.

Hank said, 'It won't do no good to see Sheriff Fulton. He's a Heart Bar Nine man, 'cause my Dad said the Heart Bar Nine elected him.'

'This Heart Bar Nine? A powerful outfit?'

The boy sobbed a little; Jamison waited. They rode along the river and Jamison smelled the muddy smell of dank water, of catfish and pike, of rushes and timber. They came to a wagon road. Jamison put his bronc on this, and the boy said, 'This is the road to Mill Iron town.'

'How far, Hank?'

'About four miles. I'll tell you about the Heart Bar Nine.'

'Shoot, pard.'

Hank told him that the outfit was owned by two people: Monica Bateman and her brother, George. George Bateman had been shot through the back and now was confined to a wheelchair.

'When did the shooting happen? Was it an accident?'

According to Hank, the shooting had occurred some months previously; it had been from ambush. The shooting of the farmer had been blamed upon the farmers. At that time there had been seven farmers in the region.

Jamison scowled. 'But I saw no farms—no buildings —when I rode off the rimrock, son.'

'The other six left and the Heart Bar Nine burned their buildings. Only me an' Dad had the guts to stay.'

Jamison nodded.

Jamison had two primary thoughts. This boy was all alone now and had a man's job ahead of him—he would have to make his own way. That in itself was a chore sometimes even for a grown man. And there seemed to be something bigger behind this, something greater in importance than mere homesteading. Jamison did not know just why he had this latter theory. Maybe it was just a hunch. But he had found, across the years, that it had paid to play his hunches.

A man had been murdered, his body then burned. And murder was a charge that sometimes brought the noose. And the land for which the murdered man had died had not seemed worth killing for. . . .

Jamison looked up. 'Here comes a rider, Hank.'

Hank also looked. Jamison saw his face pale a little, and the boy's voice was husky.

'Sig Lamont, and Sig is range boss for the Heart Bar Nine.'

'Don't tip your hand. Let me do the talking.'

The boy paused. 'All right.'

A bony man, this Lamont. Flat-bellied, craggy of face. He rode a lathered sorrel. First, he looked at the boy. And Jamison watched Lamont's bony face with the scrutiny he had acquired watching other faces—thousands of faces.

Did the man's dull grey eyes show surprise at seeing this boy? Jamison got this quick impression. Maybe Lamont figured that young Hank, instead of riding a horse, should, by all right, be dead back by the burned-down cabin?

'This rain should be good for your crops, kid,' Lamont said.

He had a rough voice.

Jamison looked at the boy. Hank would some day make a good poker player, for his young face was almost blank, held that way by rigid control.

'Yes, good for our wheat, Lamont.'

Now Sig Lamont looked at Jamison, and his voice was painfully blunt. 'Who are you, stranger?'

'That is my business.'

Lamont's lips became tight; his eyes showed suspicion. Mingled with this was a faint touch of visible anger. This ran its mark across the man's weather-browned face, giving it savage colour and life.

'Maybe a farmer, eh?'

'No plough handles,' Jamison murmured.

'We don't want farmers. Mill Iron town and this range is controlled by one outfit, the Heart Bar Nine. Me, I'm the spread's ramrod.'

'A high, high position,' Jamison said quietly.

His voice was satirical. He saw Lamont give way to anger now, the gesture moving across his face visibly.

'Don't get tough with the Heart Bar Nine outfit, stranger.'

'You leave me alone, I leave you alone.'

Lamont nodded. For a moment, then, their eyes met and held. Lamont's dull eyes by now were normal—deadpan, emotionless.

'Good logic. See that you live by it. . . .'

Jamison spoke very dryly. 'Thanks.'

Lamont used his spurs. He loped toward the location of the burned-down cabin. Jamison swung his eyes back to the boy.

'Looks to me, Hank, like he's heading back for your cabin. He gave the impression he was surprised to see you.'

'I noticed that. He figured I should have been dead back there—with my dad, I guess.'

They rode toward Mill Iron, and Jamison, riding beside the boy, gave himself over to conjecture—because of a fishing excursion, this youth was still alive. Had he been at the cabin with his father he would have died with his father. . . . Jamison remembered the man who had run through the brush. He remembered the excited face of that man—that gunman had just murdered a fellow-man.

He figured that Hank would know the identity of that rifleman, but he did not describe the gunman, nor did he tell the boy about the event. Young Hank had enough trouble without knowing, at this time at least, the identity of his father's killer. If he acquired this information, the boy might try to kill the murderer and he, in turn, might get killed.

And he was too young to die.

Jamison thought: And what about me? That question was, in one sense, ironical. He, a stranger, had blundered on to a murder scene. . . . Did this fact mark him for death? He knew one thing, and that was certain: if he stuck around Mill Iron town, he would get into trouble. The Heart Bar Nine would have to kill him because he had seen the murderer. . . . Lamont was riding out to check on his killer, to see if the gunman had accomplished his mission. Lamont would tell about meeting him and young Hank, and the killer would tell about meeting him, Jamison, there in the high wet buckbrush. . . .

If he stayed in Mill Iron, he would be a marked man.

But he had no reason to stay in Mill Iron. He was only riding through, heading across the Line for Wood Mountain.

He glanced at young Hank.

Should he take the boy with him?

Why should he be worried about this boy? He was no kin of his; no tie of flesh and blood existed between them. . . .

Jamison, you're riding through, and this boy is staying behind.

That thought settled, he gave himself over to scrutinising the town that lay in the hollow ahead. A pretty town,

B

this Mill Iron town. Lying on the south bank of Milk River on a low bluff, the town was green with cotton-wood trees, with shrubbery. Some of the buildings, though, were old, and a few could have stood some new paint. But for the most part it was a clean, pretty town.

Jamison said, 'We'd best report this to the sheriff, Hank.'

'His office is this way.'

They rode down a side street. They came to a com-bination courthouse and jail, a long frame building. A sign over the front door said, COURTHOUSE AND JAIL, BIGHORN COUNTY, MONTANA TERRITORY.

'There's the sheriff in front of his office now,' Hank said quietly.

Jamison looked. He saw a short, heavy-set man with a belly the size of a small rain barrel. He had hanging jowls, faded brown eyes, and stubby fingers now laced across the belly, seemingly holding it in and keeping it from bulging even further.

Jamison went down and said, 'Sheriff Jones Fulton?'

'Yes?'

'I'm Clag Jamison, a drifter riding through. I have the death of a man to report, and then I have to leave.'

'Who is this man?'

Hank was silent. Jamison was silent. The sheriff watched Jamison with beady, dull eyes.

'Who got killed?' repeated Sheriff Fulton.

Jamison said, 'This boy's father.'

Jamison watched the sheriff's eyes, but they told him nothing. They were vast now, the opening wide, the pupils expressing nothing. They were as moist as the eyes of a faithful St. Bernard dog. They had the doggish, unconcerned pupils of a St. Bernard, too.

'He looked for death,' the sheriff said.

CHAPTER THREE

JAMISON heard the harsh, swift intake of young Hank's breathing. He got the impression that this youth had held his temper very well and now was going to blow off steam. Sheriff Jones Fulton's negligent and unconcerned manner had broken the boy's safety valve.

'Sheriff, you—you—'

A voice said, 'What's going on here, anyway? Why, Hank, you're stuttering, you're so mad!'

Jamison turned. Hank turned. Sheriff Jones Fulton, hands still holding in his belly, showed a wide smile.

Jamison's first thought was, Good heaven, she's beautiful!

He had seen beautiful women—thousands of them. At Buenos Aires, they had crowded round his table; he had passed them on the streets of Shanghai. Usually, when they had beautiful bodies, they also had beautiful faces.

This woman had a beautiful figure and she had a face that was attractive enough. But yet deep in it was something else—Jamison sought for words to describe her face.

First you noticed her red hair—it showed from under the soft-coloured stetson. This red hair, the sun glistening on its edges, beautiful hair. Then your eyes travelled down across a high forehead and you saw her eyes.

Bitter eyes. Blue eyes, yet bitter. How old was she? Twenty-one, maybe? The eyes of a woman of fifty—a hurt, tired woman. Or was he imagining things? Jamison thought, Slow up, old boy, slow up.

Hank said to Jamison, 'Marcia Bateman.'

The blue eyes turned on Jamison. They explored him boldly; they ran over him; they probed him; they gauged him. And the full voice said, 'Who are you, stranger?' It was not a request, but an order.

Jamison said, 'One of your men asked me that back along the trail, Miss Bateman. A fellow named Lamont. I give you the same answer. Where I go and what I do is my business, lady.'

The blue eyes showed something. Jamison thought, She'd show deep feeling and those eyes would sparkle if the right man met her and loved her. . . . But that thought, winging in out of nowhere, held no significance here.

Marcia Bateman said, 'I'm sorry, sir.' She sounded sorry. She acted sorry. But Jamison knew she was not sorry.

She looked at the sheriff. 'What's the deal, Fulton?' Her tone was the tone of a woman talking to a mere hireling. Jamison was quick to notice this, and he remembered young Hank saying that this lawman was owned body and soul by the Bateman Heart Bar Nine iron.

The sheriff told her what Jamison had related. Jamison, had left out, of course, all mention of the lumbering rifleman—the man who had run through the brush, rifle in hand, his wide animal face crude and bestial.

Marcia Bateman said huskily, 'And I suppose the blame will be laid on the Heart Bar Nine, Sheriff?'

'Could have been suicide, Marcia.' Sheriff Jones Fulton's voice had a fatherly tone. 'Don't jump to conclusions, girl, before the evidence is in.'

'Everything that has happened to those farmers has been blamed on my outfit,' the woman said.

Hank cut in with, 'And that is right, and when I get the man who murdered my father—'

Jamison cut in with, 'Easy, pal, easy.'

Hank stopped. He put his hand into Jamison's. Jamison liked the feel of the boy's moist fingers. Jamison looked at him.

Hank's eyes showed tears.

Jamison said, to both the sheriff and Marcia, 'The boy has had a rough day. I'm going to feed him and get him into bed and get the doctor to give him a sedative. I'm at your beck and call, Sheriff, if you need me.'

'Your occupation, Jamison?'

Jamison looked at the lawman, then at Marcia Bateman. Her eyes were on his—did they hold a challenge, a mockery?

'I'm a gambler, Sheriff.'

The sheriff watched him closely. Was it relief that flooded his eyes? Jamison did not know. Again, he got the impression that something big, something ugly, was behind this range, pulling it the way a puppet is pulled, making it move this way that way. . . . Or was he just imagining things?

'No money around here,' the lawman said. 'Wood Mountain, though, is booming—gold. About sixty miles north of here, Jamison. Should be a good place for a man of your calibre.'

Jamison asked quietly, 'My calibre?'

'I didn't mean it that way!' Fulton blustered now, searching for words. 'I meant of your profession, sir. Don't take me wrong, please.'

Jamison almost smiled.

Marcia Bateman said, 'I'll ride out there with you, Sheriff.'

Sheriff Fulton nodded, looked at Jamison. 'There'll be an inquest, of course. The law must take its course. You'll stay in town until then, naturally?' Not a question, really; a statement—an order.

Jamison smiled thinly. 'I'll be around.'

The sheriff went to his bronc at the hitchrack. Marcia Bateman said, 'My horse is on Main Street,' and the sheriff went up, his gross body rearing with difficulty into the saddle. The sheriff said, 'I'll meet you there,' and he gave Jamison a long look before turning.

But Jamison was not watching the lawman.

He was looking at Marcia Bateman, who was walking away. She had a walk that fitted her body, he noticed.

Hank asked, 'What's wrong with being a gambler?'

'Some people figure a gambler is the devil's best friend, Hank.'

Hank said, 'My dad, he used to be a gambler once. He told me that. Back in Chicago, he gambled.'

'I thought he was a farmer back East?'

'He went farming after he was a gambler. Jamison, what the heck will I do—I ain't even got a change of clothes for my back. I ain't got a cent in my jeans, and everything I owned was burned.'

Jamison said, 'Take it easy, kid. First, we put our broncs in the livery, and then we feed the inner man.'

'Who is he?'

Jamison said, 'Our bellies, son.'

Hank grinned, a wide boyish grin. 'Guess I'm dumb, Jamison. Blame it on being a country hick, eh?'

'I was raised on a farm.'

They led their horses down the street, heading for the frame building that carried over it a time-worn legend: TOWN LIVERY BARN. They left their broncs there and went out again on to the street.

'Where do we eat, Hank?'

'Only one place in town to eat,' the boy returned. 'The Velvet Slipper Saloon, on the main drag.'

'No restaurants?'

'Only the one in the Velvet Slipper.'

The Velvet Slipper was quite a spread. Jamison wondered, Now what is such a big saloon doing in such a dinky little burg? Against yonder wall ran the bar, a long hardwood affair, with an ornate backbar, complete with mirrors, against the wall.

Jamison had expected a sawdust floor. But the floor was of hardwood—maple, to be exact—and it glistened with polish. A half-wall, just about the height of a man's shoulders, ran across the middle of the saloon. Back of this Jamison glimpsed gambling equipment: a roulette wheel, a faro bank, and card tables. Jamison looked at the scene and thought, There is some gambling here, after all.

'Take a stool,' Hank said.

The lunch counter was along the north wall. Jamison slid on to a stool beside Hank. Through the big window he could see the street outside—the street which was becoming wrapped in dusk. The rain had settled the dust, the air was clean and sweet, and night would be tumbling down soon.

Two cowpunchers, sitting on stools, were drinking at the bar, and Jamison noticed they had given him a quick appraisal before returning to their beers. There were no other occupants in the saloon and Jamison gave himself over to perusal of the menu. He was aware of a woman moving behind the counter, but he paid her no attention. He kidded Hank with, 'Can you read?'

'Heck, yes.'

The boy was looking at the menu. When he read, his lips moved, and Jamison thought, We'll have to break you of that habit, for it makes for slow reading. . . . Then he smiled. This was not his boy. . . .

Outside, a man moved into the limits of his vision, and Jamison gave him a quick look through the window.

He recognised the man.

The man was across the street. He walked slowly, but Jamison noticed that he glanced toward the Velvet Slipper. He knew also that the man could see him, perched there on the stool.

The man was the man whom he had met out there in the brush. The rifleman who had killed Hank's father.

The glance was brief. Had not Jamison been watching closely, he would not have noticed the brief sidewise twist of the ugly head. But that glance, because of its briefness, told Jamison he was in danger. Had the man not been out to get him he would have looked at him at some length—looked openly and not covertly.

Jamison hitched his .45 around.

A woman's voice said, 'You men and your guns.'

Jamison looked at her for the first time, and for some reason he found himself comparing this woman with Marcia Bateman. This woman, too, was beautiful, but it was not the hard metallic beauty of Marcia. Where Marcia's hair was red, the hair of this woman was black. It hugged her small head, sleek and compact, giving her an almost severe look—a look broken by the snappy darkness of her black eyes.

'I own this place,' she said. 'I'm Nell Robinson.'

Jamison introduced himself. She seemed to know young Hank well, for she asked about the farm. He answered in short sentences. How was his father? The boy looked at Jamison.

'You tell her, friend?'

Nell Robinson's dark eyes showed surprise. Jamison told her about the shooting and the burned-down cabin. He watched the brightness change to pinpoints of hardness. This woman, he realised, had a temper, and a will that matched that temper.

'Well, I'll be hanged!'

Jamison kept an eye on the window. The killer moved

by again, this time on the same side of the street as the Velvet Slipper, and he passed directly by the window. Again, he gave that short, sidewise look.

Then he was gone.

Jamison looked at Nell Robinson. 'Who was that man?'

'What man?'

'The one that just walked by the window.'

'I didn't look. I was doing some thinking—'

Hank said, 'That was a Bateman Heart Bar Nine rider. His name is Barney Westburg.'

Jamison said, 'Oh, I see.'

Hank asked, 'Why did you ask?'

'Curiosity.'

Hank scowled, and looked at Nell Robinson, who watched him absent-mindedly. She looked at the boy. The boy looked at her. Jamison watched them both.

'I liked your dad,' the woman said.

Hank said, 'I know you did, Miss Nell.'

Nell Robinson looked at Jamison. 'There was nothing between us but friendship. We talked and joked. He had a good sense of humour, was a philosopher.'

Jamison nodded. She was, he judged, about twenty-five. He looked at her hand. No rings. Not a single solitary ring.

'Would you live at my place, Hank? You could go to school here in town, and I'd be right glad—very proud —to have you.'

The boy said slowly, 'I appreciate it a million, Miss Nell. But I got a man to kill.'

'Hank—please—'

Jamison listened idly. His eyes were on the street. Danger stalked out there. He was wary and tough. Because of his vigilance, he happened to see the sudden lift of the rifle across the street.

The rifleman was on one knee in the narrow space between the Mercantile and the Hardware Store, half-hidden by shadows. Jamison caught the flash of the barrel as it rose.

He was already off the stool, .45 in hand. Then the rifle talked.

CHAPTER FOUR

JAMISON heard the sharp smash of glass. The window swayed, then broke loudly, and glass hit the floor. By this time the gambler was outside on the sidewalk. Behind him, Nell Robinson hollered something; he heard young Hank's bellow, too. He had been afraid that maybe the youth had been hit. For when the rifleman had pulled his sights, Hank had sat beside him, Jamison, at the counter. But the boy's yell told the gambler he was all right.

Jamison crouched, gun winking.

The rifleman had shot again, trying to follow Jamison as he ran for the door. His second bullet hit the wide edge of the door jamb. Jamison's .45 was talking, the muzzle rearing, kicking. Another rifle bullet ripped into the plank sidewalk in front of Jamison.

The town had come awake. Dogs barked, men hollered, women called. Jamison's face was bleak, lips pulled back; he emptied the .45. The rifleman screamed, the sound sharp despite the snarling of guns. He dropped his rifle and walked ahead, stunned, sick, wounded.

He screamed, 'Don't shoot no more—'

Jamison stood there, his face marked by mixed feelings; he reloaded his .45. His fingers, despite his efforts to control them, shook slightly. He watched the rifleman.

The ambusher lurched ahead, bent almost double. His fingers were laced across his belly. Jamison saw blood on his hands.

Jamison's hands were steady now. He had the .45 reloaded. By this time, the ambusher was sitting down in the street. Stunned, sick, he sat there in the mud, head down.

Jamison heard a woman's voice say, 'He tried to ambush you, Jamison. But why?'

Young Hank said hollowly, 'That's Barney Westburg, the gent that walked past the café just a minute or so ago.'

Jamison pouched his .45. 'Where's the doctor?' he asked.

Somebody said, 'He's coming.'

Westburg lifted his gaunt head. When he had broken through the tall buckbrush, after he had killed Hank's father, he had run unexpectedly into Jamison—at that time, Westburg's face had shown surprise. Now it did not show surprise—it showed fear, and death was behind this fear.

'You've killed me, Jamison.'

'Either you—or me,' Jamison said.

Westburg grimaced with pain. His lips moved in an animal gesture of fear. 'I was linin' my sights on a pigeon that was above the Velvet Slipper,' he said haltingly. 'I wanted that pigeon for supper. You came out with your gun roarin' an' I shot in self-defence.'

Jamison smiled. 'You lie, Westburg, and you know it.'

'I was drawin' my sights down on that pigeon,' Westburg repeated.

Jamison said, 'Your aim, then, was awful low, because your bullet broke the window in the Velvet Slipper.'

'I was aimin' at a pigeon.'

A man said, 'He likes dove meat. I've seen him shoot pigeons down before. Why would he try to ambush you, stranger?'

Jamison looked at the man. A tall man, bony—plainly a cowpuncher. Jamison said, 'You keep out of this, fellow.'

'Make me!'

Jamison was quick. He moved forward three steps, and he covered them fast. The cowpuncher tried to step back. As he stepped, he reached for his gun. Jamison's .45 came down with liquid ease, with metallic hardness.

The barrel cracked across the cowpuncher's head.

Then the waddy was in the mud, lying on his side. Jamison took his gun and threw it to a man who caught it.

'Keep it for him,' the gambler said.

Hank said quietly, 'You knocked down a Heart Bar Nine man, Jamison—name of Mattson.'

Jamison nodded. He had lost his temper for a moment. Westburg had tried to ambush him, and tension was thick in Jamison. The thought came that, if Westburg were low enough to try to ambush him, then Westburg had also ambushed young Hank's father.

'I'm sorry I didn't kill Westburg,' Jamison said.

Mattson sat there, tall, skinny, holding his head. Westburg was on his back now with the medico kneeling beside him.

Mattson looked at Jamison.

'Before this is over, I'm going to kill you, stranger.'

Jamison's throat was dry. 'A threat does nothing,' he pointed out. 'Only actions talk.'

Mattson's eyes were liquid pools of hate. 'Later,' he said, 'later.'

Mattson got to his feet. Carefully he watched Jamison. Then he turned, going toward a horse tied to a tie-rack.

Jamison said, 'Don't wait. Get your gun from that man and come at me. If you haven't the guts to come openly, don't try ambush, Mattson.'

Mattson untied his bronc and lifted his gaunt body into leather. He reined the horse around and, for a

moment his eyes met those of Jamison. And in them
Jamison read a terrible hate.

'Later,' Mattson repeated.

The cowpuncher turned his horse then and rode out.
Steel-shod hoofs kicked back mud and gravel.

The doctor—a short, thick man—looked at Jamison.
Jamison looked at the medico.

'He'll pull through,' the doctor said. 'Anyway, he
should live. Unless too many vital organs are punctured.
He's bleeding internally.'

Jamison nodded. 'Just another ambusher.'

'Another?'

Jamison said nothing. He returned to the Velvet
Slipper. Hank walked beside him, solemn in his youthful
way. They went into the café. Nell Robinson poured a
shot of whisky and said, 'Drink that, Jamison.'

'No.'

'Why not?'

Jamison smiled. 'I hate the stuff. I never touch it.
When a man has to lean on a crutch, he's in a bad way.'

She looked at him. 'You're an odd man,' she finally
said. 'Why did he try to kill you?'

'I don't know,' Jamison lied.

Her dark eyes showed puzzlement. She shook her dark,
sleek head. 'You men—always mysteries to us women.
I think you know but you won't tell me.'

Jamison looked at Hank. The boy's eyes were wide.
The thought came that Hank would be better off if he
never knew the identity of his father's murderer. Westburg might die; on the other hand, he might live. If
Westburg died, then he, Jamison, would tell Hank that
Westburg had, to the best of his knowledge, murdered
his father.

Jamison remembered his own stormy youth. If he told
Hank, and if Westburg pulled through—then Hank

might go against the gunman, and the man might kill the boy. So, thinking this way, the gambler decided not to tip his hand.

Young Hank still watched him. He spoke with boyish penetration. 'Seems odd, Jamison, that if he was a stranger, he'd try to kill you. . . . He weren't out shootin' doves; that was a lie. Sure you never crossed him back along your trail somewhere?'

Jamison made himself smile. He had his nerves under control now and was his old complacent self. 'He might have mistaken me for somebody else, Hank.'

This seemed to satisfy the youth's curiosity. 'Might be right, Jamison. Sure busted the window, Miss Nell.'

'He'll pay for it,' the girl said.

Jamison glanced at her. He quickly noticed the set of her thin lips. Either Westburg or the Heart Bar Nine would pay, he was sure of that.

'Chuck for us,' he said.

While Nell Robinson went back to report their orders to her cook, Jamison looked out on the main street. Two men had carried Westburg away on a stretcher obtained from the doctor's office. Hank informed him that the hotel was used as a hospital for the doctor. Jamison nodded and listened, for words floated in through the broken window. The townspeople were gathered in groups and he heard some of their conversation. They wondered why Westburg would shoot at him, a stranger. Some declared that maybe Westburg had been merely shooting pigeons after all. Somebody asked why he would shoot pigeons with a rifle with the large bore of a .30-30. Why didn't he use a small bore gun, like a .22?

Jamison heard one say, 'That's right. If a .30-30 bullet hit a pigeon, all that would be left would be a few feathers.'

'That gambler,' one said, 'is a marked man. He's

crossed the Heart Bar Nine, and he's in burning hot water.'

Jamison heard another say, 'I'd hate to occupy his boots.'

'Old Jones Fulton has his hands full,' another said loudly. 'A dead farmer on his hands—murdered. Now Westburg shot an' down. Marcia Bateman will raise the devil, too.'

Jamison said to Nell, 'Looks like this gambler should head on, Miss Robinson.'

'You'll never get out of Mill Iron alive, Jamison.'

Jamison sent her a quick look. Her face, he noticed, held determination. His lips formed one word, 'Why?'

'You've crossed the Heart Bar Nine. Marcia Bateman has a stiff, unyielding pride. Her outfit has held its rule through force. You've shattered that force. You'll have to pay, Jamison.'

Jamison said, 'I could gun my way through.'

'I doubt it.' She put food in front of them.

'A dark night,' Jamison said. 'The rimrock is rough country for trailing a man, even in daylight.'

'You won't run.'

He watched her. 'Why?'

'You have as much pride as Marcia.'

Jamison smiled. She had hit the nail with a hard hammer. 'Pride can only lead a man to a quick grave sometimes,' he reminded her.

'Pride might do that. But pride leads nations to war, and a country is only composed of proud men. When they lose that pride, something dies inside of them. Look at Jones Fulton.'

'You look at him,' Jamison joked. 'I don't like the look of him. His belly gets in the way of my vision.'

Hank ate. He listened, boyish eyes round, boyish ears peeled back. He missed not a bite nor a word.

'Fulton is only a hunk of dead meat that can still walk,' Hank said. 'My dad called him that to his face one day, too!'

From where she stood, Nell Robinson could see down the street. Now she said, 'Four riders coming in.'

Hank walked to the window. Jamison watched the boy's face. It had become hard, mannish.

Hank's lips trembled.

'Fulton an' his bunch is toting Dad into town, Jamison.'

Jamison asked, 'Besides Marcia Bateman, who rides with the sheriff, son?'

'Sig Lamont, for one. The other is Mattson.'

Jamison said, 'He rode out to report to Lamont, and to Marcia.'

Hank watched the quartet. His lips trembled harder. 'Now why did Sig Lamont head out for our farm?' He answered that himself. 'He must have known that somebody was going to shoot down my dad, and maybe he rode out there to check up.'

Jamison said, 'Go easy on that talk, please.'

Hank said, 'I'd best make some arrangements for Dad's funeral, so I'd better get down to the sheriff's office.'

The boy left.

Nell Robinson looked at Jamison. 'You had better go with him, Jamison. Of course, Sig Lamont can't pick on a boy that small, but you never can tell—if Hank gets hold of a gun, there might be some shooting.'

Jamison nodded and followed the boy.

C

CHAPTER FIVE

MARCIA BATEMAN's red hair glistened. Marcia Bateman's bitter eyes looked very tired. Marcia Bateman said, 'Maybe he shot himself—suicide. Maybe he deliberately set fire to his cabin—then committed suicide.'

Hank said angrily, 'Close your big mouth, woman! My dad said the most cowardly thing a man could do was kill hisself!'

Jamison saw anger flare in Marcia Bateman's eyes. This anger drove out the weary look and left her eyes flat and metallic. Then he saw this pass over and, when she spoke, her voice was unconcerned and dry.

'Listen to the sprout!' She looked at Jamison. 'Mattson here tells us you shot Westburg when he was merely shooting at a pigeon.'

Jamison looked at Mattson. The cowpuncher apparently was watching his female boss, although Jamison could detect the tension in the man. So the gambler deliberately said, 'Mattson, among his other accomplishments, is also a good liar, I take it.'

Mattson turned savage, bitter. 'Don't shoot off your mouth about me, you tinhorn cardsharp!'

Jamison smiled, hiding his temper. He looked at Sig Lamont, who was eyeing him with a cruel steadiness. Lamont's craggy face was flat, the planes of it broken by anger. Still, the hawkish face was under stern control. Jamison thought, He's tough—a killer.

'Your man Westburg,' Jamison said easily, 'should be taught not to shoot at pigeons with a gun as big in calibre as a Winchester .30-30. If he had hit a pigeon, the bullet

34

would have blown the poor old dove to smithereens. A
.30-30 rifle is made for shooting a man or a coyote.'

Sheriff Jones Fulton was untying the dead man from
the back of his own saddle horse. That bronc had had
a load to tote into town. Young Hank was helping them
get his father untied. Mattson moved over and helped,
too.

Sig Lamont asked quietly, 'I'd like to ask one thing,
Jamison.'

'Yes?'

'Why would Barney Westburg try to kill you? Had
you two had a run-in back along the trail somewhere
before Westburg came to work for me?'

Marcia Bateman watched, eyes wary. Sig Lamont
watched him, too—but Lamont's sunken eyes were
cagey.

'I never saw Westburg before today,' Jamison said.

Marcia Bateman breathed deeply, her bosom rising
under the silk blouse.

'I don't understand all this,' the woman said.

Claghorn Jamison sent her a quick look. If she were
acting, she was a good actor. But was she acting? The
voice of Sig Lamont dug into Jamison's thoughts.

'You get into trouble fast, gambler. And for no
apparent reason, I'd say.'

Jamison said, 'Your intelligence is limited. Don't try
to stretch it, ramrod.'

Lamont moved back a step, and Jamison thought he
would reach. Then the anger fled from the range boss's
eyes and he became himself again—competent and tough
and self-reliant. Yes, and deceitful.

'Your jokes,' said Lamont, 'are not funny.'

'Maybe it was no joke.'

Marcia Bateman said, 'Lamont, get out to the ranch.
We've had enough trouble on this grass for one day. The

last of the hoemen are gone, and suspicion, of course, will point toward the Heart Bar Nine. That's only logical. Play your cards close.'

Jamison said, 'And keep your mug buttoned,' and he said it cynically.

Lamont looked at him again, and then he turned. His boss had spoken and he obeyed, but in his obedience was a sullen streak of rebellion. Jamison sensed this and so did Marcia Bateman. Something flared in the red-head's face, and Jamison got the impression it was bafflement and not anger that lighted her pretty features. She had a job holding her tigers in check. And from what Hank had told him, her brother George was in a wheelchair, an ambush bullet through his spine. A bullet blamed on the farmers who were now all gone.

Mattson trooped after Lamont, spur rowels making a wicked song. Sheriff Jones Fulton went into his wide chair and looked at the dead man, who had been toted into his office and who now lay on the floor.

'I should cover him with something.'

Hank got a couch cover and laid it over his father. Fulton sighed and laced his hands across his belly and said, 'Thanks, son,' and his doggish eyes were on the boy. 'I want you to be a good boy, Hank. Pick up the pieces and start out again. Nell Robinson is your friend, and so am I.'

Young Hank said nothing. He swallowed once or twice but kept his mouth closed. He looked at Clag Jamison. Jamison thought, He's learning fast. Jamison spoke to the sheriff. 'Nell has a home for him, sir.'

'Good.'

Jamison asked, 'What did you find out to the cabin? In other words, what is your official report going to be —how will it read?'

Fulton wet his lips. He was an oxen tied to a burning

stall, and whichever way he turned, his tie-rope held him against the flames. He looked at Marcia Bateman. He looked at Hank. He looked last at Jamison.

'First, there was the rain. It washed away all sign—if there had been foul play. The rain effaced everything. Only your footprints were clear, Jamison—those of you and the boy. You were at the cabin after the rain, I take it?'

'We were.'

Fulton shifted, and his chair creaked. 'The body lay as you say you left it—covered with a horse blanket. The bullet holes—well, it could have been suicide. His rifle, the stock burned off, was inside the cabin, you know.'

Hank said, 'You—'

Jamison put his hand over the boy's mouth. Hank did not struggle. He leaned close to Jamison and his hands made pressure on Jamison's trousers as he twisted the cloth to gain control.

'That'll be my report,' the lawman finished.

Jamison nodded. The lawman had his point established. Westburg had had an ally in the rain. But Westburg had played his hand too far. Jamison figured that Sig Lamont and Marcia Bateman had not ordered Westburg to shoot at him. Westburg had taken that on himself.

Now he was in the hotel, shot through and through.

Jamison asked, 'When will the inquest be held?'

'Tomorrow morning. I'm also county coroner. In my office, here. Let's say ten in the morning?'

Jamison smiled. 'Early hour for a gambler.'

Marcia Bateman asked, 'Then you're heading out, eh, Jamison?'

Jamison felt the first roilings of anger. He looked steadily at her. 'Is that an order, Red Head?'

'No.'

'I might ride out,' Jamison said. 'And I might stick around awhile.' He looked at the sheriff. 'Have you any further conversation with me, Mr. Fulton?'

'Not unless you make it.'

Jamison bowed to the girl, his gesture almost cynical. 'I am at your pleasure, Miss Bateman.' He saw the flush of anger light her cheeks. 'You are even more beautiful when you are angry, Miss Bateman.'

'And more deadly,' she stormed.

Jamison shook his head. 'I disagree with you there. Women are more deadly when they are calm—they think then, and don't act on emotion. Logic is stronger than hate, and when a person is calm they hate—when they are angry, they lose their heads.'

'I called for no lecture from you!'

Jamison said, 'I could deliver one, but I won't.' He felt weary, dog-tired; humans were all the same—no matter where a man went. He had made camp that night back in the badlands and the rain had routed him out of his wet blankets at an early hour. This fact, coupled with the rainy ride with the dead man and the burned down cabin——

'Sheriff, how could that cabin burn so easily, with that hard rain falling?'

Fulton had been looking at a paper on his desk. Now he lifted his ox-like eyes, and they were rolling marbles in moist sockets.

'Fire—inside of it,' the sheriff said. 'Dry inside, and it burned inside first, and the rain couldn't hit it.'

Jamison tried something. 'I smelled kerosene out there,' he said significantly.

Fulton studied him. 'I smelled it too. But there had been a five-gallon tin of kerosene in the corner and it must have exploded in the heat. The can is burned and torn.'

Fulton looked at Hank.

Hank said, 'We had just bought five gallons of kerosene for the lamps. That was two days ago.'

Fulton looked back at Jamison. 'That's my theory,' he said.

Jamison could do nothing but nod. Marcia Bateman said, 'I'll see you in the morning, Sheriff,' and she walked outside. Jamison gave her a glance and compared her back with other feminine backs he had seen. Thousands of them. . . . She stacked up well among them.

Fulton repeated, 'That's my theory.'

Jamison moved to the door with Hank beside him. The gambler stopped then and shot out his final question.

'What if Westburg dies?'

Fulton sighed, rubbed his bottom lip. Moisture was thick in his eyes. 'A man's a darned fool for taking such a job as this. One hundred and fifty, and no beans.' He addressed himself to Jamison's question. 'I suppose if Bateman pushes me I'll have to issue a warrant for your arrest, Jamison.'

'I can prove he shot first.'

Fulton nodded. 'There'll be an inquest first. But if that jury turns in murder, I'll serve the warrant, Jamison.'

Jamison nodded. 'Your job,' he affirmed.

They went down the sidewalk. People watched and people wondered and Jamison thought, They're ugly in small towns. . . . Gossip and ugliness hidden under a cloak of supposed friendship. In a big town they walk around a dead man on the street and say, None of my business, and they go on their way. In a small town they gawk and stare and shoot off their mouths. . . .

Hank said, 'He didn't kill himself.'

Jamison said nothing.

'That kerosene smell came from their squirting kero-

sene around inside the house to make it burn better.
That's why the house burned so fast, even though it
rained, Jamison.'

Jamison said, 'You stay with Nell Robinson, eh?'

'I'll be on my own in a few years,' the boy said. 'But
until I get big enough, I have to have a home. I'll work
in her restaurant, Jamison.'

'And go to school winters?'

'And go to school,' he said. 'Although I hate the
darned school. I have no kin. My mother's family is all
dead and she is dead, too. My dad had one brother—he
told me about him—he's in New Zealand. Farming
there.'

'How about you going to him?'

'On what for money?'

Jamison said, 'I got a few dollars.'

'And my uncle has eleven kids,' the boy said. 'And
you know how he would welcome me, eh?'

Jamison smiled. 'No contest,' he said.

Nell Robinson was behind the bar. A heavy-set
middle-aged woman was taking care of the lunch
counter.

Jamison asked, 'Do you tend bar, too?'

'I own the Velvet Slipper.'

Jamison hid his surprise. He had figured she ran the
lunch counter on a percentage of its take.

'I might have to stay over a few days,' he said. 'You
might need a gambler.'

Her bright eyes pierced him. 'I might, at that,' she
said. 'What game, Jamison?'

'Anything but the wheel.'

'Poker?'

'Yes, either stud or draw.'

'I might need a man,' she said.

She took Hank back to the lunch counter. A man

came out of the kitchen, wiping his hands on a towel, and Jamison got the idea he had been washing dishes. He took off his apron and went behind the bar. Three men drank, boots on the rail, and the card tables were empty, chairs neatly arranged. Jamison wondered at the size of the establishment. This was rather a big outfit to be located in such a jerkwater town. But sometimes these little towns surprised a man. Men came from the far corners of the country, moved across this limitless range, and sometimes stopped in these little towns. They wanted diversions; they wanted liquor and they wanted cards.

Nell Robinson came back, and Jamison said, 'You'll take care of the boy?'

'Like he was my own.'

Jamison tried something. 'You've had no children?'

'How could I? I've never married.'

Jamison felt the devil tickle him. 'Too bad. Most women aim their sights on a husband first off.'

'Not this one,' she stated stonily. 'And don't get ideas, gambler. You won't be the first one with ideas and you won't be the first one to have those ideas shattered.'

'A fair warning,' Jamison murmured. 'I think we'll get along good together.'

'We could be friends.'

She accented the word *friends*.

Jamison spoke to Hank. 'You take it easy, son. I'll be at the hotel if you need me.'

'Thanks, Jamison.'

The gambler moved outside. The air was clean, the wind was good, the pine trees talked; they bent their head before the wind, they bowed and they were yielding. Across the street two riders lifted their bulk into saddles. They reined their horses around and they looked briefly at Claghorn Jamison.

Mattson's eyes were flat and mean. They went over Jamison, and Mattson's mouth twitched.

Sig Lamont's eyes appraised the gambler. They catalogued him and judged him and there was nothing in them but speculation.

Then the two turned their broncs and loped out of town.

A woman said from behind Jamison, 'Mattson remembers you knocking him in the dust, Jamison.'

Jamison looked at Marcia Bateman.

'I suppose he does,' he said dryly.

CHAPTER SIX

CLAGHORN JAMISON, free-lancing gambler, lay on his hotel bed, and he looked at the ceiling. A dirty ceiling it was, with its fly-specked and aged wallpaper, faded through the passage of time. But Jamison had no thought for the wallpaper. He was thinking of what had happened that afternoon.

And he was tired, too. The long ride through the rain, the night short of sleep, and the trouble he had ridden into—all had added up and taken their toll of his strength. He just wanted to doze and then slip off into a sound and deep sleep, and sleep all night. Even though the mattress was aged and lumpy, it still beat bunking on the hard ground. And he had a roof, too, to turn the rain, if it started to rain again.

He looked at the door knob. He had his skeleton key in the lock. But he knew that a key, if inserted from the outside, could punch his key out of the slot, and the door would be unlocked.

Cautious and on the alert, he got out of bed and took a chair. He jacked the back of the chair under the knob and wedged the door shut. Then carrying the latest copy of the *Mill Iron Crusader*, he went back to bed.

A glance at the front page told him the paper was four days old. He grimaced sourly and threw it aside.

Hands laced behind his head, he did some thinking. Outside on the sidewalk a man and a woman argued. Patently the man was drunk and the woman wanted him to go home. He did not want to go. They had argued the matter for almost half an hour, their monotonous voices seeping into the room.

The blind was low—very low. As low as it could get. He was taking no chances on Mattson. Westburg had tried to ambush him. Westburg, actually had no adequate reason for stopping to ambush him. Yet Westburg had tried to kill him.

Was there some other reason—besides the chance meeting in the brush—that had prompted Westburg's deadly actions?

What could it be? Jamison asked himself.

Or was there any other reason?

Jamison did not know. He knew one thing, and that was for sure: a man could never tell about another man. All men, though stamped in the same physical mould, differed inside—it was impossible to predict any man's actions and thoughts, even if you knew him as well as you knew yourself. And what man, Clag Jamison, knew himself? Jamison grinned at that.

He must have dozed for a while. For some reason he dreamed of a woman and a boy, and he had not dreamed of them for many days now. There had been a time when they had occupied his thoughts and his dreams, but these times were getting further and further apart due to the distance of time. The woman was named Martha; the boy, Jim. Once the woman had had his surname; the boy had been born to it.

Jim would be about Hank Sturdivant's age. He wondered if Jim would have the tough deal from life that fate had given Hank. He hoped not. Then he put his ex-wife and his son suddenly from mind.

Footsteps were coming down the hall. Footsteps that stopped in front of his door. Jamison listened and a little silence grew, a silence broken only by the hundrum voices of the couple arguing outside.

Then knuckles hit the door.

Jamison said nothing. He swung out of bed and slipped into his trousers and got his gun.

Then knuckles knocked again.

He was sure the visitor was a man. The boot sounds, coming toward the door, had told him that. Maybe Mattson was trying to trick him? Or Sig Lamont? He was in danger. He knew how Raleigh Sturdivant had died. Shot to death, burned in his cabin—and Westburg had killed him. Mattson and Westburg were friends. . . . Mattson worked also for Marcia Bateman's Heart Bar Nine. . . .

'Who's there?'

'Norman Ridgeway.'

Jamison cocked his head, his mind busy. He could not place the name of Norman Ridgeway.

'Who's Ridgeway?'

'The banker,' a man's voice said.

Jamison shrugged. Why would a banker be visiting him? This town was full of riddles. . . .

He sidled to the door, jerked away the chair, and turned the key. The lock was sprung and he flung the door open. He was against the wall, and the person who entered would not see him until he had entered the room.

'Come in,' Jamison said.

A tall, bony man entered. He wore a blue suit and polished boots and a Tom Watson stetson. His eyes were dark beads separated by a hawkish nose. His jaw was long, his lips thin; his hands were thin, too, with long fingers.

'You can put your gun away,' the man said.

Jamison gestured with the .45. 'Sit down, Ridgeway.'

Ridgeway crossed the room and found a chair. Jamison shut the door and the key turned. Jamison holstered his gun.

'What do you want with me, Ridgeway?'

Dark eyes probed him. They were needle-sharp. A thin smile touched the thin lips.

'You're a cautious man, Jamison.'

Jamison shrugged. 'Mattson for one,' he said. 'Maybe Lamont. And Westburg is still alive. He tried to kill me once. He might get out of his sick bed and try again.'

'He won't, Jamison.'

'How do you know?'

'Westburg is dead. He died about five minutes ago.'

Jamison sat on the bed. He said nothing for some seconds. He felt no pity toward the dead man. Westburg had made his play and, when the chips had narrowed down, it had been either Westburg or a gink named Claghorn Jamison.

'That means I have to stay over a day or so,' Jamison said. 'There'll be an inquest. They might try to pin a murder rap on me.'

'You were riding through?'

'A drifting gambler,' Jamison murmured. He walked the room, then began to use satire. 'I could sing you a little song about the uselessness of a gambler and his days. But I won't. I'll spare you that misery. All right, Ridgeway—' He stopped suddenly, looking at the man. 'What's the deal?'

'I don't understand.'

'Why are you here?'

The banker murmured, 'A blunt man, Jamison.' He stretched his legs and looked at his boots. 'I got money invested in this dead farmer's outfit. I'll sell my investment for half of its original cost to me.'

Jamison smiled. 'I'd never soil my hands with a plowshare. If a man can't live by his brains, he's pretty stupid in my book.'

The banker got to his boots. He wiped his knee with

his right hand. He had a bit of dust on his knees and this bothered him. Jamison watched with alert speculation. This banker had not come to try to sell him some farming land. Then why had he come to his hotel room?

'A good investment, Jamison.'

'With the Heart Bar Nine spouting gunsmoke because the farmers dared take up homesteads on their grass? I don't think that is a bargain, Ridgeway. Not by a danged sight. . . .'

'Bateman can't keep farmers away. The country is moving west, always west. Farmers will come in on graze, and that's the scheme of things.'

Jamison thought of the tumbling ranges. He saw the distant peaks, the rolling hills—the trail from the Rio Grande to the Milk was a long, long way. Cowmen had fought redskins for this grass; they had broken and obliterated the buffalo. He had this impression, and it left him, and he smiled.

'They might come in—but gunsmoke will follow. I don't care to sling a gun for a hunk of sod that means nothing but work. Some day I'll inherit that sod, but I only want six feet of it, not a hundred and sixty acres.'

Ridgeway had stopped beating his knees. He bowed and said, 'Well said, sir. Your stay in town has not been a pleasant one. May it turn out to be more congenial than it has been.'

Jamison asked bluntly, 'Why did you come here to look me over, Banker?'

Something touched Ridgeway's eyes. Was it anger?

'You imagine things, Mr. Jamison.' The banker purred his words. 'I came only on a business deal.'

'Why did you think I would buy this farm?'

The bony shoulders rose and fell. 'A man has to try. You know that from your—ah, profession, sir. One never knows until he tries, you know.'

Jamison nodded. This was not the answer. He knew that; so did the banker. But for now this answer would have to suffice.

'Good night, sir,' the gambler said.

'Good night, Mr. Jamison.'

Jamison stood there and listened to the boots go down the hall. He heard them turn the corner and go into the lobby and then their sound came back no longer. The man and woman out on the street had moved on. He was glad they had gone; they bothered him. Life had enough troubles without a man and his wife fighting. They should either agree or agree to disagree, he thought idly.

So Westburg knew the answer to the Great Secret. . . .

Clag Jamison had a brief moment of unrest—he had sent Westburg on that journey. And Westburg, to put it bluntly, had been nothing more than a stranger to him—yet he had tried to take his, Jamison's, life.

Jamison put him out of mind.

He would have to stay a day or so in this town of Mill Iron. That thought was not agreeable. If he stayed there would undoubtedly be trouble. Unless Marcia Bateman held Mattson—or even Sig Lamont—in check. But that would take a stern rein and a tough hold.

More boots came down the hall. Jamison let the man knock; his gun was on Sheriff Fulton when he ambled into the room. The fat lawman stopped, belly bouncing, and he said, 'You take no chances, gambler.'

'Sometimes it pays, Sheriff.'

Fulton sighed, and Jamison smelled garlic. Fulton said, 'Wonder if that chair will hold my weight?' and then he said, 'I'd best sit on the bed.'

Jamison watched him amble across the room. The bed sank and protested; it held, though. Jamison saw the big man wince as pain flashed across his face.

'My belly,' the lawman said. 'Always hurts.'

'That garlic would eat the bottom out of a copper tub.'

'Only thing that helps me. Stinks like fury but tastes good.' The eyes, hidden behind heavy rolls, went over Jamison. 'Westburg kicked the bucket.'

'So I heard.'

'Who told you?'

'Your banker. Ridgeway.'

Was it surprise that touched those deep eyes? 'You meet people in a hurry, Jamison. A few hours on this range and you know 'most everybody. An odd, odd man, that banker.'

Jamison had an idea. 'How long has he been in Mill Iron town?'

Fulton thought, head to one side. 'About two years, I reckon. He came back when George Bateman came back —came from college, George did. His dad died that year —his father and Marcia's dad. Great old man, Old Man Bateman. George came back to run the spread and ran into a bullet some time back. He gets around, though— likes to gamble in the Velvet Slipper.'

Jamison said, 'I see.'

Fulton looked at him. 'Why did you ask?'

'Just a question.'

Fulton hauled himself on to his boots. 'We'll hold both inquests together in the morning.' The floor creaked as he advanced toward the door. 'You'll be there, of course.' Not a question; a command.

Jamison felt irritation. This man had a heavy authoritative voice that rubbed him the wrong way.

'I'll be there,' he said.

Fulton studied him. 'Then you'll leave Mill Iron— unless you are indicted for murder?'

'I might. I might not.'

D

'I could run you out, gambler.'

Jamison said, 'You could run into a bullet, too. Smack into it with your big belly, lawman. I want no trouble. You know that, and if you want to cross me, hop to it.'

'You sound tough.'

Jamison held himself; he shrugged. 'Good night,' he said.

Again, he heard a man go down the hall. But this man, instead of being light on his boots, was ponderous and heavy. Two men had visited him this night. And the sheriff had, for some reason, expressed alarm—or was it surprise? that he had been visited by the local banker.

Now another man moved down the hall, and he knocked. Again, the .45 covered a man, and again the .45 went down. For the man was the fat doctor.

'Westburg died,' he told Jamison.

'So I heard. My bullets killed him, the sheriff says— an inquest in the morning. But why tell me?'

'I don't know if the bullets killed him.'

Jamison studied the fat man. 'Why do you say that?'

'He's turning blue,' the medico said. 'His whole body, sort of greyish blue. I was out for about ten minutes; went out for cigars. When I came back he was plumb dead. He had froth around his mouth.'

'They poison coyotes,' Jamison said.

'Even human ones, eh? I must be wrong. Who would sneak in there and force poison into him, and why?'

'He might have become delirious, Doctor. He might have blabbed out some words nobody would want him to disclose. They might have silenced him for once and for all.'

'But who?'

'I don't know. Do you?'

The doctor said, 'We're imagining things. He died from bullet wounds. But I could make an autopsy. But I can't do that until the law so orders.'

They looked at each other.

'If poison is found in him,' Jamison said, 'it might clear me of a murder charge. Ever think of that?'

'They won't hold you. He shot first. You defended yourself. Besides, Marcia Bateman don't want publicity. You're as free as you'll ever be. No, he died of lead poisoning, and I'm imagining things. But I thought I should tell you, Jamison.'

'Thanks, Doctor.'

The medico left. Jamison thought, I'm awfully popular in this burg. . . . Three men had beaten a path to his hotel room's door. He went out in the hall and crossed it and tried the opposite door. It was locked. He got his key and opened the door. The room was empty and dark. He lit a match and found a lamp and looked around. The room had not been rented out.

Me for this room, he told himself.

He left his belongings in his original room and went to bed in the other room. About midnight he came awake. He had been awakened by a man coming down the hall. The man evidently walked on tiptoe, for he made very little noise. Jamison opened the door a little and watched.

The man was bending over the lock on Jamison's room. He was inserting a key into the lock. Jamison heard the door tumblers turn, and then the man stiffened, ear to the panel.

Lamplight, dim and uncertain, showed his face, and Jamison recognised him. The man had his .45 naked in his fist. He listened and Jamison watched, and then the man opened the door.

Six-shooter raised, Jamison went across the hall on his bare feet. He came in behind the man and the six-shooter came down once. The man stumbled, grunted, and Jamison buffaloed him again.

This time the gambler knocked him cold.

CHAPTER SEVEN

Sig Lamont balanced his gaunt body on his stirrups. 'That Jamison might be a gambler, Mattson, and he might not be, either. He might be a federal man.'

'He could be,' Mattson agreed.

Lamont took off his hat and the breeze ruffled his sparse reddish hair. 'He seen Westburg come out of the brush after Westburg killed the farmer and burned his shack. Westburg told me he had run into Jamison.'

'I know that.'

Lamont said, 'He's tough, that son is. We sent Westburg against him and he shoots Westburg, and Westburg misses him.'

'I know that, too!'

Lamont grinned. But he hid the grin from Mattson. 'He kinda got the best of you, too, Mattsan.' he said with devilish intent.

'You're tellin' me nothin'!' Mattson fumed and spat. 'I'll kill him, Sig, so help me Gawd! I'll turn him inside out and look at his guts!'

'He might be just a gambler, like he says, an' not a gover'ment man, like we fear. I'd like to send Ridgeway over to look him over and see what he can find out. That banker is smart.'

'Not as smart as he puts on.'

They rode about a mile out of town. Suddenly Lamont pulled his bronc off the trail and sat a still saddle. A lanky man, wrapped in thought, his brain built this thing up, taking cognisance of the day's happenings.

'Maybe we shouldn't have killed Sturdivant,' Lamont said quietly.

Mattson said, 'Why not? He had the plates made. We have used his as far as we could. We don't need an engraver no longer. He was gettin' yeller-bellied, he was—he might have squealed.'

Lamont said, 'Blast that Jamison. I wish I knew for sure if he was a gover'ment man.'

'There's one way to find out.'

'Yeah. . . . And thet?'

'Search his belongings. Might find something on his saddle. We can split the saddle-skirts, look for hidden identification. If he's a federal man, he'll have somethin' on him or his person to prove it.'

'His saddle is in the livery barn, ain't it?'

'Sure is.'

'He gets a hotel room. Only place he could spend the night. He has to be in the hotel. There are ways to get into his room. We could slug him cold and then search, or we could kill him to make really sure.'

'Killing him would be the best.'

Lamont leaned forward, hands on saddle-horn. He did some thinking. 'What about Westburg, Mattson?'

'What about him?'

'We've used him far enough. He's no gunman. He proved that when he fouled up the deal today. He might get delirious and talk. He could foul up the nest. We put George Bateman out of the way so we could rustle Heart Bar Nine cattle. We got two good deals, brother—bogus dinero and stealing cattle. If Westburg talks he could mess up the whole caboodle.'

'We could bump him off. . . .'

'Poison,' Sig Lamont murmured, 'coyote poison. . . . Strychnine. Some in that line camp on Willow Crick, ain't they?'

'Thet coyote hunter left some there. In a can up on a shelf. I can lead you to it, Sig.' Mattson spat and grinned. 'But how we gonna git Westburg to eat it? We cain't feed it to him in a hunk of meat like they feed it to a coyote!'

'We'll feed it to him, don't worry.'

The Willow Creek line-camp was about four miles to the south. They rode there and got some strychnine, and Mattson carried it in a Bull Durham sack in his breast pocket. When they reached Mill Iron the town was wrapped in darkness. Kerosene lamps made indistinct lights.

The Heart Bar Nine outfit had a livery barn of its own for the use of Heart Bar Nine riders. This was set on the outskirts of the town. They rode in and dismounted and tied their broncs.

'You go talk with Ridgeway,' Lamont told Mattson. 'I'll meet you there later on. First, I visit Westburg.'

'What if the doc is there?'

'I'll handle this,' Lamont said stoutly. 'You worry about yourself and I'll worry about myself, savvy.'

'Sure got a sore tooth tonight, Sig.'

Lamont grinned in the dark. 'I'm going to leave this grass with about a hundred thousand dollars, Mattson. And no gover'ment dick is going to cheat me out of it. If this Jamison bucko steps in my way a bullet'll blast out his heart. Well, I'll see you.'

'Good luck, Sig.'

Mattson went down the alley toward the rear of the bank. Sig Lamont put the Bull Durham sack in his shirt pocket, the tag hanging out. He went into the hotel by the back door. The door to Westburg's room was open. Lamont saw that the doctor was inside. He slid into an empty room and watched through the crack between the door and casing. Time seemed to stand still. Finally the doctor left the room and went into the lobby.

Lamont acted, then.

He went across the hall and entered Westburg's room. Westburg grinned at him. 'Come to visit me, eh, Sig?'

'Set with you for a while.'

'Doc jes' left me. Said I'd get along okay while he stepped out for a bite to chaw on. He'll be gone about thirty minutes—Hey, what the devil you doin', Sig? Let go my mouth!'

Sig Lamont had one bony knee on Westburg's chest, holding the squirming man down. He got astraddle the sick man, pinning him to the bed. With both hands, he prised open Westburg's mouth until he got the man's cheeks in between his teeth. He held one hand inside, keeping the mouth open, and with the other he poured the poison into the man's open mouth.

He emptied the sack, then let the man close his mouth. Westburg was red-hot with anger.

'What you doing?'

'Not so loud, Westburg. I had to give you that medicine that way.'

'Medicine?'

'Yeah, some Marcia sent in with me. She said her dad used to use it—said it was the best medicine in the world —What's the matter, Westburg?'

'My—heart. . . .'

The man tried to sit up. He got halfway up, then fell back. His breathing tore from him; his muscles jumped; he tried to scream—but Sig Lamont throttled him, hand over the gunman's open mouth.

Sig Lamont watched the man's face change. He felt the strength leave the man's flesh. Only when Westburg had stopped breathing did he remove his hand. And then his fingers went down and rested over Westburg's heart.

No heart action, he thought. Stone dead, the coyote. . . .

He scurried across the hall. He went into the room

and opened a window and slid outside. He was between the hotel and another building. He closed the window behind him and walked down the alley. Behind him lay a dead man. A man he had killed. Apparently it did not bother him.

He walked up the alley and came to the back door of the bank. He rapped five times, leaving a space of time between each rap. The door opened and he stepped into Ridgeway's office. The office was dark. Lamont felt of the darkness and he did not like it, and the thought came that now Westburg was in the dark—and would be there forever. For the first time, he felt irritation.

'Light the blarsted lamp,' he snarled.

The door went shut behind him. A match came to life in the hands of Ridgeway. The lamp sprang into action. It showed Mattson sitting with his chair against the wall. Ridgeway held the burning match.

'Well, Sig?' the banker asked.

'He's dead,' Lamont said. 'He was a coyote and he ate poison.' He laughed, and Ridgeway suddenly cursed, for the match had burned his fingers. Lamont said, 'Ain't you got no sense, Ridgeway?'

'Sometimes I doubt it,' the banker said. 'Running with you sometimes appears to me to be a sign of lack of intelligence.'

'Don't rile me,' Lamont grunted.

Mattson said, 'Well, he's out of the way, men. We had a big day—we got rid of Sturdivant, too.'

'What about Jamison?' Lamont wanted to know.

Lamont looked at Ridgeway. Ridgeway looked at Mattson. Mattson watched Lamont with bright eyes.

Lamont said, 'I've done a night's work. Mattson, you go to the livery barn. Get his saddle and go through the bags, and if needs be split the skirts to see if he carries anything there.'

Mattson nodded, smoke curling from his cigarette.

Lamont spoke to Ridgeway. 'You go to his room and talk with him. Make him an offer to buy the Sturdivant farm. Sound him out and see what you think. Then come back here and report to me.'

'Okay,' the banker said.

They went out the back door. Lamont heard their boots move down the alley. He went to the banker's desk and pulled open a drawer. Methodically he searched the desk. He was looking for nothing particular, he was just passing time. He ransacked the desk and then leaned back against the spring of the swivel chair. He locked his hands across his belly.

He sat there, thinking.

Ridgeway was the first to return. He was flushed and somewhat angry, and Lamont said nothing, letting the man be the first to speak. Finally Ridgeway said, 'He's a tough cuss.'

'What did you find out?'

'I'll start from the first. Doc had just discovered his patient was dead. He told me Westburg had kicked the bucket. I made like I was surprised and I went down the hall and told this to this fellow Jamison. He had the door barred and he met me with a six-shooter in his paw.'

'Overlookin' nothin', eh?'

'He wondered if the Law would hold him. We talked, and I offered him Sturdivant's farm. He said he'd have no use for a set of plough handles. Never wanted to touch a plough, he said.'

'You found out nothing, then?'

'Not a single thing, Lamont.'

Lamont paced the floor. He dragged on his smoke. His boots made rough sounds. The lamp flickered. Ridgeway sat in silence.

Finally Lamont said, 'Maybe Mattson will bring in something.'

They sat in silence until Mattson arrived. He had gone through Jamison's saddle bags. He had found not a letter or a bit of identification. He had slit the saddle's skirts. He had found nothing between the sheepskin and the upper leathers. But he had found one little item.

'Mind how Uncle Sam runs a hoof brand on his hosses,' he told the pair. 'Well, I get down on my hands and knees, and I feel along the hoofs of his hoss. And you know what I found?'

'You probably got your hands darned dirty,' Ridgeway said cynically.

Lamont scowled at the banker. Plainly the range boss was irritated. 'What did you find, Mattson?'

'Well, his hoss has been branded on the hoof, but the brand is almost worn off. Still I could make out the top of a U and a S. So he's ridin' a government hoss.'

Ridgeway scowled and rubbed his jaw.

Lamont looked at his cigarette. 'Could prove he was a gover'ment man—and it might mean nothin'. The army has cut down its cavalry and it's sold lots of its horses. No more Injuns to fight. He might have got hold of a cavalry nag. We should have more evidence than that.'

Ridgeway said, 'He's a stranger. He has no kin on this grass. He could suddenly disappear and everybody would figure he rode out of town. We could get his bronc out of the livery and run it into Canada with the next beef herd we steal from the Heart Bar Nine.'

Mattson asked, 'How about him?'

Lamont winked at Ridgeway. Mattson did not see the wink. Lamont said, 'Your job, Mattson.'

'I'm a-hankering to tangle with him,' Mattson said, and rubbed his palms together.

Lamont shook his head. 'We don't want anybody to know you killed him, Mattson. You got to manage it so nobody will know. Slug him if you can and don't shoot —a bullet makes a lot of noise.'

'I'll slug him, we'll tote him out on the prairie, and then we'll shoot him and bury him, eh?'

'If you can slug him, do it. If it takes a pistol shot, shoot the pistol. And aim straight, Mattson.'

'He's already dead,' Mattson said.

The gunman hitched his gun around and drew it and inspected it. Then he restored it lightly to holster. 'Wish me luck,' he said, and spat. He missed the spittoon and Ridgeway glared. 'Worse than an old maid housekeeper,' he told the banker, and he went into the night.

He went down the alley and entered the hotel by the back door. He went past the room holding the dead man and he got a skeleton key out of his pocket. Ridgeway had given him the key back in the bank's office. The hallway was silent, the lamps flickering. Shadows moved and gathered, and he had a cold feeling in his belly. He moved more slowly.

The hotel was quiet. He had spent some time at the office since coming from the livery barn. How much time? he wondered. Over an hour, at least—by this time, Jamison would undoubtedly be asleep.

He came to Jamison's door.

He inserted his skeleton key. He had expected to meet resistance, for he figured Jamison would leave his key in the lock from the inside. But there was no key. He stood there, debating. Then he opened the door.

The next thing he knew, he heard a man behind him. He tried to whirl but something came down and hit him across the head.

The *something* knocked him unconscious.

CHAPTER EIGHT

SHERIFF JONES FULTON slept in his wide swivel chair, fingers laced across his sick belly. He snored deeply. He had a wife of many years, and the years had widened her gross body and had honed her tongue. He seldom went home.

Suddenly he came awake. Something had landed with a thud on the floor. He stared at the unconscious man and then looked up at the man who had toted the limp form into his office.

'Jamison,' the sheriff said. 'Up to more trouble, eh?'

Jamison grinned, hiding his anger. 'Mattson came to pay me a midnight visit, Sheriff. Even had a key to my room. And a six-shooter in his fist. But he got the wrong room and I came in behind him and introduced him to the barrel of my Colt. He's still asleep.'

Fulton was awake by now. A group of people, attracted by Jamison toting the unconscious man, had crowded into the office, and evidently their presence irritated the fat sheriff, who chased them outside and locked the door.

Fulton stood there, back to the closed door; he mopped his forehead with a palm. 'Ain't hot,' he said, 'an' by dab, I'm sweatin'. . . . He lifted his eyes again from the unconscious gunman. Another mark for the Batemans and for Sig Lamont against you, Jamison.'

Jamison asked roughly, 'Should I have stood still and let him shoot me, Sheriff?'

Fulton's eyes were dull in the lamplight. 'You want to file a charge against him, Jamison?'

'I do. Illegal entry into my hotel room, with intent to kill. And what's more, he spends the night in a cell, savvy?'

Fulton allowed himself a smile. Then this went before the rapid push of pain, and his jowls became glum and pale.

'Lamont won't like it, us juggin' his top gun-slinger. He'll go bail in the mornin' an' then Mattson will be a tiger without a leash. The best thing you could do would be to jerk stakes and drift, Jamison.'

'And leave a possible murder charge behind me?' Jamison grinned tightly. 'I leave this range and a coroner's jury will bring in a charge that I murdered Westburg. There'll be placards up from the Red River to the Milk River. I'm staying and settling a few points, Sheriff. Which way to the cell?'

'This way,' Fulton conceded.

The Sheriff led the way. He carried a lamp. Behind him came Jamison. The gambler did not carry the gun-man across his shoulder. He pulled him by the legs. Mattson slid across the slivery old floor.

Fulton said, 'Only got one cell.'

He laboriously unlocked the gate, and Jamison pulled Mattson inside, made a circle and left the gunman on the floor. Fulton shut the door with a clang. Mattson swallowed and then sat up and looked around. He had a pained, dazed look in his eyes that even the dim lamp-light revealed.

'What the blazes happened to me?'

Jamison leaned against the bars, and his smile was fleeting. 'You don't remember?' he taunted.

Mattson staggered to the bunk, head in his hands, and sat down. Finally he looked up with, 'I was coming to visit you, Jamison. Marcia Bateman was sending me over to apologise to you for havin' acted so uppity. I stuck my haid in your door to holler to you an' the ceilin' fell on me.'

'You're an accomplished liar,' Jamison said. 'You opened the door with a skeleton key and you had your .45 in your hand. You made one error though, Mattson.'

Bright eyes—feverish eyes—watched him. 'And thet error, card-slick?'

'You went in the wrong room.'

Mattson studied him. Suddenly he said, Oh, my achin' haid,' and then, after a pause, 'You was registered in thet room in the hotel book, Jamison.'

'I got suspicious,' Jamison said. 'I moved to the room across the hall.'

'And you come in behin' me, eh?'

'From behind,' Jamison said.

They looked at each other. There was hate in Mattson's flaming eyes; hate filled the pores of his body. Jamison read this hate and realised that as long as he was on this Milk River range, as long as Mattson was alive—that hate would grow and flourish and attain greater stature. There was this thought in him, and the thought was not good—still, he was forewarned, and there was the old adage about how to be forewarned was to be forearmed.

'You're a smart one,' Mattson conceded.

Sheriff Fulton watched. Lamplight showed beads of sweat on his wide forehead. Fulton watched and Fulton saw this hate, and Fulton wondered which one—if any of them—would be alive, when and if the shooting started. He placed his odds on Jamison. Even though Mattson was a fast hand with a hard gun—

'The Heart Bar Nine will bail me out,' Mattson said.

Jamison nodded. 'I'll be waiting,' he agreed.

Mattson said nothing. Jamison said nothing. There was no need for further words. Each understood where he stood with the other. Jamison turned and walked to the office with Fulton bending the floor as he plodded behind him. Young Hank Sturdivant was in the office.

Fulton said, 'How did you get in here? I had the door locked.'

'The window was open,' the boy said. He looked up at Jamison and, though his eyes were boyish and young, they still seemed to hold a stern maturity. Jamison wondered at this incongruity.

Hank said, 'Mattson tried to kill you, eh, Jamison?'

'He did.'

Hank said, 'He tied into a tough man.' His hand found Jamison's. Warm, boyish, clinging to something substantial, seeking a friend in the dark. Jamison was touched; he thought of his boy, Jim, who was about Hank's age. Life spun a fast loop. Life laid the loop out; no man knew when or where he would step into the noose. But life sure could frontfoot a man and bust him on his kisser.

Jamison said, 'You should be in bed, son.'

They went out together. Townspeople stood in dark groups, and they were silent when Jamison and the boy walked by. Their bootheels made sounds on the raw plank sidewalks, and these sounds moved into the night and were claimed and became a part of the silence.

'I got a bunk back of Nell Robinson's saloon,' the boy told him. 'She's got a few beds back there where drunk cowpunchers sleep. She gave me the run of the spread. No more cowpunchers'll sleep there; it's my room. People went by the window and I heard one mention your name, so I put on my boots and followed.'

Jamison nodded. 'You got a bed for me there, Hank?'

'There sure is. For you and me, pard.'

They walked on. The boy was silent. Jamison got the impression that something worried him. He let the youngster put his worries into words. Finally the right time came.

'Westburg killed my dad. He's dead, Westburg is. His soul was rotten; my dad said that. I guess I don't hate him now, Jamison.'

'That's the right approach.'

The boy said, 'You know, I wonder about my dad. He had no reason for becoming a farmer. He never farmed back in Ohio.'

'What did he do?'

'He was a printer. He made—oh, what do you call them?—pictures? You know, on metal.'

'An engraver?'

'That's the word.'

Jamison said, 'Maybe he wanted to get out in the open. Maybe he wanted to get to be his own boss and not hit a payroll each month.'

'He couldn't even milk a cow when he first came out here. He tried to milk our cow from the left side. She kicked him on his rump.'

Jamison said, 'Some cows are ornery, Hank.'

They turned into the Velvet Slipper Saloon. Nell Robinson wore a green dress that clung to her and accentuated her figure. But her face was not pleasant when she saw Hank.

'You're supposed to be in bed, Hank.'

Hank said, 'I heard about Jamison. I went to the jail. He beat the stuffing out of Mattson and jugged him.'

'We've heard of that.' She put her arm around the boy. 'Now go to bed and try to sleep.'

Hank said, 'Watch your back, Jamison.'

'I'll do that, boy.'

He went through the saloon and went through a door and became lost from sight. Nell Robinson looked at Jamison.

'He thinks the world of you,' she said.

Jamison said, smiling, 'Just a no-good drifting gambler. They're ten cents a gross.'

She repeated, 'He thinks the world of you, Jamison.'

She turned and went behind the bar. She said, 'Something for the nerves, Jamison?' and he said, 'Never drink.' He put a dollar on the bar. 'For your drink.'

She shook her head. 'I never touch it. And if I did, your buck would be no good. I own tons of the stuff.'

Four cowpunchers stood at the bar. Jamison moved his back against the rail and looked at the card tables. Only one was operating. Five men played there, and Jamison picked out the house-man. He had that look about him, and to Jamison he stood out as a gambler. But the gambler was not interested in the green-shaded house-man. He had, in his lifetime, seen thousands of gamblers.

As men, as professionals, they raised no interest in him any longer.

But one poker player did interest him.

First, he was in a wheel-chair. Second, Jamison knew he was George Bateman. He looked at Marcia's brother. He was a young man, this George Bateman—wiry and thin, and his dark hair was getting prematurely grey. He looked at Jamison with level blue eyes.

Their eyes met and held for a long moment.

Jamison wondered what those eyes held. He could not see them clearly and, had the lamplight been stronger, he doubted if he could have read them, and he was long-skilled at reading human eyes. He got one thing out of the gaze; this man was deep and he was quiet and he had self-control.

Then George Bateman looked back at his cards.

Jamison thought, I want to size him up from close

range, and he moved over to the table, but George Bateman did not look up. Jamison said to the house-man, 'There's an empty seat,' and the house-man said, 'Put your rump on it, Jamison.' Jamison slid down and asked, 'What is it?'

'Dealer's choice. Either stud or draw.'

Jamison said, 'I'll take a stack.'

Bateman glanced at him and shuffled the cards. He had long, thin fingers, and Jamison thought they trembled a little. . . . But he was not sure.

'Always room for one more,' Bateman said.

Bateman said, 'Stud.'

Jamison had little interest in his cards. He played automatically. Bateman won, and the house-man dealt, and then Jamison had the cards. He said, 'Draw,' and did the dealing.

Bateman peeked at his hand. 'You're a tough man with a deck of cards, Jamison.'

Jamison smiled.

Bateman said, 'And with your fists and six-shooter too.'

He was driving at something. Jamison said nothing. Bateman threw his hand away.

'Sometimes good poker players don't live long,' he told the house-man. 'I know one of the best of them all, and he died when he was only thirty-eight.'

Jamison smiled. 'A bullet?'

'Heart attack,' Bateman said.

Jamison knew the man was baiting him. He noticed that Bateman spoke good English. He had the marks of culture and education. He knew how to make words dangerous, and he could play with words and sentences. Jamison knew Bateman was warning him to ride out of this Milk River country. Jamison paid him no attention, though. There was something rotten here—stinkingly rotten. For that matter, he doubted if he could ride out.

The Heart Bar Nine was an old outfit here, and it had built up its prestige by driving out smaller outfits, just as it had driven out the farmers. He, one man, had defied this big cow outfit. He doubted if Marcia Bateman—and Sig Lamont—would let him ride north into Canada.

To uphold the prestige of the Heart Bar Nine, they would have to get him. Let one crack come in their defence, in their haughty pride—and they, as an outfit, would be through. Done. Finished.

Let one man—or one gun—defy a big cow outfit, and that outfit had to strike back. If it did not, then it was through. Cow outfits were like men. They had their pride, and he, Jamison, had rubbed sandpaper across that pride—he had flaunted the Heart Bar Nine and, so far, he was ahead.

Sig Lamont came in and stood behind Bateman. Bateman said irritably, 'Move to one side—I want no man watching my hand.'

'Okay,' Lamont soothed him, 'okay.'

Jamison looked over his cards at Lamont. 'Your man is in the clink. I put him there. He tried to visit me with a six-shooter in his fist. I got a little suspicious.'

'He'll be out by morning.'

Jamison nodded. He gave his attention back to his cards. He heard the hoarse, animal breathing of Sig Lamont. Jamison bet and raised a bet. An old man came in and his eyes were wide.

'Jamison?' he asked Nell. 'Where is he?'

'Can't you see, hostler? Over at the card table.'

The old man went over to Jamison. He seemed excited. He smelled of horse liniment and manure and hay. Jamison recognised him as the operator of the town livery barn.

'I dozed off for a while, Jamison,' he began. 'While I was sleepin', somebody snuck in an' did it.'

'Did what?'

'They went through your saddle-bags. They even split the skirts on your kak. They opened the fender leathers, too. Now why do you reckon they did that?'

Jamison said, 'Raise you two, Bateman.'

The chips went out on the green table. Two fell out, and Bateman raised, and Jamison raised.

'Why would they do that?' the old man repeated.

Jamison said, 'I expected it.' He spoke to the world in general. 'I ride an ex-cavalry horse. Bought him down at Fort Keogh out of Miles City. Got him cheap, and he's got good legs and wind. The horse has no brand on his hide. He is hoof-branded U.S., but the hoof is wearing down and the brand is almost gone.'

Bateman watched his cards.

Sig Lamont breathed deeply.

Nell Robinson listened and had her thoughts. The other players wanted none of this trouble, so they said nothing. The big clock ticked, and time ran off into oblivion and the endless centuries.

Jamison spoke to the livery barn owner. 'When morning comes have my saddle repaired. There might be a time wher. I'll make somebody pay for cutting that stitching.'

'What was they looking for?' the old man asked.

Jamison said, 'I got my ideas.' He played cards in silence. The old man left and the smell of manure left with him.

Lamont stood there silently.

Jamison did not look at the range boss. He watched George Bateman's thin hands. After a while Bateman gestured with the little finger on his right hand. The finger rose, fell, was still.

Only then did Jamison look up at Sig Lamont.

'That's your signal,' the gambler said dryly. 'You're supposed to go now, Lamont.'

Lamont snarled, 'Am I a dog?'

Jamison grinned. 'You should know,' he said.

Lamont turned and left. Jamison looked at him. 'He's so mad his boot heels are punching holes in the floor,' he said.

Bateman glanced up over his cards. He said nothing.

CHAPTER NINE

AFTER leaving the Velvet Slipper Sig Lamont went back to the bank where he talked with Norman Ridgeway. The lanky range boss was burning and the banker kept his mouth shut, for he was somewhat afraid of Lamont. He had seen him handle his gun too many times. . . .

'We'll bail him out come morning,' Ridgeway said.

Lamont was stony-eyed, and his right hand rested on a holstered gun. 'We should gun him out of that tin-can cling,' he snarled.

Ridgeway shook his head. 'We got to keep on friendly terms with Fulton,' he said placatingly. 'The best deal is to hold our tempers and wait until morning, Sig.'

Lamont's eyes were still flint. 'What if we kill him off?'

'Kill who?'

'Mattson, of course.'

Ridgeway watched him. There were times when the cold-bloodness of this man chilled the marrow of his bones. This was one of those times.

'I don't understand you,' the banker said.

Sig Lamont spoke slowly. 'Mattson knows too much. He might get soft and do some blabbing.'

'Not him,' Ridgeway maintained. 'Not Mattson.'

Lamont showed a thin smile. 'All right, all right. We'll sick him against this gambler—when we get him out.' He went to the door and put his hand on the knob and stopped. 'What about the latest shipment of money?'

'Joe took it north at sundown. The deal is the same, I suppose, up there in Wood Mountain. A thousand bucks worth of bogus bills for one hundred in gold dust. Joe carried thirty thousand.'

'And he takes back three thousand in dust, eh?'

'Unless the Mounties tie on to him,' Ridgeway said.

'They won't. Joe knows the ropes.' Lamont seemed wrapped in thought. 'I wonder if Mattson got shot to death—in his cell—if there would be some way we could pin the shootin' on to this gambler?'

Ridgeway sucked his bottom lip. He gave this thought. Then he said, 'If there's an angle there I can't see it.'

'You printing any more money soon?'

Ridgeway shrugged. 'Sturdivant printed almost a million dollars worth two or three days ago. Printed till we ran out of paper. Wood Mountain can take a lot of it, Sig, but not a million bucks worth. It might be a gold-mad town, but a million dollars is lots of dinero.'

Sig Lamont nodded.

Ridgeway asked, 'How about this Jamison? You still figure he's a federal man?'

Lamont scowled. He rubbed his jaw, the whiskers making sounds. 'The livery barn man came and told Jamison about somebody openin' the seams in his saddle. Jamison made the remark that his bronc used to belong to Uncle Sam and that he bought him down in Miles City at Fort Keogh.'

'He's probably telling the truth.'

Lamont smiled. 'Maybe he is—maybe he ain't. Thing that interested me the most was why, for no apparent reason at all, he went out of his way to tell us about the horse. But it still don't seem logical that a federal man should come in riding a horse hoof-branded U.S.'

'Can't tell for sure,' Ridgeway said.

Lamont said, 'So long,' and went outside. He gave Ridgeway a little space in his thoughts. Ridgeway and George Bateman had met back East, while George had been going to college. George had run up big gambling debts that the Old Man would not pay and he and Ridgeway had paid them with bogus currency. Then the Old Man had died, and George had quit school, and he and Ridgeway, thinking of the gold rush at Wood Mountain, had come hightailing it to Mill Iron town. And with them Ridgeway had brought their printer, Raleigh Sturdivant.

Lamont swung into saddle, and he thought. But I took over the deal from them. I worked them both ways. . . . He had put the bullet against George Bateman's back, but he had not killed the man, and he had wanted Bateman's death. Easy thing to blame it on the farmers.

For George Bateman had the pride of the Old Man, something Marcia lacked. For Marcia hated this land and its people, and he, Sig Lamont, had used this hate —he had pitted brother against sister, and he had won. Now, leaving Mill Iron town, he headed toward the north-west, angling across the Milk River basin, heading for the mouth of Frenchman Creek, about twenty miles away.

Lamont reined the blue roan towards the hills, and he rode high on stirrups. The horse was a chunky horse and tough circles had stiffened his shoulders; he bounced like a ton of rocks. Lamont put his palms on the fork of his saddle and rode his oxbows high. The thought came that, if things worked out right in the next few months, he would leave this country. Leave it with a lot of gold dust. The world was big and men were fools and a bullet could blast a man's way. A bullet didn't care whom it killed or where or when it did the killing. . . .

The roan was too tough at a trot, so Lamont put him into a slow lope. The hoofs ate up the miles and he crossed the river at the crossing, spray shooting upward.

On the far side he let the roan drink. But not too much,
for there were miles ahead; he put the roan up the
north bank. He found the sagebrush-covered prairie and
the hills came out of the darkness, and somewhere cattle
bedded down. He could not see them but he could smell
them and feel them, for at heart he was a cowman and
cattle had made up his life—lumbering, slobbering,
stupid cattle.

Lamont reined his roan to a halt.

For a moment, he sat saddle; he wished dawn were
here. He watched the dark and he felt of the dark and
then he heard a hoof move and he called out , 'Sig
Lamont, riding in.'

'This way, Sig.'

Cattle got to their feet. They moved and he heard
their sounds, but he could not see them. He rode toward
the voice. Their horses almost collided, it was that dark.
Sig Lamont pulled in.

'Jake ?'

'That's right, Sig.'

Lamont settled in saddle, one part of his ride through.
He rolled a cigarette, and the match touched the craggy
recesses of his gaunt face. The flame played and threw
light across him and then died. Only the cigarette coal
glowed with each intake of his breath.

'How many head, Jake ?'

'About four hundred odd.'

Lamont pulled on the cigarette. 'Almost ready to
shove them north in Canuck country,' he allowed.

'How many more days, Sig ?'

'Two, Jake. Then you head north. A little matter of
the Mounties, but I got a man working on that. The
Mounties move north in two days and these dogies start
in behind them.'

'The Mounties,' Jake murmured.

'They're a chore,' Lamont said. 'But there are ways to get around them. I'll ride with you.'

'See you then, Sig.'

'Two days,' Lamont repeated.

The man rode away and he sang in a low voice. A good voice it was, too—low, rich, satisfying. Sig Lamont listened to it and thought, the first calm thing I have heard or seen all evening. . . . Then he turned his horse and rode toward the Heart Bar Nine Ranch.

He let the horse hit a running-walk.

His mind was agile. He sought for loose ends to tie this thing to make it a compact ball. The only loose end was a gent named Clághorn Jamison who had blundered into something too big for him. Or had he *blundered*? Had he come in because of his own volition, and had Luck been with him when he had seen Westburg right after Westburg had murdered Raleigh Sturdivant?'

He'd take care of Jamison.

Accordingly, he pushed the memory of the gambler from his mind. His bronc was tired, but still he drove him with his spurs, and when dawn came tumbling across the Montana ranges the horse was grey with dust and a rim of lather showed under his headstall and under the rim of the Navajo saddle blanket. The ranch lay on a flat along a creek, and a guard rode out of the thick diamond willows.

'Howdy, Sig.'

'Top of the morning, John.'

John looked at the rising sun. 'Gonna be another hot day,' he said. 'Send out Duke when you get into the house. He should have relieved me an hour ago.'

'I'll do that.'

John sniffed. 'I smell the cook's coffee. An uneventful night, as the story book says.'

'Marcia?'

'In the house, I reckon. She never rode out in the night.'

'Thanks,' Sig Lamont said.

He rode into the barn and stripped his horse and watered him and tied him to a manger filled with native bluejoint grass. He poured a measure of oats into the stall-cup and threw his saddle over the rack, hooking his bridle over the horn. Then he went to the bunkhouse.

'Up and at it, men. Duke, get on your boots, cram in some grub, and go out and relieve John.'

'I slept late,' Duke said.

'We know that. Get moving.'

He went to the house. He had a foreman's house, off to the right, but he walked past it; he was sleepy, too. A man gets sleepy easier when he gets a few years added to his carcass, he thought. He entered by the back door. The housekeeper, formless in an old dressing robe, poked at the wood stove. She was about fifty and she was man-crazy and he knew this from experience. He put his arm around her and pulled her to him. He kissed her and she kissed him back.

'Where have you been?'

'Just like a woman,' he said. 'The minute a man enters, she shoots the questions at him. Where is Marcia?'

'In her bedroom.'

'She up?'

'I don't know. Go and see.'

He patted her arm and went down the hall. She stood at the door and watched, but he did not notice this. He knocked on a door and got no response, so he knocked again, and still no voice called out. He entered. He was in the darkness of a woman's room. He smelled the perfume and the other female necessities, and he crossed the room and sent up the blind. Light came in and lay across the bed. Marcia Bateman was awake and her lovely red hair spilled across the pillow. The covers did not hide her feminine appeal.

'What do you want?'

Lamont grinned. 'Nice way to welcome a sweetheart.'

'You're not my sweetheart. I play up to you because I can use you, Sig. I need you and you need me.'

Lamont looked at her. 'You never can guess for one minute how much I need you,' he told her.

'You've said that before.'

He went over and sat on the bed.

He said, 'Watch your tongue. Some day I'll own you.'

She shook her head. 'Not you—or any man. Why, I don't even own myself—sometimes I get the craziest thoughts. . . .' She changed the subject. 'How about the herd?'

'Two days and it moves.'

'More money for my sock,' she said. Her eyes got scheming. 'How about your bosom friend?'

'Which one?'

'Jamison.'

He leaned back and laughed silently. 'When the time comes we'll get good and rid of that tin-horn.'

She was deadly serious. 'If George ever finds out we are stealing the Old Man's cows, he'll shoot us both. This ranch is an obsession with him. I wonder which farmer shot him?'

He thought, I wonder how much you know, or suspect. . . . He said, 'Raleigh Sturdivant, of course. Mattson got him.'

'What is Jamison doing?'

He told her what he knew about the gambler. Her face showed doubt. 'I'll play up to him, Sig. Every man is a fool for a purty female face and a soft voice. I read it in a book once.'

He stood up. 'You read the wrong book, sister. It

didn't have Jamison's name in it. I think he'd be a tough nut for any woman to smash. He might be a gambler and he might not be.'

'What could he be, if not a tinhorn?'

'We're running cattle into Wood Mountain. Actually, we're stealing cattle from your brother. Mounties might have sent down a scout. When we cross that International Border, we move into big politics, child.'

'I'll play up to him.'

'Do that, but watch your own mouth.'

'I wasn't born yesterday.'

He looked at her. His love for her showed in his eyes. She did not love him. She did not even care for him. He was necessary and therefore she tolerated him. She had a sombre nature; he was wild, tough. Now these natures clashed and his head lowered.

'Honey,' he breathed.

She let him kiss her. She even kissed him back. There arose in her in this moment a terrible, driving anger. An anger directed toward herself. She hated him, she hated these stupid cowpunchers, she hated this cold and dead land. She wanted people and gayness and she wanted a city and she wanted the night. She would get it, too, and he would supply these things.

So she kissed him.

He drew back his head and said, 'Whewww . . .' and then he left. He walked down the hall and had his thoughts. She did not know about the bogus money. Her brother knew about that; he got his cut. George Bateman did not know about their stealing Heart Bar Nine cattle. He, Sig Lamont, was riding the middle horse; he was playing one against the other, and the net was pulling shut. He could feel the net closing, although he could not see it. A stray slip of the tongue, any misstatement; somebody might get wise.

Well, the end was near. Soon he'd have his stake and he'd pull out, but he'd make darned sure he had a woman with him.

A red-headed woman, a woman who promised much.

He went into the kitchen. He slapped the cook, and she turned around, and he said, 'How about some hot java?'

'Coming up, Sig.'

He pulled a chair close to the kitchen table. He looked at her broad back. An odd thought struck him. He could have married her any time he wanted, but he had never wanted to.

He wanted to marry the red-head.

And the red-head did not want him.

The whole thing was twisted around. Like life, he thought. He sipped the hot coffee.

'Thanks,' he said.

The heavy woman smiled.

CHAPTER TEN

CLAG JAMISON hit the sougans about three. He had won the big sum of thirty-seven dollars in the poker game. A Heart Bar Nine puncher had wheeled George Bateman down the street and into the hotel. Bateman had lost around three hundred. One of the other players had held the hands.

Jamison had pushed back his chair with, 'Me for the blankets, longside of the boy.'

'I'm locking up,' Nell Robinson said.

Jamison stretched again. 'Getting old and grey. Can't take it like I used to. Why don't you marry me and make me a home, Miss Nell?'

'I was looking for a similar deal.'

Jamison went to the back room. He did not light a lamp. He heard Hank's deep breathing, and Jamison undressed and got between the covers. The night was warm; he kicked off the blankets. He lay there and did some thinking. He would not try to run the blockade. That would be useless. Why did they fear him and want to kill him? Plainly they were mistaking him for somebody else. Otherwise they would not have cut up his saddle as they had.

But who? And why?

The next thing he knew, somebody pounded on the door. Hank sat up and stuck both fists into his eyes.

'Who's there?' Jamison asked.

'Nell Robinson. I've your breakfasts ready, if you two sleepy-heads can get out of bed.'

'Room service,' Jamison said.

Hank looked at him. 'What's room service?' he wanted to know.

Jamison smelled the air. 'Coffee, for one thing. And is that bacon we smell, boy—crisp and delicious bacon?'

Hank forgot the possible definition of *room service*. He started to dress. 'Yesterday was a bad day. Maybe today will be better.' Suddenly the sense of loss came over him. He lay down again and said, 'I don't wanta eat, Jamison.'

Jamison nodded, understanding. 'Take your time, boy,' he encouraged.

Nell knocked again.

'Coming,' Jamison said.

He heard her walk away. He heard her moving in the next room. He had not known she had an apartment in her saloon. She was quite a girl, he realised. Reliable and solid and strong. He liked her, although she wasn't going to know it. He had had one woman, and one had been enough. Not that he was still in love with her. He just did not want a wife. When he got old and couldn't get around he'd hire a big fat Mexican housekeeper. He grinned at that thought. He pulled on his boots, and Hank did not look up as he went out the door.

He was in the main part of the Velvet Slipper. The air had a stale smell—the smell of all saloons and gambling dens—and he saw the sunlight through the big windows. An old man was washing the windows. Jamison looked around and saw a door, and the old man said, 'That's her room. She's in there.'

Jamison knocked on the door.

'Come in.'

She wore a dressing robe that clung to her and emphasised her shapeliness.

'Where is the boy?'

F.

Jamison said, 'He'll be in soon. It hit him again.
'Where do I wash?'
'On the back porch.'
She went outside with him. The Montana sun was
glorious. Jamison said, 'And to think men get ugly
thoughts when the sun and morning are so good.' She
poured water into a thick glass basin. He washed and
said, 'My shaving kit is on my saddle.'
'Shave afterwards.'
He rubbed his chin. 'I won't make a very nice-looking
face across the table,' he commented.
'Even shaved, I'd doubt that.'
Jamison came back to her apartment. Clean, neat,
not burdened with too many knicknacks. It fitted her.
He found a chair.
'How many eggs?'
'Two.'
'How?'
'Wide awake.'
She broke the eggs. They made noises in the pan. He
looked at her back. He said, 'Do you do this to every
bum that drifts in and gets into trouble, Miss Nell?'
'You helped Hank. He's my friend. My boy, now, one
might say.' She did not look at him.
'I wonder,' he said, 'if I could run the blockade?'
'After the inquest?'
'Sure, not before. They might try to pin something on
me. You think I could get out of Milk River basin?
With a whole hide?'
'Don't talk so foolish.'
'What's foolish about it?'
She put the eggs on a plate and laid three strips of
bacon beside them and she served him.
'Jamison, you rubbed sandpaper into the eyes of the
Heart Bar Nine. If you get away with it, others can.

Marcia Bateman has pride. So has her brother. And so, for that matter, has Sig Lamont.'

Jamison ate slowly. 'I guess that's right, Miss Robinson. But the deal that tricks me is this one.'

'Yes?'

'Why are they after me?'

'Maybe you've seen something they didn't want you or anybody else to see. Maybe they're afraid of you. The government gave deeds to the homesteaders under the Homestead Act. Maybe they think you're a government man coming in to investigate. That could be, you know.'

'But I'm not a government man.'

She shrugged and sat down opposite him. She put her head in her hands and looked at him.

'You're the first man who has eaten at my table since my father passed away,' she said. 'It looks good to see a man eating.'

'Don't get ideas about me,' Jamison said, grinning. 'I'm a drifting, no-good son-of-a-gun of a gambler. The lowest animal in the social scale. I'll play Wood Mountain until snow threatens, and then it's Rio for the winter. I'm a wild hand with the women and I treat them rough and never marry them.'

She smiled. 'You bark bigger than you bite.'

Young Hank came in. He washed and Nell Robinson cooked more eggs. Jamison got a hunch they wanted to be alone. They had things to talk about, matters to settle —they had to know each other better. Accordingly he excused himself and left. Outside, the sun was bright and threatened heat.

Sheriff Fulton sat outside his office in the sun with the back of his chair tilted against the building.

'Sunning yourself?' Jamison asked cordially.

Fulton lifted one eyelid; his heavy eye looked up.

'They'll put me away in the dark soon,' he said. 'I'm big and the worms will have a feast. The inquest will be at ten.'

Jamison nodded. 'I'll be there. Mattson?'

'Still in my cooler.'

Jamison looked across the street. Dirty town, dusty town, ugly town. A man never knows where his bronc will carry him or the towns he will see or the women he will meet. A man never knows where his grave will be. . . . Jamison hated the town. He hated it with the sullen savage hate a person holds towards an inanimate object. He hated it although he knew the hate was foolish and futile.

'If Mattson moves against me, Sheriff, I'll kill him.'

'He might do that. And he might kill you first.'

Jamison grinned. 'Then I'll feed those worms before you do.' There was nothing more here. Not a thing. Each understood the other, each knew where the other stood; the sun was neutral. Only the sun, though, was neutral. The rest of this range, of this grass, of these hills and these canyons—they were not neutral. There were two factions here and Jamison was one of them.

'So long,' Jamison said, and moved toward the livery barn.

Fulton sat there, head down; gross flesh drank of clean sunshine. Fulton dozed and Fulton awakened, and pain shook him awake. Jamison went to the livery barn and looked at his damaged saddle. Anger rose in him, and this anger was directed towards a nameless person—the individual who had done this deed. Because he did not know the person's name, he directed his anger toward the Heart Bar Nine. And then, realising such direction was of necessity foolish, he wiped his anger away.

'Get the rig to the saddle shop and get it stitched,' he told the holster. 'And get a bottle, too.' He tossed the gold piece, and a grimy claw made a swoop. 'Your eyes look sad.'

'Thank ye, sir.'

'Don't thank me. I gave you a headache.'

Jamison went to the hotel. A look at the register showed the number of George Bateman's room, and he climbed the stairs slowly and sombrely. He knocked on the door and waited.

He knocked again.

Then a voice said, 'Who's there?'

'Jamison.'

A short silence. 'Come in.'

Jamison went into a darkened room. A blind went up, and a Heart Bar Nine cowpuncher, dressed in long-geared underwear, sat on a bunk. He blinked his eyes. On another bed was George Bateman.

Jamison found a chair.

Bateman said, 'You get out of sougans early.'

Conversation, nothing more.

Jamison nodded.

The cowpuncher dressed. He said, 'I'll get some chuck up here, George,' and Bateman nodded. Bateman doubled his pillows and got his body propped up. 'Only from the waist down,' he said. 'Above the waist I can move. The bullet hit my spine. I'll never walk again, the medicos say.'

Jamison went right to the point. 'What's behind all this, Bateman?'

Bateman's grey eyes watched him. Bateman's thin fingers lay motionless on the covers. Bateman bided his time. Then he played his cards slowly and cautiously. He played them one at a time.

'Behind what, Jamison?'

Jamison gestured impatiently. 'Get down to the point. I saw Westburg running from the burning cabin. I

pulled Raleigh Sturdivant out of the fire, dead. Westburg pulled a gun against me. Somebody cut my saddle
all up seeking identification. You know what I'm talking
about.'

Only Bateman's grey eyes were alive. 'I don't know a
blamed thing that you're talking about, Jamison.'

Jamison got to his feet. This man was tough and he
held his thoughts; he was a good poker player. Jamison
turned his hat in his hands.

'What about Mattson, Bateman?'

'What about him?'

'He works for you. He carries a high grudge against
me. Are you sending his gun against mine?'

'He's over twenty-one.'

Jamison let himself go a little. 'So are you. And so is
your sister. Yes, and Sig Lamont. And I'm over twenty-
one, too.'

'I don't follow you.'

Jamison was tough. 'You follow me all right. If Mattson runs his gun against me, I'll kill him.'

'He might not.'

'He won't—if you order him not to.'

'You over-evaluate my power.'

'He draws your wages,' Jamison pointed out.

'But I don't control his thoughts, just because I control his pocket book.'

Jamison said, 'Good day, sir,' and left. He went down
the hallway thinking of the crippled man. Bateman had
sat there, eyes alert and sparkling, and Bateman had
chuckled with inner mirth. Jamison got the impression
that the man had somehow out-pokered him. Or was he
wrong? He gave this no more thought. Bateman was
tied to the bed and the wheel-chair.

Still, a man's gun was dangerous, though not as
dangerous as a man's agile brain. The ginks with the

brains hired the ginks with the guns. . . .

The clerk said, 'Giving up your room?'

Jamison had taken his gear out of his room. 'I am. Too much company.'

The clerk was sour. His attempted smile was sour. His eyes were sour. He hated mankind.

'You owe me for two days' rent.'

'One day,' Jamison corrected him.

'Two days. Our new day starts at eight in the morning.'

Jamison smiled. 'All hotels start new days at noon.'

'This one don't.'

Jamison paid him for one day. Rage flared across the little man's eyes. He had a small man's arrogance and air of toughness.

'Double that, gambler.'

Jamison said, 'There's a fly in that ink bottle.'

The man jerked around, surprised by Jamison's sudden statement. He stared at the open-capped ink bottle. Jamison got him by the back of the neck with one hand and got the ink bottle in the other hand.

The runt tried to break loose. Jamison held him easily. The ink bottle came up and ringed the man's long nose. Jamison tipped the man's head back. Ink ran over his cheeks and covered his face.

Jamison released him.

The clerk went to his knees, sputtering and cursing. Jamison picked up his gear and went outside.

He had a little ink on his hands, he noticed.

CHAPTER ELEVEN

Jamison soon saw another set of fingers that had ink on them too. For a long, long time these fingers had known the feel of ink.

The fingers belonged to a dead man.

The coroner's jury consisted of six men. They looked at the two corpses in silence. The bodies lay on an old pool table. The cloth was old and torn and the wood was scratched. Westburg had a long, homely face. Sturdivant looked as if he was merely asleep. The thought came to Jamison that Westburg had murdered Sturdivant and now he lay in death beside the man he had killed. It would be ironic and just that they be buried in the same grave. Jamison almost had to smile at his silent jest. And he had to keep a straight face.

Fulton had sent the jury down to verify the two deaths. The sheriff had not come along—his belly was acting up. His under-sheriff, a tall dour man, had taken the jury down to the morgue. Now he asked, 'You gents through lookin' at these carcasses?'

'We sure are.'

'This place is clammy,' another said.

They all went outside. Jamison had given his testimony. Now he said, 'See you later, Under-sheriff.'

'Where you going?'

'If you need me I'll be in the Velvet Slipper Saloon.'

The tall man scowled. 'I ain't got no charge against you, so I can't hold you. Jes' don't leave town, savvy? If the verdict is against you I'll have to jug you, Jamison.'

'You know where to find me.'

Jamison went one way; the jury the other. He was a little worried about the verdict. More than one stranger had been double-crossed in these small towns. Yes, and in big ones, too. . . .

He kept remembering the fingers. Ink had been ground into them and they looked as if they had been washed in kerosene to get rid of the ink. Still, the ink had entered the pores.

Jamison stopped and went back to the morgue.

He lit the lamp. He moved close and looked at Sturdivant. He remembered the boy had told him his father used to be an engraver. Jamison lifted the dead man's right hand—it was cold and stiff. He bent down and looked at the fingers. Then he did some matching of facts. Sturdivant had been in this country for many months, and that meant months away from printer's ink. Yet this ink was fresh on his fingers. Not many days old.

Jamison went outside again. He crossed the street to the office of the *Mill Iron Messenger*.

'You want to hire a printer?' he asked the old newspaper man.

The old eyes studied him. 'Mister, you trying to be funny? I ain't got enough work for myself, let alone hiring another man. And they tell me you're a gambler, not a printer.'

'I'm looking for a job for a friend. He's a good man. He's in Denver now, but times are hard—'

'I cain't hire him. I never have hired a man since coming to this burg. This is no newspaper town. Advertisin' is slow.'

'You mean you never have hired a man in the time you've been in Mill Iron? Haven't you ever had a rush and had to put on a hand?'

'Never.'

Jamison said, 'Dull town, sure enough.' He talked a little while longer, with the old man asking questions about the deaths of Westburg and Sturdivant, and Jamison answering. Then he left and went to the Velvet Slipper. Sturdivant had ink on his fingers—fresh ink—and yet he had not worked on the only press in town, down at the *Messenger* shop.

Young Hank was sweeping out their quarters. Jamison sat on the bed and asked, 'Did your dad have a printing press out home?'

The boy stopped sweeping. He looked at Jamison, and his boyish eyes showed doubts as to Jamison's sanity.

'He never had no printin' press, Jamison. He ain't done any printin' since he left the East. What brought on that question?'

Jamison smiled. 'I don't know for sure, son.'

The boy resumed his sweeping. He seemed to have taken the shock well and weathered the storm. Jamison reasoned that the young can pull themselves back together faster than the old.

He wondered what the boy thought. Was there hate in him? Was there desire for revenge? He wondered if Nell Robinson's wise counsel had not done much to straighten out Hank's thinking. He hoped so. Nell, he decided, was a heck of a fine woman.

'Is the inquest over, Jamison?'

'Not over yet, Hank.'

The boy leaned on the broom handle. 'I know what they will bring in. They'll say my dad committed suicide.'

'Just leave it at that,' Jamison asked.

'Then they'll say that Westburg was killed by you, and that you shot to pertect yourself. Self-defence, ain't that the word?'

'Let's hope so.'

'They won't pin a rap on you.'

Jamison leaned on one elbow. 'Why are you so sure, boy?'

The broom made hard and fierce swipes on the floor. 'The Heart Bar Nine ain't askin' the Law to fight their fight, Jamison. They'll ask that you go free and then their guns will talk against you. They don't want you to walk around, because each step you take will be an insult to the Bateman spread.'

'You think of that yourself?'

'Nell an' me talked it over.'

Jamison felt the fingers of unrest pulling at him. He swung his legs off the bunk and stretched.

'We'll see, kid, we'll see.'

The boy watched him leave the room. Jamison crossed the long saloon and went outside. He moved toward the sheriff's office. When he passed the bank, Norman Ridgeway came out.

'Hello, Mr. Jamison.'

Jamison lifted his hat. 'Have you sold the Sturdivant farm yet?'

Ridgeway shook his head. His dark eyes were polished beads under thin dark brows. He rubbed his hawkish nose.

'I'm stuck with it,' he said.

'You might find a sucker,' Jamison replied. 'The world is big and man always moves across it, and some day a man will come who wants it. No matter what a person has that he doesn't want, somebody wants that particular thing.'

'Philosopher, eh?'

Jamison said, 'No, just a plain fool.'

He left the banker there. Ridgeway watched him for a moment and then wheeled and went into the bank. Jamison got the impression the man had deliberately gone out on the sidewalk to have a few words with him.

Into the category of odd people—people against him—
he had to insert the name of Norman Ridgeway. Norman
Ridgeway, banker. . . . Or was he wrong?

The town was quiet and slept under the sun. To the
south the rimrock was dark and long, running its igneous
length against the rise of the hills. Jamison looked north.
There the hills were also stretching out, reaching north
into Canada. There, in that distance, was Wood Mountain.

There arose in Claghorn Jamison at this moment, a
fierce and savage unrest, for he wanted to ride out, to
deal cards in the gold-mad town. But guns held him
here, and they were savage and deadly guns.

Or did the threat of guns hold him?

He knew this was not the case. He had in him a streak
of pride. They had threatened him and had tried to kill
him, and this was what held him—not the fear of guns.
He had analysed this problem down to its innermost
core. There was trouble on this range, and he did not
know the entire nature of this trouble. In other words,
he thought, I don't know just what I face or whom.

He was nearing the sheriff's office when the coroner-
jury came out. The jurors headed for the Velvet Slipper,
for the sheriff had paid them in cash from his own
pocket, and would later get a rebate from the county
funds. They paid no attention to Jamison; their minds
were on beer and bottles. The gambler went around
them and came into Fulton's office.

Sig Lamont loafed, shoulder to the wall, eyes indolent.
He merely nodded and Jamison nodded back, and the
room stiffened. Fulton had his hands laced across his
belly and his up-raised eyes were steer-big and sick.

'Sturdivant was a suicide, Jamison,' the sheriff said.

Jamison nodded.

Lamont rolled a cigarette and it went to his tongue.

He watched Jamison over the cylinder.

'They acquitted you,' the sheriff went on. 'Self-defence, they called it.'

Jamison said, 'No other way out, Sheriff.'

Lamont said, 'That might be so. And it might not be, tinhorn.'

Jamison turned and looked at the range boss. Lamont's eyes were cynical and dull. His gaunt and craggy face was bony and belligerent. From nowhere came a thought, and it touched Jamison, and it asked, Do you some day have to kill this man, Jamison? And Jamison wondered.

Fulton said sharply, 'Watch that gol-darned tongue of yours, Lamont. You heard me.' He had authority.

Jamison saw quick anger cross Lamont's flat face. But the range boss did not speak to the sheriff.

'I'm bailing Mattson out, Jamison.'

Jamison nodded, said nothing. He spoke now to Fulton. 'Then my hands are clean and the Law doesn't want me?'

'That's the deal, Jamison.'

Jamison spoke to Lamont. 'Bail out your two-bit gunman. If he lifts a gun against me—or even looks like he'll draw—I'll do my best to kill him and kill him sudden with one bullet.'

Lamont said nothing.

Fulton looked up, his eyes heavy. 'That will be your duty and privilege, Jamison,' the sheriff intoned.

Jamison thought, This lawman is honest. . . . He looked at Sig Lamont again. The range boss's eyes told volumes, but his lips were a thin line in his leathery face.

Jamison turned and left.

He went toward the bank. Nell Robinson came out of the Mercantile carrying a basket of groceries. 'I've heard about the verdicts, Jamison. That was the only thing the jury could turn in. You'll be with Hank in time for dinner?'

Jamisoon shook his head. 'I want to thank you, Miss Nell, but I've got some riding to do this afternoon.'

'If you're trying to leave for good, say goodbye to the boy. He thinks the sun rises and sets in you.'

'I'll be back later,' Jamison said.

She went on her way. Jamison looked at the sheriff's office. Lamont and Mattson had just come out on to the sidewalk. Mattson looked at him and Jamison watched the gunman. Lamont tugged Mattson's sleeve and they crossed the street. Jamison went into the bank.

'I want to talk to Mr. Ridgeway,' he told the clerk.

CHAPTER TWELVE

RIDGEWAY took off his hat and the wind ruffled his dark hair. Ridgeway said, 'This is a good piece of land, Jamison.'

They were in front of the burned-down Sturdivant cabin. Jamison dismounted, remembering the only other time he had been at this cabin—when he had pulled the dead farmer from the flames. The house was ashes. No printing press reared its ugly head out of the wreckage.

Jamison said, 'I want to look round.'

He walked to the hen-house and the other buildings. They were all small and none hid a printing press. Young Hank, then, had been correct. . . . Jamison looked at what apparently was a root cellar dug into the side of a hill. The cellar had a heavy two-inch plank door.

Jamison said, 'What's that?'

Ridgeway looked at the cellar. 'His root cellar, I guess.'

Jamison walked to the door. For some reason, he had half-expected to see a lock on it; no lock was there, though. He went into the room cut into the side of the Montana hill. The place smelled of earth and vegetables. The smell was clean and earthy and good.

Jamison lit a match.

He saw three bins. One held potatoes, another a few turnips, and the third was empty. No printing press here, either. He shivered, for some unknown reason, and went outside. There was no press on this property. And yet Raleigh Sturdivant had fresh ink on his cold dead hands.

The sun outside felt good. Warm and clean, washing across him, kissing the endless range of hills and valleys.

Jamison stood and let the sun run over him, and he acted like a prospective buyer who might purchase this farm. He had learned what he had come to learn. He had talked Ridgeway into coming with him for two purposes.

First to ride with him to the ranch on the pretence that he was interested in buying the spread. Second to protect him from ambush. With Ridgeway along, there would be less danger of rimrock rifles booming down on him, for he knew that the banker was friendly toward the Heart Bar Nine.

He had ridden deliberately with the banker between himself and the rimrock. He had noticed Ridgeway's deep scowl at one time. The thought came that perhaps the banker understood, too.

'How about it?' Ridgeway asked.

Jamison said, 'Price is too high.'

Ridgeway moved in the saddle, discernment on his dark features. 'Not even what my bank has invested in the property, Mr. Jamison. Well, think it over, sir.'

Jamison went into the saddle. 'I'll see you in a day or so. You might lower your price, too.'

'That I doubt.'

Jamison shrugged. 'Have to be lower if you expect to sell it to me.'

They rode back toward Mill Iron. Jamison apparently was loafing on stirrups, weight on his high leather. But he carefully watched the rimrock. Ridgeway was deep in saddle, and Jamison glanced occasionally at the man. He had tried to pull the banker into conversation. But he had found out nothing about the man's past. Secrecy was a needle stitching the banker's thin lips closed. Rather, Ridgeway had almost openly questioned him. When it came to information, the thought came ironically that Ridgeway was ahead of him.

A jackrabbit squatted in sagebrush, long ears against

his back. He was so close they could see his bulging brown eyes. They saw sagehens, too. Jamison saw the skull of a buffalo, the horns beginning to peel with time. He was warm and silent, and the mystery of the range-lands was in him. He was glad Ridgeway had not spoken. He was glad for silence.

They topped a long ridge, and to the northwest Jamison saw the lazy lift of lazy dust. This hung against the horizon in slow laziness and it marked the western horizon as a cloud marks a flawless sky.

'Cattle moving,' the gambler murmured.

Ridgeway looked at him, then looked at the dust cloud. 'Too early for fall roundup; too late for calf roundup. . . . The wind is playing across the alkali beds, Jamison, and lifting the white dust.'

Jamison nodded. 'That's right,' he said. He became lazy again. He loafed in his kak. Underneath, he did some thinking. Cattle had raised that dust. Either cattle, or milling horses—and the Heart Bar Nine raised dogies, not cayuses. Yet Ridgeway had claimed that the dust came from devil twists walking across the grey of alkali beds. . . .

Why?

Jamison let his thoughts go even further. Yet he had his gaze on the high points, watching and feeling tension within him. Why had Norman Ridgeway lied to him? Or had he lied? Maybe the dust came from the wind, at that.

Jamison looked again. No, he thought, cattle makes that, for it hangs against the sky, and devil twists flare up, turn their savage and short course, and then the dust falls and is gone. Cattle or horses moving toward the north.

Too early for beef roundup. Too late for calf roundup. Then why did cattle move?

G

There came to him a nebulous idea. He had earned his livelihood for years by playing hunches, by tying this fact to that, by reading something into a situation that at the time seemed devoid of implication. Now he did some mental work. He tied into this thing some ink, and he tied into it some dust. He let his mind toil with these two elements, mixing one with the other.

And he came out with nothing concrete. But a hunch was that way—it was dim and formless for some time and then, without warning, the air fell away and the clothes and structure of absolute form took its place. Maybe this hunch would be that way, too.

'Seems odd that a gambler would want to settle down on a farm,' Norman Ridgeway observed.

'I can't ride out of the valley, so I might just as well locate on a farm.'

Ridgeway looked at him and noticed his thin smile. 'I don't follow you, Jamison.'

Jamison smiled. 'I think you do, Ridgeway. I've crossed the Heart Bar Nine. I've killed one of their men. Legally, I'm a free man, but the Heart Bar Nine has its own sets of laws, and I'll have to pay.'

'I doubt that,' Ridgeway said.

'Loyalty is a magnificent virtue,' Jamison reminded him. 'But sometimes it gets in a man's way and he stumbles over it.'

'The Bateman spread has nothing on me,' Norman Ridgeway said.

Jamison said nothing; he merely let the subject go. He wondered how much young Hank Bateman knew about his father. The reasoning came that if the boy knew too much, he might die. There was something sinister and deadly here, and Raleigh Sturdivant had apparently been a part of it. Maybe he had unknowingly handed some danger down to his son.

Jamison decided to talk to Nell Robinson.

They came into town and they left their broncs in the livery. Ridgeway had the air of a man who had been used, and in fact, Jamison had, in a measure, used him. Ridgeway walked out of the barn with, 'See you later, Mr. Jamison,' and Jamison said, 'I'll think it over and let you know.'

Ridgeway went towards his bank.

The old hostler said, 'He looked mad, Jamison.'

Jamison tossed him another five buck gold piece. 'For another headache,' he said. He saw glee enter the old eyes. 'Hie yourself down to the saloon, young man.'

'I'll take care of your horse first, and thanks.'

'Don't thank me,' Jamison said. 'Thank the guy who minted the coin.'

Jamison went to the Silver Slipper. Young Hank was changing clothes in his room.

'Where you been, Jamison?'

'Out to look at your farm. I might buy it.'

The boy said, 'I wish you had stayed in town. They buried Dad and Westburg. The sheriff said they had to work fast in this hot weather.'

'Oh.'

Jamison could say nothing. He sat on his bunk. He had expected them to bury the pair tomorrow. Then he got another suspicion—the medico had said that Westburg had looked as if he had swallowed poison. Maybe they had buried the gunman in a hurry to keep the doc from running an autopsy on him, and then blamed the sudden burial of both men on the clinging heat and being without an undertaker to embalm?

Jamison watched the boy change to his old clothes. Young Hank was very quiet and he had been crying. Jamison walked the floor. The boy watched him. Finally the boy said, 'When I get grown I'm goin' to be a gambler like you, Jamison.'

Jamison stopped. 'If you do I'll come back and beat the tar out of you, Hank.'

The boy said, 'Gotta wash dishes. Nell says to work and work and then a man doesn't think.' He put a hand on the doorknob. 'It's an odd thing, Jamison. Nobody wants anybody to take up the job he's got. Dad never wanted me to be a printer.'

Jamison tried something. 'Your father was away from a press for a long, long time, wasn't he?'

'Yes.'

'He still had ink on his fingers.'

The boy looked at his shoes. 'You know I noticed that, too. Now where did he get that ink, Jamison?'

'Was he away from home much?'

'Nights, about once or twice a month. I don't know where he was or if he slept or gambled or what. You know, he never told me much.'

Jamison nodded.

The boy left. Jamison washed his hands and lay on his bunk and did some thinking. From the saloon proper came the sounds of voices. He had heard those same voices in thousands of other saloons. They had no owners, nor did they need owners—they were merely voices, and they babbled and said nothing.

Jamison slept.

When he awakened, dusk was thick. The room was filled with darkness. He sat up and he felt good; sleep had restored him. The thought came that he would finish this thing, and he would ride out of Milk River—or he would stay here forever. He ate at the lunch counter, and men watched him and eyes touched him. Mattson came in, surly and belligerent, and Mattson eyed him with cold belligerency. But the line was drawn across

Mattson's brain, holding his temper back. Mattson was balancing logic against temper, and logic had won. Mattson was remembering Barney Westburg and how he had fallen. Jamison knew now that Mattson would wait for the dark and an ambush spot.

Jamison ate and took a far seat back to the wall. He watched men come and go, and they wheeled in George Bateman. Bateman looked at him, and he had the open jealousy that a cripple holds for the well. Bateman nodded with a tense curtness. Jamison nodded and smiled.

Bateman wheeled himself to the gambling table, and he got his cards. Jamison watched and waited and wondered where Sig Lamont was. Also, where was Marcia Bateman? Out to her ranch? Jamison thought of the redhead, of her graceful body, her flowing red hair. After a while, he went to the table; he took a seat. He was opposite Bateman, who lost with agonising regularity. About midnight, somebody threw a twenty-dollar paper bill on the table, and Jamison cashed it with a gold piece. He knew, the minute he saw the bill, how ink had got on Raleigh Sturdivant's fingers.

For the bill was counterfeit.

CHAPTER THIRTEEN

LATER that night Jamison studied the bill under lamplight. Only an expert on paper money could ever have detected that the bill was a phony. Jamison, who had gone through the tough school of gambling, knew all the angles—only a man trained as he was trained could have made this discovery.

Young Hank rolled in bed, forearm over his eyes.

'Turn out the lamp, fellow, and let me sleep.'

He turned his back to Jamison.

Jamison extinguished the lamp. Bateman had thrown the bill on the table. That had been the only paper money in the game. Bateman had lost his gold and silver, and this bill had come out of his pocket.

Jamison knew now why they had cut his saddle to pieces and why Mattson and Ridgeway had come to visit him. By accident he had ridden a horse that formerly had belonged to Uncle Sam, and they figured he was a government man. Jamison smiled at this thought.

This had started as a little thing. One point had collided with another, one thought had moved into conjunction with another, and now he had this much information. They had not shot Raleigh Sturdivant because he was a farmer. They had shot him because he was a printer and an engraver—and they were through with him. And if young Hank knew anything about his father's lawlessness, then he would die too. . . . But then logic told Jamison that in that case they would have killed the boy before this.

Young George Bateman had come home from college

when his dad had died. He had been followed by Norman Ridgeway. Then Raleigh Sturdivant had arrived. This much he knew by the old process of keeping his ears open and his eyes wide and his mouth shut.

Three men, tied together—now, only two.

And Sig Lamont, too.

Was the red-head in on this? Jamison gave this matter thought. He lay there in the dark, listening to the boy's deep breathing, listening to the gaunt and far stillness of the dark Montana night. He thought of Marcia Bateman. He thought of her in a slow and detached manner, thinking not in terms of the fact that she was a woman—rather, he thought in symbols, and she was only that, and nothing more. There was still some conflict in his mind. The whole thing, he realised, centred around a town he had never seen, Wood Mountain. There was gold there, and bogus dinero could be passed there, for it was in Canada, and an American dollar was worth twenty-five per cent more than a Canuck buck. This was a cagey scheme. He had blundered into it. Had they left him alone he would have left them alone. But they had run guns against him and they had threatened him and he could not leave. He wondered where their printing press was located. Not at the Sturdivant farm. The afternoon ride had shown him that. The bank was evidently the clearing house. Then maybe the press would be in the rear of the bank? He remembered the low-pulled blinds. Ever since he had been in town the blinds had been down. He added this to what he knew, and he figured he knew the location of the press.

He wondered if he should tell Nell Robinson about his find. Then he realised he did not know her very well and he had best keep his knowledge to himself. She might even be in on the scheme. Still water, so the old legend said, ran deep. And she was still and calm.

He slept.

When daybreak came, Nell again had breakfast for them, and Jamison felt the wild push of unrest.

She said, 'You won about five hundred last night, I believe.'

'You keep track,' he said. 'Five hundred and eight dollars and thirty-five cents, to be exact.'

'Don't be so cynical.'

Jamison felt the tightening of the apron strings. When they got to know you well they started with their feminine wiles. He stood up and bowed from the waist.

'I beg your pardon, Miss Nell. I did not mean to be cynical.'

She jumped to her point. 'I need a good gambler. I offer you the job, Jamison.'

Jamison did not want to hurt her. He did not want to come out flatly and tell her what he thought of this dinky, dusty little burg. He didn't want to tell her he'd rather be dead and buried than to spend time in such a one-horse town.

'I'll think it over,' he murmured.

Young Hank went out. Nell Robinson arose from her chair. Jamison put his hand on her bare forearm.

She didn't move. She looked at him. 'Well?'

'How about that boy?'

Her eyes searched his face. 'I don't quite understand, Jamison.'

Jamison said, 'There's danger here. His father was murdered. He was killed because they had used him and wanted him no longer. Maybe the boy knows something he should not know. They might try to kill him, Nell.'

Her eyes were industrious. They went over him, tested him, felt him, pushed into him. What did they hide? If anything. . . .

'I think you imagine things, sir.'

Jamison shook his head slowly. 'I do not, Miss Nell. Watch him close, please. Do that for him.'

'I don't understand you. Why was his father murdered, as you say he was? And who murdered him and why? Raleigh Sturdivant was only a farmer, Jamison.'

Jamison thought, She doesn't know a thing about this. Either that, or she should be on the stage, legitimate or otherwise.

'Just watch the boy, please.'

She had a puzzled look. Jamison went to the livery barn. A sudden hunch hit him and he turned into the bank. Ridgeway looked up from his desk. He said, 'Good morning, Mr. Jamison,' and he looked down. He had some papers on his desk.

'I'd like to break a twenty-buck gold piece,' Jamison said.

Ridgeway motioned to his teller. Jamison gave the bank the once-over twice. A door led to a rear room. The room with the low-pulled blinds. Jamison got four five-dollar pieces and thanked the clerk and started to leave.

Ridgeway asked, 'Made up your mind?'

'No sale,' Jamison said.

Ridgeway nodded. His eyes were small and his darkness showed through. 'Sorry, Mr. Jamison.'

Jamison got his bronc and rode out of Mill Iron. The northern hills were shimmering under sunlight. The rimrock stretched along them, dark and igneous, and Jamison knew for sure they had riders posted there. Bateman had made a slip. Or had he intentionally thrown out that bogus bill?

Either way, it was part of their plan.

Jamison lifted his horse to a trot, eyes on the rimrock. Noon was on the land, hot and close, when he rode into the Heart Bar Nine. No guard challenged, but he knew there were guards; he rode to the hitch-rack in front of the long house and went down.

Sig Lamont moved out of his foreman's shack. Behind him Jamison saw Mattson, standing in the doorway. Lamont said, 'Something you want, gambler?' and his tone was not pleasant.

'Talk to George Bateman.'

'He's still in town. At the hotel.'

Jamison knew that, but he acted ignorant. He said, 'Well, I'll be darned,' and then he looked at the door of the ranch house. Again, he got the impression of her beauty, and the dressing robe she wore, pulled close to her, only enhanced this beauty.

'What do you want to see my brother about?' Marcia Bateman asked.

Jamison's hat came down. He looked at Sig Lamont. For a moment the man's guard was down, and his love and longing for Marcia showed in his eyes.

'Our business,' Jamison said.

She said, 'Come in,' and Jamison entered the long room. Flagstone floor, an immense flagstone fireplace, and beams coloured by time and oil. He took a seat by a big window. She did not let Lamont enter. She said, 'All right, what do you want to see him about?'

'I said,' Jamison repeated patiently, 'that it is our business, and nobody else's. But it concerns a twenty-dollar bill he gave me last night in a poker game.'

'A twenty-dollar bill. . . . What do you mean?'

Jamison shrugged. 'I needed a ride, to limber my muscles. I wanted to look at a lovely woman. A piece of paper money is very rare here in Montana. Across the Line I understand it is paper and very little gold. I thought he might like to buy the bill back, for plainly he was keeping it as a good luck piece. Or so I would guess.' He got to his feet. 'But maybe I rode out to see a pretty red-head, and kept the bill just as an alibi.'

He was smiling.

She wasn't.

She seemed puzzled.

Jamison said, 'But I can sell you the bill.'

She shook her head. 'That's his business.'

Jamison shrugged. 'All right,' he said. 'All right.'

He went to the door. She followed him. 'Sometimes I doubt your good sense,' she said.

Jamison agreed. 'So do I—sometimes.'

The yard was without humans. A calf bawled in a corral. A chicken cackled over a new egg.

Jamison said, 'Good day, madam.'

'What you have to settle with my brother is his business and your business, and is none of mine.'

Jamison mounted. 'With that attitude, you'll make some man a wonderful wife.'

'But not you.'

Jamison essayed surprise. 'Why, the thought never entered my little head, Miss Bateman. I'm glad you brought it to me.'

He was in saddle. He glanced at the window. There was a flower bed below it. Bootmarks were in the soft earth. He had done his duty. He had performed what he had ridden out here to bring about. She was not the only Heart Bar Nine person who had heard about the twenty-dollar bill.

Jamison turned his bronc.

He glanced back once as he entered the timber along the creek. She was entering the house. He glanced at Lamont's cabin. Lamont watched from the window. Then the cottonwood trees hid the house.

Jamison let his horse hit a running-walk. The heat was too great to make an animal hurry. Jamison thought of the red-head. She had not offered to buy back the bogus currency. That meant, then, she did not know about this counterfeiting. Had she known, she would have wanted the bill in her hands. But she had not wanted it. Her brother was in on this mess. Apparently she was not. Lamont would be in on it, too. He associated with Ridgeway. Lamont knew now about the bill. Jamison did some reasoning. Maybe Bateman had had orders not to pass the currency on this range. But he had passed it.

He and Bateman were both in danger. Bateman, for passing the bill; he, for letting Lamont know he had it. Lamont was no fool. He would know why he, Jamison, had ridden to the Heart Bar Nine.

Throw a red flag in a bull's face, Jamison, and the bull will go wild.

He apparently was riding for Mill Iron town. But, once in the hills, he did some fancy work; he cut back and he headed northwest. There were complications to this thing, and Lamont and Ridgeway held the strings, he knew. George Bateman could not ride range. A bullet —a farmer's bullet—had put him out of commission. The Heart Bar Nine had an enormous range. Tumbling miles and miles of grass. A man in a wheel-chair cannot ride. So then what does he do? He trusts his foreman.

Jamison remembered dust. Dust, lying long and low against the far hills. Cattle moving? Devil twists on alkali beds?

Maybe.

Jamison rode toward that dust.

CHAPTER FOURTEEN

NORMAN RIDGEWAY stopped and looked at Sig Lamont. 'So he rode right out to the Heart Bar Nine—big as life and twice as tough—?'

'And he offered to sell her a twenty-buck bill,' the range boss said.

Ridgeway stopped walking and put his jaw in his hand. For a moment there was no sound but the clock on the desk. 'What does it all add up to, Sig?'

Lamont had his boots on the desk. His spurs were digging into the varnished surface. He knew that Ridgeway did not want him to put his boots on the desk. So he did it just to make the man mad.

'He's a gover'ment man, like we figured. Bateman got so mad from losing so steady he pulled out this bogus bill. Either that, or he forgot.'

'Could have been either.'

Ridgeway continued his pacing. He put his hands behind his back. He looked at the ceiling. Lamont watched him and had his thoughts. The time had come for George Bateman to go. He had outlived his usefulness. Sig Lamont thought of the man in the wheel-chair. He thought of him in a detached and irrelevant manner, as a man thinks about a steer going to slaughter and how much he will bring in beef, tallow and hide. . . .

'Where is Jamison now?' the banker asked.

Lamont said, 'He drifted north, so the scout said. Maybe he might try to run the blockade. We'll get reports back later, I figure.'

'You having him trailed?'

'I had a man on him. But the man got turned back in the badlands. Bullets. Rifle bullets.'

'Suspicious cuss all the way, eh?'

'Uncle Sam's man,' Lamont said.

Ridgeway sat on the edge of the table. He pushed Lamont's boots off the desk. The range boss's justins hit the floor with a bang. Lamont leaned forward in his swivel chair, and he controlled his anger.

'A man of quick decision,' Sig Lamont murmured.

Ridgeway said, 'And I can use a gun when and if the occasion demands.' He grew thoughtful, his face darker than usual. Lamont's dull grey eyes watched and showed nothing.

Lamont said, 'I tried to get rid of Bateman. I flopped. The time has come, Ridgeway. He goes.'

'We don't need him any longer.'

Lamont got to his feet. He brushed his knees. 'Mattson and me will tend to him. He's' in the hotel, I reckon.'

'He's in the same room he had yesterday.'

'We'll fix him—for good.'

'How?'

Lamont smiled. 'Like we fixed Westburg. We got some more coyote poisonin'. We know how to use it.'

Ridgeway nodded.

Lamont stopped at the door. 'There's another one I'm afraid of. He might know too much.'

Ridgeway looked at him. 'Who?'

'The boy.'

'Young Sturdivant?'

Sig Lamont nodded. 'The same. His old man might have told him about this currency.'

'We kill him and the range will go wild. They'll rise up and gun against us, Sig. He's just a kid.'

'He might know. If he does, he goes.' Lamont was

determined. 'And nobody need know how he went or who did it.'

'We'll talk that over later. Where the blazes is this Jamison gent?'

'Maybe jes' ridin' out for the heck of it.'

'Wonder where he is?'

'You said that before. The cattle move tonight. I'd planned to help move them to Wood Mountain. The red-head had planned to go, too. But I'll stay here. Keep an eye on Jamison. The danger is here; not on the Line.'

'Marcia going?'

'I don't know. I don't care. But George Bateman has to go, Ridgeway. And the time is now.'

'I'd still give my eyeteeth to know where Jamison is.'

'He can't run out. Our rimrock guns will turn him back. He's as good as dead now. He knows it, I guess. He'll have to gun his way out of this, and we got too many against him.'

'Maybe.'

'No maybe about it. He's a goner.'

Ridgeway nodded and said nothing. Sig Lamont went out the door that led to the alley. He glanced at the drawn blinds. Mattson moved out of a shadow and asked, 'Well, Sig?'

'George. He goes.'

'Now?'

'Yes, now.'

Mattson fell into step; they went down the alley. Dust and gravel ground on boots, spurs made their music, leather gear creaked.

'Wonder where he is?' Mattson asked.

'Who do you mean by *he*?'

'This gink Jamison.'

At that moment, Jamison was on a high hill. Hidden by underbrush and wild service berry bushes, he was watching an interesting scene. Cattle were on the flat below him. He could see them clearly, and the smell of their sweat and dust came to him. He heard their low distant mooing.

He had his field-glasses from his saddle-case. He focused them and brought the heard in close. He read the brand: Heart Bar Nine. Fat steers, all of them; good beef. A beef herd. . . . And why a beef herd at this time of the year?

He could get only one answer.

They were going to be moved north into Canada. They were going to run the Canadian Line and make beef for miners in Wood Mountain. This much he knew. Was Lamont stealing his home outfit's cattle? While George Bateman was gambling, and while Bateman was tied to a wheel-chair, did Sig Lamont and Mattson steal Bateman cattle?

Was Marcia in on this thievery?

He had figured, for some time, that the brother and sister had split, for little indications had pointed in that direction. He spent the rest of the day on the hill. About dusk Marcia Bateman rode out. She got the crew to work pointing the cattle toward Canada.

Dust rose and cattle bawled and horns clashed. Jamison figured the herd consisted of about two hundred head. Maybe more. He was no judge of cattle. He knew cards, and he knew men, but there were two things he did not know—one, cattle; two, women. And this woman was a riddle.

She did not go with the herd. She had two men to haze them north. Then she wheeled her sorrel and loped back toward the Heart Bar Nine Ranch. Jamison had a hunch: he would angle in and intercept her and talk to her. . . . But to do so would tip his hand, he knew.

He stayed on the hill until the cattle were out of sight.

Then he looked toward the Heart Bar Nine home ranch.
He could not see Marcia. Dusk had come in; it held to
the grass, it quieted the earth. This was the hour of
peace, the hour when the sun became lost, when the
world started to lose its strict heat. At this hour, the
world was calm; earth prepared for the night. Still, there
was no peace—not on this grass, at least.

Jamison went to his horse and he wondered if George
Bateman knew about this rustling. He knew that a fierce
and savage pride in the Heart Bar Nine was in the gun-
crippled man. Sheriff Jones Fulton had told him that.
Fulton had swivelled his moist and ox-like eyes, and he
had told of the pride Bateman had had in his dead
father, how he worked and fought to keep the outfit
running and strong. From what Fulton had said, Jamison
figured that never would Bateman let Sig Lamont—yes,
and his sister—run prime Heart Bar Nine cattle across
the Line. For they would not draw top prices there. The
Canucks knew they were illegal cattle, and the Canucks
could buy at their own price—a Mountie always rode
in the background. . . .

He decided he would talk with Bateman. He would
bargain one point against the other, and maybe he could
ride out. For Jamison knew that superior guns faced
him. He knew ambush was nothing on this range. The
murder of Raleigh Sturdivant had told him that. There
were two games—two dangerous games—being played
here. Stolen beef, and bogus paper money.

He had half-expected to see either Sig Lamont or
Mattson hazing the cattle. But neither had ridden north
with the herd. Where were they? He let his thoughts
dwell on Mattson. Where was the killer?

He did not know that, at that particular moment,
Mattson and Sig Lamont were in Banker Norman Ridgeway's office, a whiskey bottle on the desk and three

H

glasses around it. Ridgeway drank sparingly. Lamont barely touched his whiskey. But Mattson seemed to have found a great ally, a wonderful friend, in John Barleycorn.

'To the dead,' Mattson toasted.

Lamont said, 'Watch it, Mattson.'

Mattson looked at him. 'They walk across my dreams. They kick at my sleeping carcass. I meet a beautiful woman and she turns into a man I have killed. God in heaven, what a man does to pervert his life!'

Lamont smiled. 'You're not ruined yet. You still have never been married. You've shown some sense.'

'I wonder,' Mattson said. 'I wonder.'

Mattson leaned back; his chair spring squeaked. He had a happy, satisfied feeling. Part of it was caused by the whiskey. He was a big shot, seated in a banker's chair; he walked and talked with kings. George Bateman was dead. Blue he was, for the poison had turned him that colour; still, he was dead. No more cards could be held in those fingers, no more curses could be spewed from the blued lips. He, Mattson, had a hundred bucks —in gold, too. He had a future. He did some remembering. Flies buzzed against panes. The air was drowsy and the air was good.

Mattson said, 'His guard—he was gone— We came in, and he was in his chair, and his back was toward us, and he said, "Thet you, Smoky?" 'cause he figured we was the guard. We wasn't the guard though, eh, Sig?'

'For blazes' sake, shut your mouth!'

Mattson studied Ridgeway. 'Lamont has chicken nerves. He's cute and purty but his nose doesn't like gunsmoke. Well, we come in then. I gets him from the back—both hands over his eyes—and he kicks. He opens his big mouth to yell, and Brother Lamont goes to work.'

'Forget it, Mattson!'

'He's still got itchy boots, Ridgeway. Mother Lamont's youngest son Sig gets tired easy. The gunsmoke is ahead, Sig. Buck up. So he gets a spoonful of this coyote poison in his mug. Afore he knows it, he's swallowed it. I just hang on to his eyes.'

There was a silence. Only the flies broke it. They tried to push out the pane. They had tried it for days. They never learned.

'I jes' latch on to him like he was my ornery long-lost brother,' Mattson went on. 'You know, Lamont timed him, right to the second. How many seconds till he went limp on us, Sig?'

'Sixty-three,' Lamont said.

Mattson turned his glass. The ring it made on the desk fascinated him. He stared at it.

'Little over a minute. From here to across the bar, and I don't mean the one in a saloon. Didn't somebody once write somethin' about somebody crossin' a bar?'

'He didn't mean a saloon either,' Ridgeway pointed out.

'Tennyson,' Lamont said.

Ridgeway turned sharply and stared at the range boss. 'By Hades, you knew—you knew. You surprise me.'

Lamont showed anger. 'I can surprise you other ways, fellow,' he said with meaning. 'Bateman is out of this. Dead, a carcass. But what about this Claghorn—cripes, what a handle—Jamison?'

Mattson said, 'My meat, Sig. My pork chop. My sirloin. Name the time and place—and slip me five hundred. Dust, not that no-good dinero.'

'Later,' Sig Lamont murmured.

Mattson looked at him. 'Why later?'

'The time,' said Lamont, 'isn't here yet.'

Mattson scoffed. 'You're a stupid fool, Sig,' he said.

'The time is here—but you ain't got sense enough to know it.'

They glared at each other. Two wolves bound together by synthetic friendship, their union cemented by necessity and not by honour. They circled each other, ears back; their fangs clicked.

Ridgeway came in and held them apart. 'Don't be a couple of fools,' he panted angrily. 'Save your guns for the enemy!'

That held them apart.

CHAPTER FIFTEEN

Jamison pulled off his boot. Somebody knocked at the door. Jamison held the boot and said, 'Come in.'

His gun lay beside him on the bed.

The door opened and Nell Robinson came in. She closed the door and stood with her back to it, her left hand on the knob.

Jamison asked, 'Where's the boy?'

There was something about her manner, her quietness, that disturbed him. She seemed to be holding back a secret.

'The boy?' Jamison demanded. 'He all right?'

She nodded. 'He went over to visit with a friend. Jamison, you imagine things—who would hurt him, and why?'

Jamison skipped that point. 'What's on your mind, Nell?'

'Bateman. George Bateman.'

Jamison watched her. A devilishness came into him. 'What about him, Nell? You aim to marry him or something drastic?'

'He's dead.'

Jamison dropped the boot. It hit the pine floor with a sharp sound. Jamison spent a moment looking down at the boot. But he was not interested in the boot. He had his thoughts.

The boot was only a camouflage.

The gambler looked up. 'What happened to him?'

She spoke quietly and slowly. Behind her a man made noises in the saloon. Jamison thought, They'll holler from

here to eternity. . . . The minute a man is born his big
mouth goes open. He listened to her words.

'He was alone in his hotel room. Smoky was out—
Smoky is his man, you know. He wheels him around
and takes care of him. Well, Smoky came back. George
Bateman was dead in his wheel-chair.'

'Suicide?'

She shook her head. 'He suffered no bullet wound. He
was just—well, dead. Doc examined him. Doc said his
heart had kicked out. He was a young man, too. But I
guess a person never knows what his inside looks like.'

Jamison picked up the boot. He put it on. He had forgotten his hot and aching feet. This added something
new to the whole thing. Bateman was out of this for
good and always. And why?

Because of a bogus twenty-buck bill?

Jamison wondered about that. Two men had died
under mysterious circumstances. Barney Westburg first;
now, George Bateman. Or had the man—or the men
—died a natural death? Jamison remembered the
imprint of boots in the flower bed out at the Heart Bar
Nine. Either Mattson or Sig Lamont had hunkered there
and had listened under the window.

He asked further questions. Had anybody been seen
entering Bateman's hotel room? Nobody had. But what
did that have to do with a man who had suffered what
was apparently a heart attack? Jamison asked no more
questions. She was not involved in this; he was sure of
that.

The thought came that she was the one clean person,
outside of young Hank. Jamison felt at this moment a
sort of kinship toward her. Not because he was clean of
this, for he was not—he had shot and Westburg had
fallen, and now the gunman lay in his grave. But she was
clean and good and strong, and she was made of brittle

and clean dust. Jamison stood up and said, 'Too bad.'
He looked at her sharply. 'What about his sister?'

'Marcia?'

'Yes, what about her? She's lost her father and
mother. George was her only close living relative, was
he not?'

'He was. She'll get along.'

Jamison asked, 'Was there ever one woman who liked
another?'

'Let's not go into philosophy.'

Jamison followed her into the saloon. He glanced at
a gambling table and its green top, and the thought
came that George Bateman had not a bit of interest in
cards at the present. He felt a feeling of loss, for the
man had been a rather good poker player, one who
used logic and not hunches. But he had felt this same
emotion upon losing other good players either by death
or because they moved to another table. And this feeling
soon left.

He went to the sheriff's office.

Fulton was big in his chair; he filled the seat; he
overflowed the arms. He raised his great shaggy head,
and suffering was in the lines of his bloated ugly face.
His hands were laced across his gigantic belly.

'My belly—it hurts. All the time, it hurts. Jamison,
what the devil is inside of a man like me?'

'I don't know what is inside myself.'

'Doc don't know, either. Or if he knows, he won't say.'
He lowered his steer-thick eyes. 'Bateman is over the
Ridge. He's on the other side. About this time one of the
Celestial Clerks is signing his name on the Supernal
Ledger. Then the other clerks will look up his records.'

Jamison nodded.

'Wonder if a man has a few days to look around?
Once back East I started to a college. Gonna be a smart

gink, poor dumb me. They gave us something they called
"orientation". Took us around the campus for a few
days to kinda get our horns rubbed off an' a smell of the
new pasture.'

Again, Jamison nodded.

'Wonder if they do that across the Ridge, Jamison?'

Jamison shrugged. 'I can only guess. We'll know
some day—soon. But what about Bateman, Sheriff?'

The head lifted. Momentarily pain left before the
push of curiosity. 'What about him?'

'He's dead, they tell me.'

'Heart attack. In his room. But you've heard the
details, I suppose?'

'I have.'

'Heart attack,' the lawman repeated.

Jamison moved toward the door. 'What if it wasn't a
heart attack?' he asked.

The head went down. Did the sick man want to hide
his eyes and facial expression? Jamison wished he knew.
The gambler watched the lawman. There were a few
moments without words. Outside, a horse neighed, and
the sound was shrill and keen. A man called to another,
and the sound of the horse was clean against the vile
cursing of the human. This registered dully on Claghorn
Jamison.

'What do you mean, Jamison?'

'You know what I mean. Somebody might have murdered him. He was helpless from the belly down and
they could have strangled him.'

'They could have, but they didn't. Doc says heart
trouble. And if *they* were to strangle him, who the blazes
is *they*—and why would *they* kill him?'

Jamison thought, He's either out of this, or a darned
good actor. He shrugged, said, 'Just a thought.'

'Better keep such thoughts to yourself.'

Jamison controlled his anger. 'A warning, Sheriff?'

This time the immense head lifted. The eyes were dull and watery in red sockets. 'Not a warning, Jamison. Merely a suggestion. Why, I couldn't punch my way out of a Sioux tepee.'

Jamison smiled.

The sheriff watched him. Jamison watched the lawman. Jamison almost told him then about the bogus bill and the stolen herd going north. *Stolen herd*? Yes, stolen from a dead man, George Bateman.

'How will her brother's death hit Marcia?'

'I don't think it will faze her, Jamison. George was a holy terror. Still, he loved that ranch—he had a fierce, savage pride in it. Heaven help a man who had stolen a Heart Bar Nine steer—if George Bateman could have got his hands on him. He'd kill him with his bare fists.'

Yes, Jamison thought, stolen beef.

'What will she do?' Jamison was persistent.

'Nothing. Just keep on running the spread. Why do you ask so many questions?'

'My father,' said Jamison, 'was a newspaper reporter.'

Fulton lowered his head. 'My blasted belly,' he said painfully.

Jamison felt a sort of pity for this lawman. He was convinced by now that Fulton was honest. He knew that the safe-keeping of this town and this country had long been entrusted to this man's hands. Fulton's belly throbbed and ached, but his real pain was mostly mental.

Jamison left, closing the door slowly. Dusk was moving in, touching the hills, bathing the cottonwood trees. He went toward the Velvet Slipper Saloon. When he was passing the doctor's office the medico called to him.

'Come in, sir.'

Jamison went into a room becoming dark. The medico had a cot in his office and he lay on it against the far dark wall. Jamison could hardly make out the man's outlines and he could not see the man's face.

The room smelled of medicants. Chloroform and iodine and other smells. Jamison did not like the smells. He did not like the closed and dark atmosphere of the room. For some reason it reminded him of a tomb.

'What do you want to see me about, Doctor?'

'George Bateman is dead.'

'So I've heard.' Jamison stood in the dusk and gave this thought. 'Heart attack?'

'He turned blue,' the doctor said. 'A kind of a greenish blue.'

'The same as Westburg?'

'The same.'

Jamison asked, 'After a heart attack does a body normally turn bluish-green, medico?'

'No.'

'What does it mean?'

'Not a thing,' the doctor said. He sat up, and now Jamison got another smell—the odour of whiskey. 'Want a snort, gambler?'

'Never drink it.'

'I never touch it myself, Jamison. I drink it so fast it never touches me.' The medico laughed at his joke.

Jamison thought, Bateman was poisoned. He wanted to say it right out, to come out in absolute terms, but he's afraid. . . . Or am I reading something into all this? But he had some reason for calling me. . . .

Jamison said, 'Good evening, sir.'

'Watch your back, Jamison.'

Jamison spoke seriously. 'Thanks for the warning.'

The man drank and wiped his lips. 'Warning? I don't follow you.'

Jamison smiled and went outside. He stood outside the door and gave the town a slow and careful scrutiny.

He looked at the Mercantile, the Saddle Shop, and at the Velvet Slipper Saloon. Two boys came out between two buildings, and he recognised young Hank Sturdivant. Young Hank hollered, 'Hello, Jamison,' and Jamison answered. Still, the gambler watched.

Two horses—Heart Bar Nine horses—stood tied to a hitch-rack. Jamison knew they belonged to Sig Lamont and Mattson, for Nell Robinson had so told him. He looked at the bank. Lamont had come out of the door, and he stood long and tall in the dusk, and Jamison saw that the man watched him. Lamont was about fifty yards away. Lamont said nothing; Jamison said nothing. There was something sinister here, something unravelling; Jamison knew it concerned him. Lamont leaned against the bank and took out his bandana and wiped his forehead; the air now was cool.

This gesture, out of place in the coolness of the evening, was a warning to Claghorn Jamison.

Jamison wheeled, and he faced the Velvet Slipper Saloon.

CHAPTER SIXTEEN

MATTSON had come out of Nell Robinson's saloon. He saw Jamison and he moved out of the doorway. He was thin and crouched; the dusk hid his face. But his intent and purpose was there for all to see.

There was this—and the silence.

Jamison walked out two paces. Somebody hollered then, and the sound was high, and it was a siren luring people out of houses and stores. They came out and there were not many of them, and each knew the other's secrets, for this town was only a pinpoint on the sweep of the prairie.

Behind him Jamison heard the doctor move in his office. He heard steel click and he realised the man had put a cartridge into a rifle barrel. He was aware of the medico in the doorway. He did not turn his head, for his eyes were on Mattson; he felt the proximity of the medical man.

'For me, the rifle? Or for Sig Lamont?'

'For fair play,' the man said.

Down at the sheriff's office, a man had come rushing in, but Fulton could not make it out of his chair very quickly. The man helped him, and the sheriff stood up. He stood there and he listened to the snarl of the guns. He heard three shots, and they came together as one. Then their echo died and a voice cried, 'He got Mattson! And Mattson started to pull first! He put two bullets through Mattson's black heart! Hey, are you shot, gambler?'

Fulton got to the door then. He moved outside, and

the planks creaked, and he carried his bulk ahead, and
his gun was in his hand. He came first to the medico
and he said, 'Put that rifle away, you drunken fool of a
quack!'

'Sig Lamont,' the medico said. 'I'm watching him.'

Fulton wheeled and stabbed a glance at Sig Lamont.
Norman Ridgeway had come out of the bank and he
was behind the Heart Bar Nine range boss. And it was
to the banker that Sheriff Fulton spoke.

'Watch Lamont, Norman.'

'Okay, Sheriff.'

He was sick, and the worms would soon dine, but he
mastered this situation. He wheeled his gaze from the
gunman and looked at the medico. 'Put that Winchester
on its hooks. It might go off and kill you.'

'That would be all right with me.'

'Put it away!'

Again, he spoke with authority. And the doctor
obeyed. Then the sheriff looked at the man who lay on
the sidewalk, up ahead of Claghorn Jamison who stood
with his back against the wall, looking at both Ridgeway
and Lamont.

'Mattson jump you, gambler?'

Jamison said, 'He pulled first,' and his voice, despite
his efforts, was shaky. His fingers were still, but the flesh
along his right forearm twitched and jumped. He shifted
his gun to his holster. Still, his forearm jumped.

The sheriff said, 'Stand where you are.'

Jamison stood there, and he looked across the street
at young Hank Sturdivant, who came across the dust
and stood beside him.

The boy said, 'Friend, did you get hit?'

Jamison shook his head. He put his hand down and
found the boy's. He thought of his own boy. It would
be hard to leave the boy behind. Then the ironic thought

came that perhaps he might not go. As a matter of fact, he had been lucky to come out of this alive.

He watched Sig Lamont. He watched Norman Ridgeway. They stood close together, and they were bound together—this he knew. Fulton went to one knee and he knelt beside Mattson, and his breathing was coarse and animal as it whistled through his wide nostrils.

'Jamison, come here.'

Jamison said, 'Okay, Sheriff.'

Hank went with him. They stopped and Fulton looked up, his breath hacking. 'He's dead,' he said. 'One bullet, through the high ribs. You shot twice?'

'I did.'

'One missed, then.' Fulton got to his feet with an effort. Still, he breathed deeply. 'Your first one must have hit him.'

Jamison asked, 'Can I look him over?'

The question puzzled the sheriff. He turned his heavy eyes on Jamison and looked at him.

'Go ahead,' he said at length.

Jamison knelt and went through the dead man's pockets. From the bank Ridgeway watched; Sig Lamont watched; the town watched. Jamison came out of one side pocket with a poke. He untied the buckskin sack and poured out gold and put the gold under the sheriff's' nose.

'You have gold around here—free gold?'

'None that I know of.'

Jamison poured the gold back into the sack. His hands were steady now. He said, so only the sheriff would hear, 'That came from the gold fields across the Canuck Border—from Wood Mountain.'

'How do you know?'

'It was either traded for stolen cattle—or for counterfeit money.' Jamison tied the sack neck together; the long buckskin thongs hung free. He said, 'He was paid this to try to kill me.'

There was only the breathing of Fulton—heavy and dead and shrill. Only this, and Lamont, standing there, watching, waiting, playing his cards close.

Yes, and banker Norman Ridgeway.

'You're crazy,' Fulton said throatily. 'You pistol-whipped him and he wanted his revenge. You knocked him cold with your six-shooter and he wanted to build up his rep. again.'

'He was paid,' Jamison said flatly.

Fulton looked at him, and then the sheriff wet his lips. 'What are you hiding from me, Jamison?'

Jamison did not answer. He swung the poke, holding on to the buckskin tie-thongs. The thongs were solid to the poke. He turned and went to where Sig Lamont stood. He carried the poke in his right hand, letting it swing from the straps. He moved toward Lamont. Lamont watched him come; the town watched, too. The town wondered what was going to happen, and why— but Lamont knew. This knowledge put a sharp thin light in his dull eyes.

Behind Lamont stood Ridgeway. The banker wet his lips, and Jamison noticed the gesture; his smile was slow and easy. He came up to Lamont, and then he stopped about a yard away. He let the poke hang at his side. Its belly was thick and heavy with gold dust.

Jamison said, 'You sent him against me, you two.' He made it a mere statement. He watched only Lamont. 'You paid him in dust and then had him match his gun against mine.'

'Dust?' Lamont asked.

'Yes. Gold dust.'

Ridgeway moved and settled down. He had stepped from behind Lamont. Lamont noticed this and his scowl was a savage groove across his forehead. Ridgeway stopped and became compact.

'Where would I get gold dust?' Lamont asked.

'Canada,' Jamison said. 'Wood Mountain.'

Lamont's nostrils moved in and out. 'You talk like a fool,' he said slowly. 'I'm a cowman, not a miner.'

'A gunman,' Jamison corrected him.

Jamison had himself in hand by now. The shock had left and the memory of the roaring guns was falling back. Later, in the still of darkness, it would return to him; he would fight his inner battle then, not now. The press of action was pushing these thoughts into the discard.

'Don't rub my fur, Jamison.'

Jamison swung the poke. It made a sharp hard arc and it hit Lamont across the jaw. Too late the gunman tried to lift an arm for protection. The heavy gold hit him solidly, like a thick fist coming out of nowhere. It dropped him and he sat down, his back to the bank. He was stunned and sick, and his illness was not only physical; it was mental. The town had seen this gambler out-guess him and knock him to the sidewalk. And the town would talk and look at him in derision.

Fulton moved in, and he had Sig Lamont's .45. Fulton stuck the gun under his wide belt and stood there and watched. Lamont said nothing. He held his jaw and sanity came to his eyes.

Lamont started to rise.

Fulton said, 'Keep sittin', Sig.'

Sig Lamont looked at the lawman. He sat there. He swung his gaze over to Claghorn Jamison. But the gambler was looking at Norman Ridgeway. The banker was a little taken aback. One minute his gunman had stood solid and big; the next, he was sprawling on the worn plank sidewalk.

'You moving in on this?' Jamison asked of Ridgeway.

Ridgeway shook his head. Shock had left and a sly craftiness had taken its place.

'Not my fight,' the banker said.

Jamison said meaningly, 'Are you sure?'

'You talk in riddles.'

'You understand me,' Jamison replied.

'You still talk in circles, gambler.'

Jamison said, 'This afternoon I rode the hills. I had a run-in with a rifleman. His job was to keep me from leaving the Milk River valley. Are you sure that rifleman wasn't under your orders, Ridgeway?'

'Not my gunman, gambler.'

Claghorn Jamison looked at Sig Lamont. 'Maybe he was acting under your orders, Lamont?'

Lamont got to his boots. He said, 'You're crazy in the head,' and he got his gun from Fulton, who had unloaded it. 'You don't make friends fast, Jamison. And you've made no friend out of me.'

Jamison said, 'I knew that—from the minute I saw you. I'm sick and tired of your dinky, dirty little town. You've penned me in with your guns, but I'm getting out real soon!'

Fulton said, 'What's behind this, men?'

Nobody supplied any information. The obese lawman was in the dark and he was reaching out; his fingers touched nothing but darkness. He was getting riled and this showed through his eternal pain. It touched his jowls and made them hanging bunches of muscle.

'When you feel lucky—' Lamont said.

Jamison said, 'Any time, any time.'

There was nothing more to say. All had been said. Jamison turned and said to the sheriff, 'Another inquest, huh?' and Fulton said, 'Tomorrow morning, Jamison.' Fulton sighed then, and pain took over again. 'My big old belly has a red knife in it.'

Jamison went down the street. They had taken Matt-son to the makeshift morgue. Somebody had thrown a bucket of cold water over the blood on the planks. A broom made vigorous sweeps across the splintery surface, washing away the last physical traces of a drifting gun-man named Mattson. It occurred to Claghorn Jamison that, to the best of his knowledge, he had never heard Mattson's given name.

But he did not dwell long on this fact. It was mean-ingless and without import. Hank Sturdivant came in close to him and said, 'Nell has coffee ready for you, Mr. Jamison.'

'Thanks, Hank.'

They walked into the Velvet Slipper. The few occu-pants regarded Jamison with casual glances, but curiosity was uppermost in their minds, if not in their eyes. Jami-son and the boy crossed the long room with its gaming tables and long bar. They came to the door to the woman's apartment, and Jamison lifted his knuckles against the panel.

'Come in, boys.'

He went into her kitchen and saw that she looked pretty wearing a housedress and apron. The mystery of this dark-haired woman was a deep and stirring thing. She could run a saloon, deal out drinks, gamble with the best; still she was essentially a woman—there was softness about her, a tender femininity. Jamison stood and looked at her and had his thoughts. She would eventually find her man, and they would live a good life—but he was not that man. He had one woman and he had lost her because of a clash of wills, and one had been enough.

She said, 'Sit down.'

Hank said, 'I don't want coffee.'

'You may go,' she said.

He left then. Jamison found a chair and pulled it

close to the table. He played with the edges of the table-cloth. 'Did you crochet this, Miss Nell?'

'Yes.'

He looked around the kitchen. Spotless. He looked back at her. Suddenly he put his head on his arms on the table.

She came over, and he felt her stroke his hair. She said, 'Take it easy. Nerves are tough creatures, at times.'

Jamison kept his head down.

Her hand stroked his hair. 'Men are like boys—sometimes. Remember when you were a kid? How you wanted to grow up and be big and walk proud and tough and make your mark? I was that way. I never knew that even when I was big, sometimes I could and would still cry in the night.'

Jamison lifted his head, his nerves under control. She looked at him and then went to the stove and returned with the coffee pot. She poured his cup and said, 'A spiker?'

Jamison shook his head. 'Thanks just the same.'

The coffee made him feel better. She poured her cup and sat opposite him.

'What is this all about, Jamison?'

Jamison shook his head. 'You'll probably know soon, Miss Nell,' he said. He reached for a piece of toast.

'I'll butter it for you,' she said.

CHAPTER SEVENTEEN

JAMISON stood with his back against the wall. Lamplight glistened off the mirror and there was a faint perfume in the room. Jamison stood there, and then the door opened and she entered.

She wore a dressing gown. The belt was tight around her thin waist and her red hair was almost to her belt. She stopped and looked at him. He had figured she would be surprised. But she was not surprised. Her eyes were tired and bitter, and they did not belong in a face so young and beautiful.

'Well, Jamison,' Marcia Bateman said.

'I came in through the window. I wanted to talk to you—alone. I slugged your guard and tied him down. I gagged him.'

'You tell me nothing I have not already guessed.'

'Your brother is dead.'

'I know that. I was dressing to go to Mill Iron to claim his body.'

'Heart attack?'

'The doctor said so.'

Jamison shook his head.

She asked, 'What do you mean?'

'You know what I mean, Miss Marcia. Right now a Heart Bar Nine herd is moving north. It's going to Wood Mountain in Canada and there it'll be sold for beef for the miners. Stolen beef. Beef run across the Line against the laws of the U.S. and of Canada.'

'Not stolen beef, Jamison. *My beef.*'

'Stolen,' he repeated. 'Stolen—from your brother.'

She studied him.

'I don't understand you, Jamison.'

He moved closer. He took her by the shoulders and spun her, and she landed sitting on the bed. He sat beside her and took both her hands and he held them firmly.

'I'm going to tell you something, young lady. Something you think I don't know. You and Lamont have been stealing Heart Bar Nine cattle. Selling them for high prices in Wood Mountain. Stealing them from your brother.' Jamison tried something. 'Why do you suppose they poisoned your brother?'

'Poisoned him?'

Jamison forced her back on the bed. She lay on her back, hair spilling on the counterpane, eyes on him. Bitter eyes. Old-young eyes. Eyes which were tough and hard, not womanly. No femininity in them. Jamison did not like her eyes.

Jamison looked down at her.

'Doc says he might have been poisoned. For that matter, the same holds true of Westburg. They killed your brother to get him out of the way. They killed Westburg to silence him.'

'They?'

'Lamont. Ridgeway.'

Her eyes searched his face. 'You know a lot. Yes, we've been stealing cattle. My brother had one pride in his life—this ranch. My father slaved and worked and killed himself by working for this ranch. George thought my father was God. But what about Westburg?'

'Paper money. Counterfeiting.'

'You back on that again?'

Jamison nodded. 'You're in danger, woman. You know it and so do I. I tried to sell you a twenty-dollar bill. I did that for a purpose.'

'And that purpose?'

He couldn't tear his gaze from those eyes. Hard and metallic, and not a bit of softness. What had happened to her back there along her few years? Greed? Hunger for a good man? Hate? Fear? Or just life? Good old tough old Life. . . .

'To see if you were in on the scheme.'

'What scheme, Jamison?'

Jamison spoke slowly. 'Your brother came from college. He had been in trouble there—gambling. He took men with him to this town. They did not come in together—they broke up and came in separately. One came as a banker.'

'Ridgeway?'

Jamison nodded. 'He had to have a banker to handle the money. Handle it through his bank. So Norman Ridgeway came and bought the bank and they had that pivot point. Then they had to have a printer. Somebody who knew engraving and printing as a fine art.'

'Who was he?'

'A man parading as a farmer. A man named Raleigh Sturdivant.'

Her hands clenched and opened. Her lips trembled. But her eyes were the same. Always the same.

'They had Westburg kill Sturdivant?'

'That they did. Then they killed Westburg. Silenced him forever. They were through with both of them, so they killed them.'

'Sturdivant wasn't useful any longer?'

Jamison nodded. 'I'm sketching in some of the scenes. They printed money and evidently took it to Wood Mountain and sold it for raw gold. Mattson had raw gold on him when I killed him. Gold from Canada, paid to him by Ridgeway and Lamont, to send him against me.'

She was silent. He felt her silent scrutiny.

'They worked me,' she said slowly. 'I had the small end of the stick. Cattle, and I thought they were my friends. All the time, my brother and they worked the big game—and here I was, waiting for a stake to head out of this blasted country. I hate it here.'

Jamison sat on the edge of the bed. He looked at her in the mirror, and she returned his gaze.

'Why do you tell me this, gambler?'

'For two reasons.'

'One, to start with.'

'They might kill you. They killed your brother—or at least sign points that way. If they can get you out of the way the whole thing is theirs. They'll buy this spread for a dime on a dollar.'

'They don't dare kill me!'

'So you say. . . . They're greedy and ugly and selfish. I wouldn't want your blood on my hands. Therefore I rode out to warn you. You've had that warning. From here on out, act as you see fit. I've done my duty.'

'Thanks.' She was ironical.

He used irony, too. 'Double thanks.'

'And the second?' she asked.

'They got me penned in. With what I know they can't let me live. I blundered into this, and it built up, and now it's got me in its tentacles. The second thing is just based on hope, one might say. I don't think it is worth mentioning.'

'Go ahead.'

'Order them to lay off me, Miss Bateman. Let me ride from this valley in one piece and unmolested, and I swear that I'll never reveal their secret. All the signs have pointed to me as being a government agent, even to the cavalry horse I bought down at Fort Keogh. Go to them and make this proposition to them and let me ride out of this valley.'

She bit her lip. Her bitter eyes roamed over his face. 'You're a good-looking man,' she said. 'Have you ever married?'

Jamison said harshly. 'Don't pull that old stuff on me, Miss Bateman. You're just a beginner; I've been worked on by experts. Can you influence them?'

'Why do you want their promise? Are you a coward?'

Jamison showed a tired smile. 'I'm no fool. I want to live. Gold means nothing to me. I've won it one night, lost it the next. I like to breathe good air. I like to admire a lovely woman. They might kill me. They've sent two gunmen against me—by luck, I'm still alive.'

'I could order them to lay off you,' she said.

'Would they obey you?'

'No.'

Jamison got to his feet. She stood up and looked at him.

Jamison said, 'I've warned you. You can go over with them or stay neutral. But watch their guns—and their poison.'

'And you?'

Jamison shrugged. 'The same path. When they move, I counter-move; when they shoot, I try to shoot faster. I can tell you this for sure.'

'Yes?'

'I'm making my final play. Those cattle of yours will never reach Canada. I'll see to that. Their counterfeiting scheme will come out in the open. That will be my chore, too.'

'When you expose the cow-stealing, you expose me.'

'That will have to be. I've offered you my proposition. I have nothing more. It's on your neck—and mine.'

She was very, very close. Her lips were open, her eyes almost closed.

'Jamison, a man hasn't kissed me for a long, long time.'

'That's because of your own stupid pride. Love isn't a one-way street. You have to walk down that street. What have you got to offer a man—besides conceit and a magnificent body?'

'Isn't my body enough?'

'No.'

She said, 'Kiss me, Jamison. Don't go. Talk to me—Jamison.'

He shook his head.

He looked into her eyes.

'Good night,' he said.

He did not leave by the window. He went down the hall and through the kitchen and out the back door. He stood there and listened. The Montana wind was moving lazily and slowly; the Montana night was calm. He went across the clearing and he went up to the guard. He was still tied and still unconscious. Jamison untied the man and ungagged him and then he realised the man was dead. Whether the blow over his head or the gag killed him, Jamison did not know. He did not particularly care. By this time too many men had died. One dead man was a tragedy; three dead men a matter of grave-digging.

Jamison found his bronc and mounted. He turned the horse and looked back at the Heart Bar Nine Ranch.

The light was gone from her window.

Did she lie there alone in the dark, hugging her pillow and crying? Did she lie there alone with stony eyes that looked up at the dark ceiling without a tear?

He favoured the latter.

He rode toward town. He thought of Lamont and Ridgeway. At that moment, the two were in Ridgeway's office. The blinds were down and the lamplight made shadows dance, for the chimney was dirty and the wick uneven.

Lamont had his boots on the desk. His spur rowels gouged deeply into the hardwood. This time, though, Norman Ridgeway did not notice the damage done by the spurs. He stood over by his safe.

'Where the devil did he go?'

Lamont said, 'He might have tried to run the blockade. If he did the boys will get him. We should get a report soon.'

'I doubt if he did that.'

'Why doubt it?'

'He knows he can't make it. That brush he had this afternoon with our man told him that.'

Sig Lamont rubbed his jaw. 'What if he goes to Fulton, Ridgeway? Fulton don't know a single thing so far. He's honest, the fool.'

'We got to get him,' the banker said. He turned to the printing press. 'We got to get that money out of there, too. And do it soon.'

'What'll we do with it?'

'Take it out somewhere,' the banker said, 'and bury it.'

'When?'

'Soon,' the banker said, 'right soon.'

The lamp continued to flicker.

CHAPTER EIGHTEEN

NELL ROBINSON was tending bar. One of her bartenders was out sick. He had drunk too deeply and had a head the size of a barrel. She was wiping glasses when Hank Sturdivant came behind the bar.

'You are not supposed to be here, young man.'

'I know that. But he sent me. He's in our room and he wants to see you right pronto.'

'He?'

'Jamison.'

The woman undid her apron. 'Tell him to come to my apartment.'

The boy returned to the rear apartment. Jamison was sitting on the bunk; he looked up when the boy entered.

'She's going to her apartment,' the boy said. 'She'll meet you there.'

Jamison nodded. He started for the rear door. He did not want to go through the saloon and enter her apartment; he would go through its back door. Young Hank started to follow him.

'You stay here, Hank.'

'Ah, Jamison!'

'I said stay here.'

The boy sat on his bunk. He wore a disgusted look. Jamison went into the alley, took a few steps to the right, and was at the rear door of Nell's apartment. He knocked and she called to him:

'Come in.'

She had a lamp lit. She was slender and dark and her small head was perched bird-like to one side as she watched him.

'Hank said you wanted to see me, Jamison?'

'Sit down, please.'

She sat on the bed. She brushed the front of her dress. She was collected and poised.

'Yes, Jamison?'

He paced the room. 'Fulton?' he asked. 'Is he honest, Nell?'

She watched him. 'Yes, I think so. He's been sheriff since I was a child. His wife has a tongue that's honed on a razor strop. His pride is in keeping the peace. But since he's been sick—Yes, he's honest.'

Jamison nodded.

'Why ask?' she wanted to know.

Jamison stopped and pounded one fist against the other. 'I'm taking a big chance. I'm judging you to be an honest person. I don't think I'm wrong. I have a brother in Chicago, Illinois. His name and address are in my saddlebag. If they kill me I want you to notify him.'

'That all?'

'No, it isn't. The boy is in danger. I want to tell you something. They think I'm a government man—but I am not. This town and this range are sitting on top of dynamite. They're ready to blow its fuse.'

Her eyes followed him.

'I want your opinion, Miss Robinson.'

She nodded. 'Tell me.'

Standing there, he told her the entire story. He watched shock change and transform her, giving her added colour and character. Step by step he unfolded his story. What he did not know for sure he filled in through deduction. It was the same story he had told Marcia Bateman.

'And I sat here—and all the time this was going on? Even Fulton doesn't know. I'm sure of that.'

'Why are you sure?'

'Because if he knew he would act. I mean that, Jamison. He'd move against them, even though Lamont is foreman of the Heart Bar Nine, even though Ridgeway is the local banker.'

'You're sure of that?'

'As sure as I'm alive.'

Jamison spread his hands. 'That's the deal,' he said. 'I'm caught in it and I've got to gun my way through. I wanted your opinion on Fulton. You say he is okay. If he is all right in your estimation, I'm going to him and tell him all this and get him on my side.'

'He'll be with you.'

Jamison said, 'I want to thank you for your help, Miss Robinson. Take care of the boy and raise him to be a good man. I know you'll do that. If I get through this alive I'll ride out to Wood Mountain. I'll think of you and the boy and I'll write to you sometime.'

'Once a month, Jamison?'

He smiled. 'I'll do that. Now I have to see Fulton.' He bowed and took her hand. 'And you will keep this our secret until this is over?'

'I shall, Jamison.'

Jamison held her hand. He found himself comparing her with Marcia Bateman. The red-head fell short in the comparison. This woman ran a saloon and she heard men curse and she had seen them fight and kill. Still, this had not touched her—she was still sweet and girlish and good. Greed had not touched her, either—it had not made her eyes bitter or her lips twisted, as greed had done to Marcia. They were two splendid examples of two types of woman; they stood on opposite ends of the scale.

'Good luck,' she said.

'I'll need it.' A boyish smile.

She stopped at the door. 'I have a Winchester behind my counter. If the fight is on the street, I'll have the rifle covering your back, Jamison.'

'No, you stay out of this!'

Her eyes were serious. 'Try and keep me out,' she said. She went out and closed the door. The sounds of the saloon entered and then died. Jamison stood there and had his thoughts. He kept remembering her. She reminded him rather vaguely of Martha. Where was his ex-wife? Was she keeping house for her new husband, and had his boy half-brothers and half-sisters? Jamison had a heavy feeling. It was not lonesomeness for his ex-wife and his son. They had moved out of his life and he would never see them again. He did not want to see either again. To see them again would bring back old ideas, and old ghosts would walk. Better that the living dead be buried against the dim horizons of Time. A man walks a lonesome way. He has company, and yet he is alone; some day it will end, Jamison. Will it end here in this dinky, dirty little cow town? When you rode on to that burning cabin the name of Milk Iron held no significance. Just the name of a town, nothing more. But now it held power and hate and fear, and death walked the dusty streets. The rain would pound down some day, and the rain would wash sod, and the earth would sprout flowers. Jamison had these thoughts. He was a little afraid: no man can reconcile himself to Death. He wanted to live. There were two of them. He would have to get Fulton to help him. He turned his mind to practical things.

He tried to think things out from the viewpoint of Lamont and Ridgeway. What would their plans be?

They would be intent on two purposes. One, to kill him. The other, to get all evidence out of the way. He wrestled with this latter hypothesis. Then logic told him they could not get the printing press from the back room out of town on a moment's notice. Too big and too heavy. And what about the paper money? They would have to get rid of it. And if they got rid of it he would have no evidence against them. The plates would be gone from the press and the press alone could prove nothing—newspapers were printed on presses. Yes, and checks were printed, too—or so Ridgeway could claim.

He went toward Fulton's office.

He went down the alley. He stopped as a rider came at a running walk down the main street. Lamplight from the Velvet Slipper fell over the rider as he dismounted and tied his bronc to the tooth-gnawed hitchrack in front of the saloon. Jamison recognised Marcia Bateman.

All the ingredients of trouble were in this town. The only thing needed to mix them were a few words and a few bullets.

Jamison stood in the darkness and held a one-man debate. Marcia Bateman might be killed this night. But would they dare kill her in town where possible eyes might watch? No, they would do it out on the range, or in some dark room—their style was the midnight style, and open deeds were not their habit. If she stayed around people, she would be all right.

What did she mean to him?

Nothing, Jamison told himself.

He went down the alley. Ahead, he saw a man move; then he was gone, for shadows had claimed him. Jamison stood there and realised he had drawn his .45. His skin was wet and he was solid and stiff. His nerves were raw and he did not remember pulling his gun.

Jamison continued toward the sheriff's office.

The town was quiet. People had gone to bed. This was a Saturday night town, Jamison realised. Cowpokes and country people came in on Saturday to do their

buying and usually they stayed over to dance and drink
and gamble. On this night, which was a week-day evening, there were in town only the people who lived here,
and they were not many.

Jamison came to the sheriff's office. He leaned against
the back of the building and gave the alley a long and
intent scrutiny. He saw nothing dangerous, so he went
along the side of the building and came to the front
sidewalk. He stopped there in the darkness and looked
at the street. The thought came to him that he was indeed a hunted man—a furtive creature trying to slip
unnoticed through the dark. This rankled him somewhat.
He was a man who had up to now walked openly down
whatever streets he trod, and those streets had been in
some of the far-thrown reaches of the world. Rio, Singa-
pore, Johannesburg, and Sydney, just to name a few of
the towns. And yet here in this dirty cow town he kept
to alleys. The thought made him smile, but the smile was
not a happy one.

There was no sound from inside Sheriff Jones Fulton's
office. Still, a lamp was lit; Jamison saw yellow lamplight tumble out the one big window to lie across the
splintery plank sidewalk. Fulton was inside. He had
another thought: Maybe they had already got to the
sheriff and had killed him. Poison, the way they had got
Bateman and Westburg: or had it been poison? Jamison
realised he was working on lots of assumptions and
theories. Some of these, he figured, would prove wrong.
But he had the solid core in his hands. And that was
what counted.

He saw no danger on the street. The bank had a low
light and it glistened from under a low-pulled shade. The
back room where Jamison figured the printing
press was located, the room where the money was
printed, was dark also. Jamison watched it, and after a

while he thought he saw a tiny pinpoint of light through the blind, but he was not sure.

The window was securely blacked out.

A dog trotted across the street, hunting garbage cans. He came toward Jamison and did not see him until he was very close; then he scooted away, for man had ground fear into him through boots. Jamison realised he and the cur were kinsmen on this night. Neither dared travel in the light. Again, this made him angry, for this was the first time he had shunned the lamplight in the night. He thought of cattle moving north and he thought of George Bateman, who had died because of those cattle. Man made nefarious schemes.

He came openly on the street, expecting a bullet to hammer across the night. But he moved quickly. He darted around the corner and went into the lawman's office without knocking.

Fulton sat in his chair, legs out in front. His gigantic head was down, his hands hung at his sides. Jamison went to the window and quickly lowered the blind. He stood there and looked at the lawman.

A sudden fear hit him. Maybe they had already got to Fulton? Maybe he was dead, his body loaded with poison? Maybe he was not asleep—maybe he was dead? Jamison looked around the room with methodical slowness. Then he moved forward. He stood beside the lawman, who still had his gross head down on his wide chest.

Jamison said, 'Fulton.'

There was no answer. Again, fear hit him. Again, he said, 'Sheriff Fulton.'

No answer.

Jamison reached down and put his lean fingers in the sparse hair. He lifted the immense head. The head came up and then the great eyes opened. Sleep filled them, and with sleep was pain.

K

'I'm a sound sleeper,' the lawman said.

Jamison took his hand down.

'You sure are,' he had to agree.

The lawman stretched, and then pain hit his face. 'My belly—it won't let me sleep. I can't sleep at home— my wife—So I get one good night's sleep about each week—and you have to break it. . . .'

'Sorry.'

By now the lawman was wide awake. He looked at Jamison. 'Now what the blazes do you want, Jamison?'

'I got something to tell you.'

The lawman's eyes were puzzled. 'Go ahead,' he ordered.

CHAPTER NINETEEN

Boots pounded across the floor. Polished boots. High priced justin boots. They moved, and the silent room took up their sounds and absorbed them. The man stopped. He cocked his head and he listened. He seemed to be waiting for somebody—or something.

He sat down.

But he didn't stay in his chair long. He was too restless. He walked again, and the room knew motion and sound. He stopped and took out his six-shooter and rolled the cylinder. The ratchet made a clicking sound, Satisfied, he pouched the gun; he let it ride high and handy in its oiled holster.

He went to the back room. He lit the lamp and looked at the printing press. It was dark and squat; it hugged the floor. He looked at it, and then he put out the lamp and returned to his office. He locked the door leading to the print room. He tried the knob to make sure it was securely locked.

Then he continued his pacing.

Outside, the night was calm. Mill Iron town lay in silence. Then the howl of a dog broke this stillness. Norman Ridgeway stopped and cocked his head and listened for want of something to do. The dog was answering the coyotes. The wilderness called, but civilisation had softened the dog; if the coyotes got him in the brush they would hamstring him and kill him and eat him. Other dogs took up the howling. Under cover of it a man came to the back door.

Sig Lamont knocked.

'Who's there?' Ridgeway asked.

'Lamont, you fool!'

Ridgeway scowled and unlocked the door. He did not lock it behind Lamont. The range boss stood and blinked in the lamplight. His dull grey eyes showed nothing and told nothing. They glistened a little in the lamplight; that was all. Nothing more.

'Well?' Ridgeway asked.

Lamont crossed the room and went to the wall cabinet. He came down with a quart of Old Crow. He got a glass.

'Drink, Ridgeway?'

Ridgeway shook his head. 'I need a clear head and a steady hand,' he said. 'Don't be so secretive. What the devil did you find out?'

Lamont poured a drink. He recorked the bottle and restored it to the shelf and shut the shelf doors. He wore a tight smile that went well with his dull eyes. He plainly wanted to worry this banker.

Ridgeway watched Lamont drink. The man wiped his lips and put down the glass. Then he went into the chair.

'It's ahead of us, Ridgeway. Tonight, too, I'd say.'

'Let it come! Let it come! What do you know, Lamont?'

'We played second fiddle, Ridgeway.'

'How come?'

Lamont spoke slowly. He seemed to possess all the time in the world. 'Well, he was out to the Heart Bar Nine, but I got there behind him. I never met him coming toward town, either. He must have swung out and followed the rim of the rimrock. He's cautious and he's tough.'

'How do you know he went out there?'

'The cook saw him. He went out the back door. She had her bedroom door open and she saw him walk down the hall. Big as life, she said. One of the boys found the guard in the brush. Gagged and slugged—and plenty dead. He'd been in Marcia's bedroom.'

'Where is she? '

Lamont looked at his knuckles. He seemed interested in his hands. He made a steeple by placing finger against finger. And his smile was amused and slow.

'She's at the Velvet Slipper right now.'

'Didn't you meet her coming to town, either?' Ridge-way's voice was a little hoarse. 'Are you blind and deaf, Lamont?'

Lamont allowed his mild smile to die. 'She must have swung off the trail,' he said, 'for I didn't meet her. He's contacted her and she knows the truth now. He's a smart one.'

Ridgeway cocked his head and did some thinking. Then he came up with a logical answer.

'She won't talk to nobody but us. She's found out about the counterfeiting. But she's in on running cattle across the Border. That's a federal offence. Her mouth is gagged by her own sins.'

'She'll jump on us.'

'Let her jump, Lamont. She'll find us no soft cushions to land on. Let the red-head shoot off her mouth!'

Lamont gave this adequate consideration. 'She won't tell nobody,' he finally said. 'She'd put her own neck into the noose. Where is Jamison now, Ridgeway?'

'How would I know?'

'You been here in Mill Iron. I been out on range. He must be somewhere here in town.'

Norman Ridgeway stopped pacing. He put his clean-shaven jaw into his thin hand. Then he came to a conclusion.

'We got to get this bogus money out of this bank, Lamont. Take it out and get rid of it. Bury it or burn it.

The printing press is no evidence against us. Lots of banks have their own presses. Print check blanks and forms on them. But the dinero has to go.'

'How about the plates?'

'They're too heavy to carry. We'll put those under the floor. Good thing I made that cellar under there.'

'Why not put the dinero there?'

Ridgeway shook his head. 'If somebody finds the plates we can claim we knew nothing about them—I bought this bank, remember?' The banker showed a twisted smile. 'My predecessor could have hidden the plates there. The government men can tell how old the paper money is and its age would pin its printing on to me. But they couldn't do that with the plates.'

Lamont nodded.

Ridgeway pounded a fist into a palm. 'We do that right pronto. Right now. I'll get the stuff in a sack. You get our horses ready down at the barn. Get moving, man.'

'Don't order me around, banker!'

Lamont's voice held a snarling, ugly note. Ridgeway turned and his hand went to his gun. They stood there and glared and measured each other. The thought hit Ridgeway that both of them had rough-edged nerves and they were acting like a couple of school kids with chips on their shoulders. Lamont gave orders, because he was the ramrod of the Heart Bar Nine; he didn't take orders.

Ridgeway softened with, 'Sorry, Sig. Excuse me, please? We got to stick together, Sig, for we got a fortune ahead of us, when this blows over. And it'll work out all right even if we have to kill this Jamison gent.'

'He's a gover'ment man. The gink with the long whiskers will move in. We kill him an' Washington, D.C., will be down on us.'

'We won't be here to be down on,' Ridgeway said. 'We'll jump the country if we have to kill Jamison.'

'I'll get the broncs ready,' the Heart Bar Nine boss said.

'I'll meet you in the alley.'

Lamont stopped, hand on the doorknob. 'Wonder where Jamison is right now?' he asked.

'I'd like to know where he is, too,' Ridgeway said.

Lamont went outside. For a moment he hunkered against the dark side of the bank. He gave the alley a deep and penetrating scrutiny. Where the dickens was this Jamison dick—this government agent? Lamont moved down the alley. He did not know that Jamison was in Sheriff Jones Fulton's office. Jamison was telling the sheriff about the bogus money and the cow thievery. Fulton could hardly believe his ears. He stared at the gambler, forgetting momentarily his eternal pain. When Jamison had finished the sheriff said that his explanation and deduction were very logical. Fulton got to his feet and waddled down the cell corridor in the back of his office.

Jamison followed.

A cowpuncher was in a cell. Jamison figured he had been booked as a drunk, for he still looked bottle-happy. The big under-sheriff slept on a bunk in the rear of the cell block. Fulton shook him awake. The rawboned man sat on the bed and Fulton talked to him.

'You get a horse and head for the Line. Contact the Mounties and spread out a blockade and stop those Bateman cattle this side of the Line. Don't let them or a cowpuncher get to Wood Mountain, savvy.'

'Are you sure Marcia is stealing her own cattle?' The man seemed to doubt his superior officer's words.

Jamison said, 'I saw them roll out.'

The man swung out of bed and started to dress. Jami-

son and Fulton went to the front of the building. The
drunken puncher was singing in a low voice. Jamison
said, 'That's terrible.'

Fulton said, 'He couldn't carry a tune in a ten-pound
lard pail.'

Suddenly something happened in the cell block. The
song ended and a body hit the floor. Jamison glanced
back. The lamplight showed the rawbound under-sheriff
standing in front of the cowpuncher's cell. The cowpuncher was on the floor. The under-sheriff rubbed his
knuckles and returned to his clothes on his bunk.

Fulton said, 'What's the first move, Jamison?'

'They should try to run out,' Jamison said. 'You go
to the bank and get Norman Ridgeway. I'll go to the
barn and watch their broncs. A rider trailed me to the
Heart Bar Nine. I think it was Lamont. Just a hunch
it was, nothing more. But he should be in town by
now.'

Fulton pulled his gun around. The holster rode in
front of him, hanging over his bulbous belly.

'I'll take Ridgeway,' he said.

'Good.'

They looked at each other. Jamison heard the under-
sheriff dressing back in the cell block. Another dog
talked to a coyote. This howling died and there were
only the sounds of the under-sheriff dressing.

'Good luck, Jamison.'

Jamison said, 'Same to you.'

Jamison turned to leave. The sheriff said, 'If we settle
this pronto don't pull out on me tonight. Tomorrow we
got the inquest over Mattson, you know. You have to
be there.'

'I'll be there—I hope.'

Jamison went out on the sidewalk. Sheriff Fulton
would leave by the back door and go down the alley.

Jamison walked down the street. One horse was tied to the hitch-pole in front of the Velvet Slipper Saloon. The bronc belonging to Marcia Bateman. Jamison wondered about the woman. He knew she was afraid, and she faced prison, and yet she was here in town. Where was she now? This question was soon answered, for she spoke to him from the darkened doorway of the Mercantile Store. He stopped and pulled back, his shoulders against the rough wall. He looked at her. He could barely see her in the dark.

'You're looking for Lamont, Jamison?'

Jamison said, 'It's time, woman.'

'He just went down the alley,' she told him. 'He went toward the town livery. He was alone.'

Jamison said, 'Did you talk to him?'

'Am I a fool? Do you figure I want to get killed? He'd kill me without blinking an eye—his back is to the wall and his gun is in his hand.'

Jamison said nothing. They stood there for a moment. The wind was slow and lazy, the night was dark and clean, the stars lifted and looked at the earth. Jamison remembered the first time he had met her. He remembered her red hair, her graceful body, and then he remembered her bitter eyes. How old was she? By chronological time, she was young; by feminine time, she was ages old. Jamison felt unrest and he felt the touch of fear. By now Fulton would be knocking at the rear door of the bank. He had better move on. He lifted his hat and said, 'Good night, Marcia.'

She said, 'Jamison.'

He stopped. 'Yes?'

'If I get to Rio—or Buenos Aires—will I see you there —maybe?'

Jamison said, 'If I met you in Rio I wouldn't know you. I'd look past you and not see you. But you won't get to Rio unless you leave this town pronto. Fulton knows about you.'

'You told him?'

'Yes, I told him the whole dirty story.'

Her voice was a low whisper. 'I can't leave now. I've got to see how it comes out. Then I have to go. If you and Fulton win, then the law will arrest me. If they kill you both, then they'll kill me. With you and Fulton gone, this range would be no place to live—no law.'

'Remember that,' Jamison warned.

He turned again toward the livery barn. A lantern hung over the wide door from an extended beam. He had taken but a few steps when a man came out of the barn leading two saddled horses. He mounted one horse, and then Jamison heard the woman whisper, 'That's Lamont!'

Jamison stood there, feeling everything drain out of him. He was conscious of fear, and he was aware of the night—it was calm and the wind brushed him, and the wind was cool. He was aware of the woman standing behind him. He was aware of the dark false fronts of the buildings, of the lamplight from the Velvet Slipper.

He had many thoughts. Some were pertinent and some were irrelevant. He thought of young Hank. Was he in his bed in his new room? He had lost his parents. His lot was his own; an unknown woman guided him. He thought of Nell Robinson. He thought of her in a detached way, not in the mood of a lover. She was dark and self-sufficient, and a man could not intrude upon her private heart; she was herself and herself alone. She was not selfish. She could marry a man and be with him, and yet she would be herself, own her own personality. Jamison thought of this as he watched Sig Lamont ride toward him.

'He's got bravery,' Marcia Bateman's dim voice said. 'He rides no alleys, Jamison.'

Jamison did not answer. She was right; this man had courage. But he used his courage and his strength the wrong way. The gambler watched him ride closer. He came at a walk. His horse kicked up puffs of dust; the horse he led dragged hoofs through the dust. Jamison moved ahead, a dark shadow in darker shadows. He loosened his gun as he walked. The thought came to him that soon he would either ride out of this Milk River country or he would remain here in one small room forever. He remembered something, a bit he had long ago read—did it come from Shelley or did it come from Keats? 'Already I feel the roots of the flowers. . . .' Keats, he was sure; the poet had told this to his doctor when he was dying. What difference did it make: Shelley or Keats? A man rode this street, and his way was treacherous, and his gun was close, for he looked for a man named Jamison. The thought came to Jamison then that Lamont had deliberately taken the street instead of the alley. For what purpose? To take him, Jamison, into the fight—so he could listen to yammering, snarling guns. To ride out or meet the dust.

And so Jamison moved forward. And so Sig Lamont rode forward. He rode into the wide square of lamplight coming from the window of the Velvet Slipper. He rode into this and Jamison came into it, and the lamplight lay across them.

Jamison said, 'So you aim to run out, eh, Lamont?'

Lamont reined his horse down and let the reins sag around the saddle-horn. The saddled horse he led came to a stop. The yellow light played across his jaw, showing the hardness of the muscles there. His craggy face was clear, the eyes a little too small. Jamison wondered

what those dull eyes held. Fear? No, not fear. Hate?
Yes, maybe hate. . . .

'I pulled in out of the dark, Jamison. You fell for the
deal.'

Jamison said slowly, 'Fulton is visiting your friend
Ridgeway. We figured you two would jump out of town
right soon.'

Lamont said, 'Who's that behind you?'

Jamison did not turn. He thought at first that the
range boss was trying to trick him—the trick, he knew,
was old.

But Lamont repeated, 'Behind you, I mean.'

Jamison said, 'In the doorway?'

'Yes.'

Marcia Bateman said, 'Only Marcia, you two-bit
thief! Just watching, but with a gun in her fist!'

The words were clear. Somewhere a man called, for
danger was seasoning this dust, and he had suddenly
become aware of it. Jamison paid the voices no heed. He
watched Lamont.

Lamont said, 'So you're against me, too, Marcia. . . .'
It was more of a lament than a statement.

Jamison ordered, 'Get off that horse—'

Then, without warning, guns sounded. Muffled guns.
The roar pounded against the walls of the bank. Jamison
could see them there—Fulton, big and heavy, his .45
talking; Ridgeway, bony, tall, dark-eyed, his hawkish
nose smelling gunpowder. And so the guns talked.

Then the shooting stopped as suddenly as it had
started.

Jamison repeated, 'Fulton and Ridgeway, Lamont.'

Lamont moved his weight on his right leg, and he
made his draw. He settled in his saddle, and Jamison
shot and Lamont shot. Lamont's horse jumped and
Lamont left the saddle, and his second bullet hit the

dust. Jamison hit him with his second bullet, shooting the range boss as he was leaving his saddle. Jamison hit him solidly in the chest. The horses stampeded and ran away with roaring hoofs, trampling on their reins.

Lamont sat there. He still had his gun. His head was down, and Jamison came forward. The gambler was alert and tough and ready. Lamont raised his head. He looked beyond Jamison at Marcia Bateman.

'I never got you in life,' the range boss said, 'but I'll get you in death.'

Before Jamison could shoot, the range boss had shot. Jamison heard Marcia Bateman scream. She tried to run, and another bullet hit her; by now Jamison had shot Lamont through the head. The bullet caught her and turned her around, and she crashed into the side of the Mercantile. She stood there and screamed and then she was silent; she slid along the building's side to the planks of the boot-pounded sidewalk.

And Jamison stood alone his gun smoking.

He stood there for some time. Young Hank came out, wearing a long nightgown, and he hugged Jamison's leg and Jamison put his hand in the boy's hair. It was Nell Robinson who took the gun gently from the gambler's hand. It was Nell who got his elbow and said, 'Come with me, please, Jamison.'

He said, 'Marcia?'

'The doctor says he killed her.'

Jamison thought of the red hair. He would never see it is Rio, or in Paris, either. The bitter eyes, he thought, are not bitter now. He tore his hand from Nell's.

'Fulton' he said. 'In the bank.'

'I'll go with you,' Nell said.

'And me, too,' the boy said.

They went to the bank. The front door was open. Ridgeway had opened it. He had not had strength enough to walk outside. He sat in a chair, and blood was on his shirt, and he lifted his bony face.

'You win, government man,' he told Jamison.

Jamison corrected him, 'Just a gambler.'

'You're a government dick,' the banker claimed. 'It was a good game while it lasted.' He lowered his head. 'Unlock the gates of Leavenworth for me,' he said. 'I been there before.'

Jamison was not listening. He went to where Fulton sat with his back to the wall. There was blood on the floor and a sack of paper money lay there, open with the bogus bills sticking out. Jamison glanced at them, and then he went to one knee beside the big sheriff.

He turned the man's head. The muscles were limp. Lamplight was reflected in the gigantic, dull eyes. They had no pain now. They were serene and out of this world, and now he walked across the clouds. His belly did not hurt him. Jamison had this thought: His belly doesn't hurt him now. A man walks a long way from the spot of his birth to the spot of his death. Jamison stood up and swore for he had liked the big man.

Nell said, 'Let's go to my apartment.'

Jamison moved, and strength came to his legs. The doctor was working on Ridgeway. Jamison thought, He'll live, but that thought held no significance. They went outside into the Montana night—young Hank, Nell, and Jamison.

Stars moved, receded, shimmered.

People talked in the darkness.

Jamison slowly took his hand out of Nell's. She said nothing. The apron strings, he realised, were pulling close. She would know why he moved his hand away.

But he held Hank's small hand.

He walked, and they walked with him and the stars talked. They showed the rimrock trail leading north. Within hours, he would ride that trail, in peace. Never again would he see this town and this Montana valley.

Jamison breathed deeply.

'The air is good,' he said.

BOOTHILL BRAND

ONE

Ric Williams was playing cards with three of his farmers
when he heard the loud and angry voices out on Black
Butte's rainswept Main Street that afternoon of May
fifteenth, 1899.

Whist game forgotten, Ric got hurriedly up from
his chair. "Somebody's arguing out on Main Street!"

His farmers also had risen. They were in Ric's
living-quarters tied onto the back of his land-locator's
office. They hurried across the office to peer out the
two windows looking out on Black Butte's two-block
long Main Street.

"Looks like trouble ahead," one farmer said.

"You said it, Mullins." Ric spoke slowly, heart
hammering.

He'd located homesteaders as a Federal Land agent
for a year on this grass and sooner or later he'd figured
hell would break loose between his few homesteaders
and this country's last remaining big cow-outfit —
Greg Mattson's Half Circle V.

And now that trouble had arrived. . . .

Two men stood across the muddy street on the
plank sidewalk in front of Victor's barber-shop. Their

163

loud voices had brought almost all Black Butte's citizens out.

For Black Butte was celebrating. This was Founder's Day. For thirty-odd years ago Ric's father — Bill Williams, now dead — and Greg Mattson's father, also gone forever, had driven thousands of wild Texas long-horns onto Black Butte's tall buffalo grass — and had started the town of Black Butte.

Streamers hung across the mud from false-front to false-front. This celebration also was in honour of the rain which had fallen steadily for over a week — the first real rain in two long dry years.

"The one in the yeller slicker is Jim Young," one farmer said.

"Sure hope he don't pack a gun," another farmer said, "'cause everybody's seen how fast Kid Hannigan can handle his pistol."

This was the last day of the three-day celebration. This forenoon there'd been a shooting contest.

Cans had been saved for months for the competition. Three guns had come out in the finals. One gun had belonged to Greg Mattson, one to Ric Williams — and the other to Kid Hannigan.

Each six-shooter had held five bullets. Each gun had had three tries. Greg Mattson and Ric had scored fourteen out of fifteen to tie for second. Kid Hannigan had hit with all fifteen bullets.

Ric and his farmers went outside to stand under the wooden awning.

Ric heard Kid Hannigan say, "After this watch where you're walkin', sodbuster! You damn' hoemen don't need the whole damn' sidewalk!"

The gunman had emphasized the words *hoemen* and *sodbuster*. Since barbwire and windmills had started invading central Montana's once-free-and-open cow-range cattle the two words had become more of

164

an insult than *sonofabitch*.

Ric said slowly, "I better get over there. Jim might have a pistol on him and might be foolish enough to try to use it."

"He tol' me he was three years on the Detroit police force afore he come out here," Mullins said, "so he might be able to use a short-gun good."

Hess and Mullins and Griffin stayed behind. Until the coming of Jim Young those three were the only farmers Ric had located on homesteads, and the three had arrived last August, too late for planting.

The past winter had been terrible. Some claimed it worse than the winter-kill winter of '86-87, if that were possible. Nevertheless, the three farmers had managed to somehow live it out on a diet of jack-rabbits, cottontails, a razor-thin deer. By now the buffalo was gone. Uncle Sam's sharpshooter had seen to that.

Mud sloshed around Ric's boots. He was sopping wet by the middle of the street.

Kid Hannigan's boss — Greg Mattson — stood with his back against the barber-shop, big and wide-shouldered in his dark-coloured raincoat. Two of his Half Circle V riders stood on his right, another two on his left.

"Here comes the land locator," Mattson told Kid Hannigan.

Hannigan said, "Keep an eye on him," and didn't even look at the advancing Ric Williams.

"I'll do that," Greg Mattson said.

Mattson and Ric were the same age. They were the only get of two Texas cowmen who had trailed long-horns into this area — two men who had died within the last few years, as firm in friendship as the day they'd tumbled the first Texas cow onto this high grass.

But not so their sons. . . .

Nobody knew why but Greg Mattson and Richard Williams had apparently hated each other the first moment their eyes had been laid on each other. Both had gone to grammar school here in Black Butte.

They had fought fistfight after fistfight through all eight grades. They had fought over nothing. They had fought just to be fighting. Old Bill Williams and Matt Mattson had decided to thrash their sons, but two weeks later they were at it again.

The two cowmen had given up.

Now Greg Mattson's gray eyes met Ric Williams' blue eyes. Hate and contempt lay in the young cowman's eyes, plainly visible.

Ric stepped up onto the planks. He spoke to Jim Young. "What seems to be the trouble here?"

Greg Mattson answered for the farmer. "None of your damn' business, Williams."

Jim Young looked at Mattson. "I can answer my own questions, cattle-king! I don't need your help!"

Greg Mattson laughed. His cowpunchers made snickering sounds. With difficulty, Ric Williams overlooked this. He looked at Jim Young.

Young was one of those men who retained their youth longer than others. Despite being married and father of two he looked like a boy of eighteen or thereabouts. He was unsteady in his high-laced boots. Plainly, he'd been drinking — but drinking was nothing new on Founder's Day here in Black Butte town.

Young spoke to Ric. "I'm over twenty-one."

Ric nodded. "I grant that. But you sure aren't sober."

"Sober as I ever will be."

Ric tactfully changed the subject. "What happened?"

"Hannigan here deliberately crossed the sidewalk to shoulder me," Jim Young said.

Kid Hannigan snorted. "Damn' farmer's lyin', land-locator. He was so pie-eyed he staggered into me an' almost knocked me into the mud!"

"My man's right," Greg Mattson hurriedly said.

Ric Williams again disregarded his old-time enemy. "Come with me, Young," he said.

"Why?" Mattson asked.

Ric said to Mattson, "I wasn't talking to you, Greg. Why don't you at least act a little civilized and speak only when spoken to, like your father told you when you were a kid."

Ric heard a few women titter at this, but the watching men remained silent.

Mattson said hotly, "Another one like that, Williams, an' you an' me tangle again, savvy!"

Kid Hannigan spoke to Ric. "This is between me an' this farmer, land-locator. Not between me an' you. He bumped me, not you."

Ric looked at Kid Hannigan. Short, bearded, blue-eyed, muscular, legs bowed from the barrel of a horse. Typical drifter, a drifting gunman. Hannigan had come onto this range last year about the same time Ric's three farmers had shown up and staked out homestead claims.

Greg Mattson had immediately hired the man. And not, some said, as a cowpuncher.

Rumours floated around the tough personage of Kid Hannigan. Some claimed he fled north out of Wyoming after a rustler-cowman war. Others said he was a Texas renegade wanted by the Rangers in the Lone Star State.

Ric said slowly, "Everybody's celebrating, Kid. A little drunk, most of us — so why not blame it on the booze and the celebration and let it go at that?"

A woman said, "Amen to that, Ric."

Ric looked at the woman. She was almost as wide

as tall. Her strong body wore bib overalls and a blue cotton shirt. High heeled cowpuncher boots encased her big feet. His eyes travelled to the young woman standing beside Kitty O'Neil, long-time owner of Black Butte's only saloon. This woman had been in town only a week or so.

This woman stood about five feet four and had blonde hair. Ric judged her about his age, or a year or two younger. Her name was Melissa Wentworth and she dealt poker in Kitty's saloon. She was Black Butte's first lady gambler. Ric had been coming out of the post office the day she'd stepped down from the northbound stage that ran north into Timber Mountain, Saskatchewan, Canada, some forty miles away.

He stopped and stared like a country bumpkin. She'd seen his awkward gawkiness and then had looked away, plainly amused.

He'd dreamed of her that night. Now her deep green eyes seemed to tease him.

"I sent Sonny Horner for Ike Ratchford," Kitty O'Neil said. "That lazy fat old sheriff should soon be putting in his appearance." She spoke with a bit of Old Sod brogue.

"Here comes the sheriff now," somebody said.

Kitty O'Neil said, "And on the double, too. And he don't look too drunk, either — settin' aroun' the office in Jones' barn playin' pinochile with those other ol' bats."

For almost thirty years the female saloon-keeper and Ike Ratchford, the man who'd become Black Butte's first and only star-toter, had kept up a running banter, but let somebody say something bad about Sheriff Ike — or, for that matter, about Kitty O'Neil in the lawman's presence — and hell was soon to break loose.

Ric felt relief touch him at the sight of Sheriff Ratchford's figure barging toward him. Ratchford had bounced him on his knee when he'd been a mere boy. For that matter, he'd done likewise to young Greg Mattson, too.

Ratchford read the problem at a glance. He rudely shoved his big body between Jim Young and Kid Hannigan. Anger flushed Hannigan's beefy face, but he made no objections. Ric wondered why until he glanced at Greg Mattson and saw Mattson nod slightly.

"No fightin' here," the sheriff said shortly. "This is a day of celebration, not of fightin'. Greg, you watch this gunman of yours, savvy?"

"Gunman?" Greg Mattson asked.

"That's what I call him," the sheriff answered shortly. He spoke to Kid Hannigan. "You get your hand on thet gun in my town, mister, an' you go to one of two places — my jail or the morgue!"

"Who says so?" Kid Hannigan demanded.

"I do, mister. An' don't forgit it, either."

Ric noticed Hannigan discreetly kept his hand away from his holstered pistol. He remembered Kid Hannigan's fast gun and deadly accuracy.

"You talk awful rough, Ike," Greg Mattson said.

Ratchford clipped, "I've said enough. Now clear the street, all of you."

Kitty O'Neil said, "Get movin' all of us."

Greg Mattson said, to Ric, "You deliberately settled this new farmer on my best Sage Crick grass an' water, Williams."

"He didn't settle me there," Jim Young hurriedly corrected. "I picked out that one hundred an' sixty acres myself on his big wall map."

Ike Ratchford said, "Did you hear me? I tol' all of you to clear the street."

Mattson and his hired gun turned and went toward

169

Kitty O'Neil's saloon, the other Half Circle V hands following. Ric's three farmers then crossed the street.

Ric spoke to Young, "You'd better stay close to us others, Jim. Or go home, but not alone, understand?"

"Ambush?"

Ric shrugged. "Not from Greg Mattson. He's the son of an old cowman and so far as I've known he's always played fair and above the table — but that Kid Hannigan rat . . ."

Young nodded. "I understand."

Ric looked at the three other farmers. They were all three ex-cowpunchers who'd tired of rodding the other man's dogies at a mere two bucks and found a month.

"I'll stick with you boys," Young said.

"I'd admire a slug of red-eye for my cold belly," Jake Mullins said. Mullins was a stocky man of around thirty. His nose had once been broken and had been set a little crooked. "But the only saloon is Kitty's an' I don't want no trouble with them Mattson men."

"Same for me," George Hess said.

Ward Griffin said, "Me, too."

"Ratchford's going into the saloon," Ric said, "and Greg Mattson has known Kitty ever since he can remember — and he'll respect her place. He won't let his hands start trouble in Kitty's."

George Hess said slowly, "So what's holdin' us back, men?"

"Nothing that I can see," Ric assured.

They started up-street. Kitty and Melissa were just entering the saloon. Mellisa's raincoat hugged her small waist like it had been glued to her hips.

Ric liked what he saw.

Suddenly, he noticed a young woman standing out of the rain in the Mercantile's front. The woman had noticed Ric's admiring glance. Her lips showed a small, amused smile. She was small — not over five feet — and young and pretty — a wholesome prettiness that came from rain and sun and this endless land.

Ric felt irritation.

Her name was Martha Stewart. She'd been born and reared in Black Butte, her father having for years been the town's only school teacher. Malcolm Stewart had resigned his teaching job last spring. Next year Martha would preside over the town's school children. She had just been graduated from the state normal school.

She and Ric and Greg Mattson had gone to grammar school together. She'd gone to Malta for high school, as had Ric — but Greg Mattson had quit school after the eighth grade to work on big Half Circle V.

Martha tossed her head, wheeled, and entered the Merc. She too showed a small waist and nice hips, Ric noticed.

Stocky George Hess had caught the play. "She's mad an' she's after you, Ric," he said.

Ric only smiled.

TWO

Rain still fell when the Black Butte rodeo-finals began at one that same afternoon. Malcolm Stewart and Ric were judges in the woman's relay race.

Three women riders had made the finals. One was Martha Stewart, another was Jennie Queen, a town's girl, and the third was none other than blonde Melissa Wentworth, gambler.

Each woman rode four horses. Each horse ran a quarter mile. When the horse had finished his lap his rider left him on the dead run, taking the saddle with her. She then ran to her next mount, held by her handler. Up went the saddle, the cinch was caught, slipped into tackaberry buckle — and the rider swung up, the end of the latigo in hand, the cinch being tightened on the dead run.

Martha and Melissa were neck-to-neck on the fourth and last horse, Jennie Queen a pace behind. Ric was surprised to see Melissa — whom he'd considered a town's woman — handle a horse and saddle with such lightning ease.

Martha and her four running-horses had won the woman's relay race for a number of years, now —

but this time the young school-teacher had plenty of competition.

School-teacher Malcolm Stewart looked at his stopwatch. "They're grinding it out in record time, Ric."

"Miss Wentworth surprises me," Ric said.

Stewart smiled softly. "You're young yet, Ric. When you get my advanced age what a woman does — or can do — will fail to surprise you."

Ric glanced at the school-teacher. This man had caned him and held him after school for fighting with Greg Mattson but yet he admired and respected the thin, gray-haired man very much.

He knew Greg Mattson held the same feelings toward this sagebrush scholar, as did the entire range and town of Black Butte.

"Advanced age?" Ric joked. "Dad said you were only twenty when he and Scott Mattson picked you out of cowpuncher ranks and said you'd have to be the local school-teacher. That's make you around fifty, old man Stewart."

"Right you are. There they slant the near curve. This mud — makes for slippery riding. Jennie is gaining."

Malcolm Stewart was correct. Jennie Queen's last horse — a big sorrel — was fast and sure-footed, shod all around. He'd eaten up the distance and when the three horses stretched out for the far stretch his head was pounding the flank of Melissa Wentworth's bay gelding.

Melissa rode Mattson Half Circle V horses. Apparently she'd soon learned the speed and ability of her broncs, for she handled them like a veteran.

"Jennie's pulling up," Malcolm Stewart said, again glancing at his watch. "That sorrel she's on is a tough horse. I'm just praying that none slide in the mud on that far turn."

"Lot of mud there," Ric said.

Ric's blood thrilled. No wonder it's called the Sport of Kings. He held his breath as the three lunging Montana horses began the last quarter-circle before heading into the home-stretch.

Now the three running-horses were on the stretch's outermost point. His breath caught. Jennie's sorrel made a slight slip. For a moment Ric thought the horse would lose his footing and go down.

But the horse held his footing. He ran on gamely, but the losing of his stride might cost him the race — and besides, the town-girl rode on the outer edge. Martha's horse held the rail. Melissa's bronc was between Martha and Jennie.

The girls made the bend and their horses came in on the final stretch, Martha's horse a half-head in the lead, Melissa's Half Circle V horse a pace behind, with the big sorrel of Jennie Queen closing in slowly, running his loyal heart out.

"By gosh, that sorrel might do it," Malcolm Stewart said. "This will set a new stampede record, Ric."

"It'll be a hard one to judge if they finish like this," Ric said.

"Take a lawyer to make the decision, Ric, and you're one. I should never have been picked to judge this, seeing my daughter's in it. I hereby and now appoint you sole judge, thus eliminating myself."

Ric Williams grinned boyishly. "Thanks," he said.

He spurred over to the finish tape. The three running-horses came in in a bunch. The tape broke and the three thundered past.

Ric spoke to the school-teacher. "Miss Wentworth's by a horse's whisker," he said.

Malcolm Stewart nodded. "Appeared that way to me."

"Jennie and Martha a tie for second," Ric said.

"I go with that, too." Again the thin teacher looked at his watch. "Record time, Ric."

The announcer rode up, megaphone in hand. "Results, judges?" Ric told him. The three women sat, their horses in a bunch, waiting. The announcer spieled off the names of Martha and Jennie. "And the winner in a new record time, Miss Melissa Wentworth!"

Ric noticed the cheering for Melissa was not its normal length and loudness. He understood. A stranger had ridden in and captured the prize that up until now had always been won by a home-town girl. These people were very clannish and always backed another townsperson. That was only normal. Most had been in Black Butte for years. Some had been born here and spent their lives here.

Malcolm Stewart was rodeo-manager, a position he'd held for years because of his high social standing as the town's only teacher. He and Melissa loped around the arena with Jennie and Martha riding behind.

Ric did not make the triumphal tour. He and Malcom Stewart would team-rope next. They'd have tough competition in Greg Mattson and Kid Hannigan. George Hess and Ward Griffin, two of the farmers, had also made the team-roping finals, Hess roping heads and Griffin the hind legs.

Hess and Griffin were fast and sure ropers, too. They each roped three calves, working against the stop-watch. When it came to the last calf the farmers were ahead by a few seconds and Half Circle V and Ric Stewart almost in a tie, Mattson and Kid Hannigan a flick ahead.

Ric coiled his wet catch-rope. With the school-teacher in this event the announcer — fat Mike Weldon — was timer and judge. Ric tossed his kinky, stiff lariat to a tender.

"Something new, Henry."

The tender tossed up a new maguey rope. Ric shook his head and tossed it back. "No soapweed. I can't handle that as well as manila."

This time he received a thirty-five-foot manila lasso. He shook out a loop, especially noticing how easily the rope ran through the hondo. "This'll do," he said.

Melissa Wentworth pulled her horse in close to his. Ric looked at her blonde loveliness and said, "Congratulations."

White teeth showed. Green eyes were full of life. "Thank you, kind sir."

Ric glanced at Martha Stewart who sat her saddle between him and her father. Maybe he was wrong, but he was sure that she'd been watching him and Melissa, but now she was apparently seriously engaged in conversation with her father.

Ric hid his smile. Naturally he'd escorted Martha to various social functions such as local country dances. So, for that matter, had Greg Mattson. Such was only logical. Eligible and single women were scarce here on the frontier. Both had also at one time or other gone to such with Jennie Queen, one of the few other girls in Black Butte.

Jennie's father owned the Mercantile, Black Butte's only community store. Ric's father had started the emporium a few months after arriving in this area with Scott Mattson and their wild Texas longhorns.

But running a ranch and a store had been too much and within five years he'd sold the Merc to Jennie's family.

"You've ridden relay before, I take it?" Ric asked.

Melissa shook her head. "First time, Ric. I practised on the sly since coming here. Greg asked me to represent Half Circle V so I promised, not even guessing at what I was entering."

Ric had liked her calling him Ric instead of the usual Mr. Williams. But when she called Greg Mattson by his first name with such familiarity he soured somewhat.

"You ride good," he said.

"Thank you. And you rope well and ride broncs in first-class manner."

"Tough competition, Miss Wentworth."

Miss Wentworth scowled slightly. "I like Black Butte. It makes me feel at home. I guess it's because I was raised in a small Nebraska town. But as long as I'm here, why not call me Melissa?"

"Melissa it is, then."

She smiled. "You know what Melissa means?"

"You can't stump me. Greek One, Doc Myers the teacher — Montana U. Means honey."

"Yes, and means a bee, too."

Ric tried something. "Have you a stinger like a bee?" He realized instantly he'd overstepped. Her face told him that. The irritation caused by the Jim Young-Kid Hannigan ruckus was still on him. It coloured his thoughts with its danger and lay always in the background. "Forget it," he said shortly.

She looked at him. "Forget what?"

"I went too far. Sometimes a joke — if that could be called such — blows up in one's face. Well, time Malcolm and I rope."

He and Malcom Stewart reined their horses in on each side of the rope barrier, loops built, both tied hard-and-fast to saddle-horns. When the calf came roaring from the chute he'd hit the barrier, knock the rope down, and then he was their game.

Ric glanced at the chute. A big husky longhorn calf wrestled with himself in the barrier, tail up and ready to go.

The rodeo-manager said, "All set, ropers?"

Ric nodded. Malcolm Stewart nodded.

"Turn him loose, boys."

The chute gate opened. The calf hesitated not a moment. He leaped out, tail up, hoofs hammering. He hit the barrier. It went down. Two roping horses leaped forward.

Shod hoofs threw back mud. The school-teacher's loop sang out, hung in front of the calf's head, came back, settled, caught. Ric's loop went singing out, flat, the calf's hind legs went into it — but Ric was slower than usual, and he knew it.

His whole attention hadn't been on his rope. Kid Hannigan and Jim Young's troubles lay in the background. The calf went down, roping horses pulled him out flat, and the announcer bawled out the roping-time.

Flankers came out, loosened ropes. Stewart and Ric coiled lassos. Stewart said, "Slow time," and let it go at that. All in the game, Ric thought.

Greg Mattson and Kid Hannigan roped next. Their combined time was less than that of Ric and Stewart. Then came the farmers, Hess and Griffin. They roped with hard sureness.

It was beautiful to watch. Ric guessed both were Texas men. Down in Texas you had to lay out your loop fast and sure. That was brush country. You ran your stock into a small clearing. You had to catch there or maybe-so never get another chance again.

He tried to remember back. Had either of these two farmers ever told where they'd come from? Here in Montana you asked few questions, if any. Many Montanans were wanted men in other states. They'd come to the raw wilderness to lose their identity and be safe from the law.

A few inquisitive souls had asked questions. They'd

received answers in form of bullets.

The farmers won. Half Circle V was second. Ric and Stewart were third. Stewart said, "Well, we got in the money, anyway." Ric was sure his voice held short disappointment.

"My fault," Ric said.

Greg Mattson and Kid Hannigan rode past. Neither glanced at Ric or said hello.

The three of them — Mattson, Hannigan and Ric — were in the saddle-bronc riding finals. Usually this was a bitter contest between Greg Mattson and Ric but now a new figure was in it — the shadow of squat, gun-throwing Kid Hannigan.

The Williams Bar Diamond Bar ranch so far had taken a beating. Ric then corrected this: the Bar Diamond Bar, as a cattle-ranch, was no more, and hadn't been for the last four years.

Ric had discovered it was impossible to run the big ranch and attend college at the same time. He'd laid out fall semester and staged one of Montana's biggest cow-roundups.

For three days Bar Diamond Bar had shipped cattle out of Malta, Saco and Hinsdale, down on the Great Northern rails. He'd homesteaded the ranch buildings, stationed a caretaker there, and had returned to Missoula and the U for the spring semester.

Bar Diamond Bar wasn't taking a beating. Bar Diamond Bar no longer existed except for the strong stone buildings his father had built years before for his Texas bride.

Ric looked at the sky. Clouds scurried across it. Rain fell steadily. Creeks and rivers ran banksful. The soil held all the water it could hold. From now on all rain would be run-off water.

The arena was a quagmire. Muddy water stood in small, deceptive puddles. None of the bucking-horses was shod. A horse could come out of the chute, begin pitching — hit a muddy puddle, and go sliding down, pinning his rider under him.

THREE

The three bronc-riding finalists drew to see who would ride first, then second, and then come out of the chute last. Much to Ric's disgust, he drew first ride.

This wasn't good. No matter how well the first bronc-rider rode — or how hard his bronc bucked — usually the excellence of his ride would be lost on the crowd before the last rider hooked his way out of the chute.

The three then drew slips for their horses. Here again Ric found a bit of disappointment for he drew Red Cloud, a sorrel gelding — a bronc not known for his hard bucking. Greg Mattson drew Mad House, a big bay. Mad House was a tough bucker. Ric had come out on Mad House last year to win first money over Greg and Smoky Smith, a Half Circle V roughrider.

Hannigan drew the choice horse, the best bucker. The bronc was a big buckskin named Yellow Hell.

Hannigan spoke to Ric. "Yellow Hell? A tough bronc?"

"The best of the three," Ric said. "I'll gladly trade

you."

"No trades, cowboys," Malcolm Stewart said. "You ride what you drew, and no other."

Hannigan merely shrugged.

Martha Stewart spoke to Ric. "I'll pick you up, Ric. Which side you want me to ride — right or left?"

"My right," Ric said and added, "Thanks."

Martha smiled her nice smile. "Think nothing of it, cowboy. I like money. You've got a few thousands stashed away, I understand."

She was joking? Or was she?

She referred, of course, to the big sum he'd made by selling out Bar Diamond Bar's ten thousand head of cattle. Ric guessed it was a race between him and Greg Mattson as to who was the richest man on this grass.

Melissa Wentworth sat her horse a few feet away. Naturally she'd heard Martha's joking. She was going to ride pick-up for both Hannigan and Greg Mattson.

When you rode pick-up you put your horse close to the bronc-rider's bronc and he went from his saddle to yours. These rodeo rules put no time limit on how long a bronc-rider had to stay in saddle.

These rules said you either rode your bronc till he stopped bucking or you were piled.

"Hard earned money," Ric said, grinning.

Ten minutes later he lowered himself down into the saddle on Red Cloud, the big gelding bunching muscles under him. Cautiously, his boots found the oxbow stirrups. Carefully he shifted weight, testing the solidness of the cinch. The Hamley saddle was screwed down securely. He'd seen to the tightening of the latigo from the ground outside before climbing the chute. The flanking strap was in place.

All three rode the same saddle. Thus none of the three could gain an advantage through using a different hull. This was a flat-plate rig with free and easy stirrup movement.

That meant you could use your spurs high, then rake tough behind — as the rodeo rules demanded.

Ric glanced up. Greg Mattson and Kid Hannigan sat on the corral's top rail some thirty feet away. Both watched him go into the saddle. Ric wondered if this were not the first time he'd seen Kid Hannigan without his gun and gun-belt. You can't keep a gun in holster on a bucking bronc unless you had a tie-down string across its hammer. Otherwise out of leather it would fly.

He saw the gunbelts and guns of Greg Mattson and Kid Hannigan hung over a corral post at Hannigan's right. An amusing thought hit him. Hannigan wasn't far from his weapon.

"Here's your hackamore rope, Williams!" The chute tender snapped his words. "Time you kicked this reprobate outa here!"

Ric twisted the hackamore rope around his right hand, making sure his grip was at least six inches above his saddle's horn. For if either of your hands touched the horn or the saddle-fork during your ride you were automatically disqualified.

Ric smiled sourly. Butterflies flittered in his belly. His heart beat rather wildly.

He lifted both spurs high, saddle-leather creaking. He felt the big horse's muscles bunch. The horse knew what was ahead.

"Turn him loose," Ric said.

The gate opened. Red Cloud and Ric Williams met in combat but inside of three lunging jumps out of his bronc Ric knew he was astraddle anything but a winner in this big sorrel.

Red Cloud did his best, but his best wasn't good enough.

He bucked toward the grandstand. Ric rode him with disdainful ease. The horse began to run.

Martha rode in close. Ric put his weight on his right stirrup. He put his arms around her slenderness.

He kicked out of his stirrups. Red Cloud ran on with an empty saddle, stirrups flapping. Ric slid to the ground. "No money in that bronc," he said.

"Points," Martha said. "You got quite a few for the other two days. They add up, you know."

"But not high enough, school-teacher."

Standing there in the rain, Ric Williams bowed to the grandstand. He gauged the applause. Not too much. The grandstand knew a good bronc. The people there were turning thumbs-down on Red Cloud.

He spoke to Malcolm Stewart. "Could I get another bronc?"

Stewart's horse pawed mud. "No other horse, Ric. New rodeo rules this year."

Ric said, cynically, "We live by rules, eh?"

Stewart shrugged. "You should know. You're a law school graduate." He reined his horse around and rode to the bucking chutes where Greg Mattson was testing the cinch on the bucking rig.

A cowboy had ridden in and snagged Red Cloud by the hackamore rope. Another cowboy had pushed close and unsaddled the bronc and had ridden back with the saddle.

When Ric came up Greg Mattson said, "Damned if that poor buckin' horse didn't almost pile you once or twice, Williams."

Kid Hannigan sat on the corral's top rail with a yellow slicker over his shoulders. He smiled.

Ric said, "You looking for trouble, Mattson?"

"Always," Greg Mattson said. "Always, Williams."

For a long second, violence again hung between Ric Williams and Greg Mattson. Anger and disappointment was in Ric because of his poor roping and his having drawn a poor bucking-horse. He needed something or somebody to vent this on and Greg Mattson's big jaw was as good a target as any — but then Malcolm Stewart roweled his horse between them.

"This is no prize-fighting ring," the school-teacher said sharply. "Afterwards you two fools can kill each other, if you want — but right now, Mattson, you got a horse to kick out of that chute, and a few thousand people that have come many miles to see you do it!"

"You don't say, schoolmaster," Greg Mattson's voice dripped sarcasm. Mattson climbed the chute.

He went roughly into leather. His boots found stirrups. He took the hackamore rope from the chute-attendant. He took wraps around his right hand, held his left hand high, raised his spurs and said, "Cut this wolf loose, gentlemen," and Mad House left the chute on a driving, piston-like run, a rough bucking horse.

And Greg Mattson rode him like the bronc-rider he was. One hand high, the other allowing a loose hackamore rope, a Texas trail-drive yell breaking from his leathery throat.

And the grandstand roared.

Mad House swallowed his head. He sunfished, bucked straight out, bucked sidewise, squealing all the time in rage, ears back, grass-green teeth showing. Mattson scratched high ahead, then raked his spurs high behind, the big bronc kicking at the flanking strap. Ric Williams watched in admiration. Here was a good bucking horse straddled by a born bronc-rider. Between the two, they made a point-gathering combination.

Eventually Mad House ran out of steam. He bucked in front of the grandstand and then stopped, completely beaten.

Greg Mattson swung a leg over the saddle-horn and landed on both feet, bowing to the roaring crowd, a wide grin on his sun-tanned handsome face.

He bowed three times, then turned and bowlegged his way back to the bucking chutes, boots grinding mud. He looked at Ric and said, "That'll win first money for me, lawyer."

"Don't count your chickens before they're hatched," Ric said.

Greg Mattson laughed.

The crowd was silent. An air of expectancy held the rainy day. The last bronc-ride was coming up.

Kid Hannigan would come out of Chute Two on Yellow Hell. This ride for the first money was narrowing down.

Ric had won first money the first day on Lost Lady. Greg Mattson had won first the second day bucking-out Loco Gentleman. The second day Ric had won third. The first day Greg Mattson had placed third. Thus Kid Hannigan had won second two consecutive days. He'd openly grumbled he could easily have won first dough each day had he had a good bucking horse.

Now Hannigan had drawn the range's top bucking-horse. And Black Butte awaited anxiously to see what Hannigan and this bronc would do.

Kid Hannigan slid off the corral-rail to land on his heels in the mud, Garcia spurs jangling. He tugged at his short beard, grinning. "Time this boy put his head under the guillotine," he said jokingly. He handed his hat to the sheriff.

"If'n this bronc kills me," Hannigan said, "thet Stetson is yours, sheriff."

Sheriff Ike Ratchford grinned. "Too small for my big head."

"Then see it lands on a head it fits," Hannigan said

grinningly.

"You'll come back," the sheriff said.

The gunman hitched up the belt of his Cheyenne leather chaps. He took his cigarette down, went to throw it away, then apparently thought otherwise, and put it back between his wind-cracked lips.

He swaggered over to the bucking-corral where wranglers were forcing the big buckskin Yellow Hell into a chute. Once they had the horse penned in, a man dropped a bar behind the horse's rump, imprisoning him.

Yellow Hell had been through this before. He knew full well what lay ahead. Wisely, he saved his energy. His job was out there in the muddy arena.

Kitty O'Neil and Sheriff Ike rode back to their stations. Each judged from a different side of the bucking horse and rider. Malcolm Stewart said, "Time's running by, Kid. They're waiting."

"So is Death."

Tenders were lowering the saddle down on Yellow Hell's broad back. Hannigan caught the cinch as it came swinging in and threaded the latigo strap through the big ring, pulled it tight, and made his tie.

"Don't you want the cinch tighter?" a wrangler asked.

Hannigan shook his head. "He needs room to breathe good. Then he can fight harder. You tend to the flankin' strap, pal."

Hannigan climbed the chute. He lowered his chunky frame into saddle. He fitted his boots into stirrups. He pulled his boots free. "Stirrups need to be shorter," he said.

Stewart reminded, "They're waiting, Kid."

Hannigan had no reply. Handlers hurriedly unlaced stirrup leathers, adjusted them, re-laced them. The gunman tested the length of the stirrup leathers. "That's just right," he said.

Somebody handed him the hackamore rope. For the first time Yellow Hell moved. He put his head down slightly. Hannigan tested the length of the hackamore rope.

"Jus' right."

Stewart said, "Kid, I hate to say it, but —"

"Then don't say it," Hannigan said.

Hannigan lifted both boots high, spurs ready to come down hard on the buckskin's sweaty and rain-wet neck.

Hannigan spoke to the buckskin. "You do your best, ol' boy, an' I'll do mine. We need day money and rodeo money. Gotta feed the kitty in Kitty's house." Then, "Turn him loose, men."

The chute gate slid open.

Ric watched in wonder. He was a bronc-kicker. He'd been reared on a horse. So had been Greg Mattson. Greg was an a-number-one man in the saddle. But never had Ric Williams seen a man ride like the gunman, Kid Hannigan, that rainy, miserable day in May, 1899.

Hannigan came out in savage fury. Yellow Hell matched his rider's coldness, inch by inch. Man and horse fought and no quarter was asked or given. Not a trace of daylight showed between the gunman and the seat of his Hamley saddle. His spurs worked in automatic precision. He rode high on the buckskin's shoulders the necessary five jumps. The he raked both high in front and high behind.

Ric full well knew that when a man scratched high behind he automatically loosened himself somewhat in his saddle. He was solid in leather on the shoulder hooking, for he had the saddle-fork in front of him, but when he scratched high behind, the saddle's cantle offered little — if any — support.

A rebel yell broke from Kid Hannigan's lips. It was blood curdling, the cattle-trail scream of the Civil War, of the cattle-trails — a sound that had sent terror through the hearts of white and redskins alike.

It had sent terror rippling across the blood-stained grass of Gettysburg. It had been the wild yell of John Wesley Hardin when that Texas gun had made Wild Bill Hickock eat crow and run out of town that Kansas night.

Now it rang across the watching, silent crowd. It washed back from high Black Butte — the rocky northern pinnacle that had given this pioneer town its name.

Kid Hannigan rode with his left hand held high. Never for a second did his hackamore-hand dip even close to the saddle-fork. He and Yellow Hell fought in the middle of the area, the horse's bare-hoofs slapping mud and water.

Once Yellow Hell slipped. Ric saw the horse start down, then catch his balance, and break into wilder bucking. Without thinking, he rode his horse close, intending to pick Hannigan from saddle when the bronc stopped bucking.

And then, Yellow Hell stopped. He stood, head down, defeated. The crowd went crazy. Never before had Black Butte seen such a bucking horse or such a bronc-rider. For one long moment, horse and rider were cast in damp bronze, outlined motionless against the Montana rain. And, at this moment, Ric Williams rode in, said, "Kid, you did it, you Texas son."

Hannigan looked at him with small eyes. "Texas, did you say?"

Ric was caught aback. He realized now it had not been his job to pick Hannigan from this buckskin. His admiration for Hannigan as a bronc-rider had overswayed his judgement.

Ric said shortly, "Texas or hell? What the hell difference does it make?"

Hannigan threw back his head. He laughed ironically. He said levelly and clearly, "You can go to hell, Williams."

Then Hannigan swung his right leg over the saddlefork to land lightly on his boots in the mud.

He looked momentarily at the howling crowd. Greg Mattson rode in. Hannigan said, "Bunch of damn' idiots." He then spoke to both Ric and Mattson. "That should get me top money for all three days."

He turned and walked through the mud toward the bucking chutes. Once there the first thing he did was buckle on his gun.

Ric Williams scowled.

Kid Hannigan had kicked out of the bucking-chute with a Bull Durham cigarette between his wind-cracked lips. He'd ridden a killer bronc to a standstill.

And he still smoked the same cigarette. . . .

FOUR

Ric Williams split his rodeo-winnings two ways: half to the school, half to the church. Later he heard Greg Mattson had done the same. This did not surprise him.

He and Greg had won money in the annual rodeo since kids on ponies running the barrel-races. Each time their winnings had gone half to the school and half to the town's only church.

Kid Hannigan said he'd deposited his winnings with Kitty O'Neil and was drinking the sum up. Ric had his doubts about this. Hannigan drank, of course — what man didn't? — but he was never seen drunk.

Kid Hannigan was a man of mystery. Despite his bronc-riding, Black Butte did not accept him. Ric figured this normal. These people were clannish and a man had to live within their ranks for twenty years or so to come anywhere close to acceptance. Or else be born in this area.

Ric Williams figured that soon this clique would be broken — and forever. The West was becoming civilized. Each day hundreds of European peasants landed in Atlantic ports, lured to the United States by the promise of free land for the asking and personal freedom — especially from terrible, never-ending wars.

The West was becoming settled. Barbwire and windmills — the two signs of homesteaders — were moving in, encroaching further day by day upon the grass of the cowman and sheepman.

The influx of settlers had begun down in Texas and was working itself north to this section of Montana — only forty miles or so south of the Canuck Line. These settlers had driven big cattlemen out of Texas and southern Colorado. Barbwire and windmills had forced thousands upon thousands of bony — almost worthless — longhorns north.

Some big cowmen had not given up gracefully. They'd turned gunmen themselves — or hired gunmen — and met the homesteaders in gunsmoky battle. Always the homesteaders won. For one thing, there were too many of them. One got killed off and a dozen more took his place. Also, the cattlemen did not own the land they claimed as grazing-land.

This land belonged to Uncle Sam. Cattlemen had moved in free after the rifles had eliminated the millions of buffaloes and forced the redman onto reservations. What redskins that hadn't wanted to be penned in and robbed of their liberties were ruthlessly slaughtered, following their meal-ticket, the buffalo, into oblivion. And most of the owners of the big Western cattle-spreads had never seen their ranches or the livestock those ranches sported for the owners were in many cases Englishmen and Scotsmen.

Most didn't even know where their big ranches were located. They responded only when the big checks came in each fall for cattle-sales.

Now all this was changing. Down south in Wyoming big cowmen had shipped in a trainload of guns that had gone down before the farmers and social pressure in what is today known as the Johnson County war.

On getting out of high school, Ric Williams had seen this coming. He'd pointed this out to his father who had said no settler would ever set boot on this Black Butte range.

Grizzled old Bill Williams had shaken his head. "Never happen here, son. We're too far away from the railroad. Great Northern is over forty miles south. Nearest shippin' point out is Malta."

"Farmers are settling all along the Milk River along the rails," young Ric had pointed out.

His mother had died of smallpox three years before. Since then old Bill hadn't been quite normal — or so his son had thought.

"Too far away to haul wheat an' supplies in an' out, son."

"Only to where there's freight to be shipped in and out and the only freight comin' into Black Butte is the bit for the store — and cattle walk out on foot to the cars in Malta."

School-teacher Malcolm Stewart had talked Ric into going to Missoula far west in the Rockies and the state university. Ric raised no objections. He didn't like cattle and the cow-business. Leave that for that sap Greg Mattson.

Now he had a law degree, had passed the state bar exams, was U.S. Land Agent — and still no friend to Gregory Watson Mattson, who still nursed cattle along. And who apparently had been unaware of the menace of barbwire and windmills — until Ric had moved in his three original farmers. George Hess. Jake Mullins. And Ward Griffin.

And now, Jim Young, another farmer on Sage Creek Meadows. . . .

"Damn it, sheriff, can't Greg see how things are? How they're going to be?" Ric and Sheriff Ratchford sat in Ric's office.

"Greg's no stupid ass, Ric. He's got plenty upstairs."

"I know that. He got better grades than I did in grammar school, by far."

Sheriff Ratchford bit off a fresh chew. "I've talked to him about this thing called *free range* which never was free except it was considered so in the average cowman's brain."

"You have? What did he say?"

"He said he'd buy me another drink."

Ric's face fell. Greg Mattson had clever ways of evading questions. Most of the time he answered a question by asking another question in true politician fashion.

"There's room for cattle and there always will be," Ric said.

Sheriff Ratchford's faded eyes studied him. "You're dealin' in contradictions, son."

Ric shook his head. "No, I'm not. The world cannot exist without livestock. Bovines are livestock. But the longhorn —" He shook his head.

The lawman nodded. "I understan'. Longhorns eat more forage than two Herefords and produce about one-quarter the meat, if that much. You can fatten two good-blooded Herefords where you can keep one longhorn skinny and almost worthless for the market."

"And cattle can graze on land that isn't fit for farming or is too rough to farm," Ric said.

"Greg's trailin' in some full-blooded polled short-horn bulls."

Ric's brows rose.

"From Candy," the sheriff said.

"He tell you that?"

"That he did. Should be in sometimes next week. Aroun' twenty odd head, he said."

194

"Why from the Canucks?"

"Closest place they is such. He had to dicker quite a bit with the Canuck officials, I understand. They don't want what little hot-blooded stock they got leavin' their country."

A cow needed nine months from breeding to calving. Usually a cow in this cold country threw her calf in April or May — or maybe even in late March, but March was risky for a late blizzard might hit and freeze the little newcomer to death.

Most cowmen turned their bulls out with their cows in June. Thus cows threw calves in early spring. By fall the youngsters were big enough to shift through the winter without their mother's milk and with a handful of hay now and then.

The terrible winter of 1886-87 had taught both Bill Williams and Greg's father that the cattle-business could not be carried on this far north without an outfit cutting hay in the summer to tide cattle through the long and terribly cold Montana winters. That winter had completely wiped out Teddy Roosevelt on his Little Missouri ranch just outside of Montana's eastern border. The politician from New York State had immediately given up the cattle-business as a bad job and retired to being no more than a politician.

Some northern cattlemen after that terrible winter had even sold off what few cattle had survived and stocked their rangelands with sheep on the premise that woollies could stand hard winters better than longhorns.

This had proven a grievous error. This logic had been based on two points: the thick woollen coat of the sheep and the fact that sheep could eat grass closer to the roots than cattle.

Their thick wool protected sheep, yes — but sheep could graze no closer under heavy snow than a cow.

195

A horse would paw down to earth and find what little grass there was. Neither a sheep nor a cow will do this. They will graze only what grass — if any — rears its top through the snow.

Stockmen soon learned that sheep would drift with a blizzard until they piled up against a cut-bank or hill and eventually were completely covered by snow. Sheep for some reason froze to death faster than a cow.

Also woollies were fair game for wolves, coyotes, bobcats and mountain lions, not to mention roving grizzly bears. Cattle fought off predators. Sheep stood and offered no resistance when being killed by wild animals.

Sheep had one advantage over cattle, though. A ewe created two incomes a year for its owner while a cow created only one. The cow produced a calf, and there its value ceased — but a sheep had wool for sale and in the fall the lamb — if a wether — went to market.

And the price of mutton — and wool — was very unstable. Australia and other nations began to produce wool and mutton, sending the market price down — and some former cattlemen got rid of their woollies and went back to cattle.

"I don't want any trouble with Greg and his Half Circle V riders," Ric told the sheriff. "I go on official record here and now on that point, Mr. Ratchford."

"You don't need to have such, Ric."

"How come you say that?"

"Well, let's say Greg makes a move. It won't be against you personally. Unless I'm cockeyed it'll be against the farmers."

"I agree," Ric said, "but I'm responsible for those hoemen, as Greg calls them. I got them in here. I settled them on homesteads. I surveyed and marked off the limits of those homesteads. Any blow against the farmers is automatically a blow against me."

"I understand. . . . I'll talk to Greg."

Ric shook his head. "Won't do a bit of good. He and I have already discussed this problem."

The sheriff's brows rose. "Oh. . . . Where, might I ask — and when?"

"In Kitty's saloon. He was in a poker game with Melissa Wentworth; her table."

Sheriff Ratchford listened.

"Greg and I had some conversation — not much — across the table. I asked him to visit me in my office. He just grunted something, no more. I told him I'd gladly ride the ten miles north to Half Circle V to talk to him. He told me not to waste my horse. Things started to freeze up. Vern Wood was in the game. He pulled out. I got out, too — or I'd have broken up Melissa Wentworth's table, and I didn't want to do that."

"Greg claims Half Circle V's been losin' cattle."

Ric Williams studied the lawman's rugged face. "I've heard that rumour, too — but not direct from Greg, but from others. Do you think it's true, sheriff?"

"Greg's an honest man. He's like his father, Scott Mattson. If Greg says his spread's been losin' stock, I'll say it's been losin' cattle."

Ric mulled this over. Greg Mattson had just finished his spring calf-branding routine. Greg evidently had also run a count on his cattle — cows, steers, bulls and calves — during the gather.

"What did he find out, sheriff?"

"Greg took a tally last fall when Half Circle V did its beef-gather. He compared that count to the one this spring. About six hundred head short, he tol' me."

Ric whistled softly. "Hard winter, though — and

lots of winter-kill."

Sheriff Ratchford shook his grizzled head. "Yes, lots of stock went under, 'specially after that late March blizzard. But Greg told his cowboys while on circle to tally all the dead carcasses they ran acrost, which they did."

"What did this tally show?"

"Far from six hundred."

Ric scowled. He played with a pencil. "All right, let's do a little surmising, sheriff."

"Go ahead."

"Wouldn't be much of a chore to get hold of cattle during a winter as rough as the last one."

"Get a hayrack ahead full of hay — dole off a forkful now an' then — an' every cow in the Black Butte area would foller you to where you wanted her to go."

Ric got to his boots. He went to the sink and turned on the faucet and got a tincup full of clear water. Black Butte town was one of the few small towns in this section that had running water in its houses.

His father and Scott Mattson had seen to that. On the south base of Black Butte hill was a spring that never went dry. Directly below the spring the two pioneers had built a rock and concrete reservoir.

They'd then piped from the spring into the reservoir and then had run pipes down hill to the town they'd laid out and built.

Ric drank of the cold water, hung his cup on the hook, and looked out the window. The rain was slacking off. He was glad of that.

Ric turned. "All right, let's say — for the record — that Greg Mattson's been losing cattle. Where would they go?"

"Feed the Indians on reservations, mebbeso?"

Ric considered that. Within a radius of fifty miles

there were three or four Indian reservations. Two were big ones with quite a few inhabitants — the Assiniboine and the Gros Ventres.

Army sutlers bought beef for these many hungry mouths. And an army sutler didn't care what type of beef the redman ate as long as he — the sutler — bought that meat cheap and sold it dear to unsuspecting Uncle Sam.

Rumour was that the sutler cut in the army officials on his profit. And the Indian got the boniest, oldest beef that could be bought — a far cry from the juicy thick buffalo steaks of just a few years ago.

"The army books are open to the public," Ric said. "All a man had to do was ask and he'd see."

The lawman laughed shortly. "That's what the law says, yes — but when you look at a ledger, how do you know it tells the truth?"

"You mean the generals — and the sutlers — sometimes keep two sets of books?"

"They sure do. An' they give you the doctored one — the one they submit each year to Uncle Sam."

"They have to skin cows before eating them," Ric pointed out. "A man might be able to get hold of a hide and see its brand."

"I doubt that. Those boys are smart. I gotta hunch they'd get rid of them hides right off the bat. Either bury them deep, burn them up with acid — or get them outa the country in a hell of a hurry."

"Or change brands? Half Circle V could be easy turned into a Circle Diamond. Complete the half circle, put a V over the first V — and presto, Circle Diamond, sheriff."

The sheriff nodded.

"Where else could stolen cattle go?" Ric asked.

"Across the Line. Canady."

Ric thumbed his bottom lip. "That's right. Miles

and miles of unmarked territory and not a U.S. man or Mountie in sight. . . . Rebrand like I said and drive north. As simple as that."

Ric sat down, nerves restless. This was a new land. It had a long, long way to go to become a legal, law-abiding country. Although the people — some of them, that was — tried to bring in law and order, it was an uphill fight.

It all depended on the people.

Newcomers could — and would — tip the balance either way. If evil-minded newcomers arrived, evil would remain dominant. If good people homesteaded and settled, peace and order would win out.

Most of the homesteaders were good, church-going people who wanted to eke out a living from the land and live with their families in peace. Ric's mind went to his three cowpuncher-farmers.

Evidently the sheriff's mind had taken the same turn for Sheriff Ratchford said, "Naturally, Greg's suspicious of those three farmers you settled on Hell Crick last fall."

"Hess, Mullins and Griffin?"

"That's the three. What'd you know about them?"

Ric considered this momentarily. "Nothing besides that they paid their filing fees and I found the section-line markers."

"This past winter? You kept an eye on 'em?"

"Not in the way you refer to, sheriff. Should I have?"

"I don't know. I'm a lawman. I've been a law-officer since a young man. And to an officer of the law each person is guilty until proven innocent, the reverse of normal procedure."

Sheriff Ratchford stopped just inside the open door. "I've talked to a couple of eye-witnesses to that Young-Hannigan trouble. A couple wouldn't commit themselves but the others say like Hannigan — that this Young button deliberately staggered against Hannigan."

"He's no fool. At least, he doesn't seem a fool to me. So why would he be anxious to commit suicide?"

Sheriff Ratchford shrugged. "Let's leave that rest for a while, Ric. We're in an area of homestead boundaries and the Homestead Law. God bless Honest Abe for making that federal law. Who owns the land the town sits on?"

"The town does. It's incorporated and the land patented. My father and Greg's dad saw to that immediately. Nobody from outside can touch it. Each householder owns the lot his property is on."

"But your father and Scott Mattson are dead."

"That makes no difference. The patent reads that with their deaths the property remains intact in the name of each and every householder — original householders, that is."

"What if newcomers come in and want to build?"

"They buy from the town council. You're a member of that. The money goes into the Town Improvement Fund."

"You still own Bar Diamond Bar buildings. Did your father ever homestead the land the buildings sit on?"

"He sure did. Dad missed nothing. He homesteaded that one hundred and sixty the first year he was in those buildings."

"How about Scott Mattson? Did he homestead the land where Half Circle V has its buildings?"

"I don't think so. I could check by getting word to the U.S. Land Office in Great Falls. Seems to me I remember Dad saying he'd tried to get Scott Mattson to homestead and Mattson said this land would never be homesteaded — that it was worthless as farm-land

and no farmers would ever come in.''

"That sounds like ol' Scott. Bullheaded as a long-horn bull. Then if it isn't homesteaded a man could stake out a claim where Greg's buildin's are — and claim the land and buildin's, an' all?"

"That's right."

"Somebody should ask Greg to make sure he owns the land where his buildin's are. Those buildin's are worth money."

"Anybody try to homestead that land and it would mean bullets," Ric said.

"Not while I'm the law. An' if all is legal. Why don't you question Greg about this?"

Ric laughed shortly. "You want a gunfight in your bailiwick? Old Doc Myers at the U once lectured on the breakdown of social relations. He said that when means of communication were gone, there was nothing left but violence."

FIVE

The rain stopped. The sun came out. Grass sprang up. What had been only bare earth suddenly became green and verdant.

Creeks and rivers went down to normal. Meadowlarks sang. Wild flowers stuck heads up through thick grass. Crocuses, wild sweet-peas, blue-bells. Meadowlarks built nests in sagebrush.

Soon young sagehens appeared. When they were approached by man or another peril the mother clucked her chickens into hiding and flew away as if a wing were broken in an attempt to lure the danger away from her new family.

This ruse did not fool an experienced and wise coyote. The coyote knew she had full use of both wings and was only pulling danger away from her young. He put his nose to the ground, went to work, and soon had the chicken between his jaws.

A similar fate was met by many a young prairie chicken. The grouse was smarter. She built her nest in the brush along creeks and rivers. And the coyote didn't like brush. He'd get tangled in the wild rose bushes and thorny buckbrush. So he stayed on the sagebrush and greasewood-covered land — where nested the sagehen and the prairie chicken.

Within a few days the sides of Black Butte turned from brown to green. Three days after the rains quit three lumber-wagons — laden with various household goods — pulled laboriously into Black Butte.

Ric stared at the wagons, his heart picking up beat. Plainly the three wagons belonged to three would-be farmers. Each wagon carried a cast-iron cook-stove. Yes, and some old furniture, too. A table, some chairs, a cupboard, things like that.

All of Black Butte came out, not to welcome but to stare. People appeared in doorways and on the plank sidewalks. The wagons ground in halfway to the hubs in drying earth and all stopped in front of Ric's land-office and law-office.

The man on the lead wagon said, "You perhaps is Mr. Richard Williams, sir?" He spoke in a soft drawl. The *sir* became *suh* in his bearded mouth.

"That I am," Ric assured.

"My name's Smith Jones. The man on the second wagon there — the one ahin' mine — is John Rogers. An' the tail wagon's the property of Bob Winston, Mr. Williams."

"Please to meet you, Mr. Jones."

Ric went from wagon to wagon, shaking hands. Jones was short and solid looking with a beard. He and Kid Hannigan were the only two bearded men in this area.

Ric wondered why he had this errant thought. Then he remembered Kid Hannigan and Greg Mattson riding into town about half an hour ago.

Mattson had not looked at Ric, standing in his office's open door, but Kid Hannigan had ironically lifted the hand holding his reins, the usual look of cynicism on his bearded lips.

Ric had lifted his hand slightly in return. The two had gone into the post office — which was in the Merc — and then had boot-hammered their way downstreet to Kitty O'Neil's saloon.

John Rogers was a lanky man with a prominent adam's apple. Bob Winston was the youngest, Ric figured — a redheaded burly man of around thirty with many freckles.

"We come out to get located on homesteads, Mr. Williams," Winston informed.

John Rogers said, "We shipped our junk into Malta. Mr. Maresh there tol' us to come out to your town."

Clarence Maresh was U.S. area land agent in the county seat down on Great Northern rails. He was a busy man with many settlers arriving each day to settle on river homesteads along Milk River.

"He couldn't locate us along the river 'cause all thet land there is took up," Smith Jones informed. "He said you had some good lan' along a crick called Sage Crick you could locate us on."

Martha Stewart left the Merc and stood beside Ric. Ric was glad she'd come to his side. He'd felt rather alone and lost for a long moment.

That morning the stage had gone south on its run down from Timber Mountain, across the Canadian Line, in Saskatchewan Province.

The stage had carried south to Malta a letter Ric had posted the afternoon before addressed to his boss, Mr. Maresh, in Malta. This letter had outlined the trouble extant in Black Butte and had asked the senior land-officer to send no more settlers north to Black Butte until this trouble had been settled, if it ever would be. The letter would reach Malta this evening. These men had apparently left Malta yesterday morning. Ric figured the trip north had taken

205

them two days because of the rutted road and the distance.

"Oh, lord," he said under his breath.

Martha heard him. "Why say that, Ric?" She spoke so softly nobody heard but Ric.

"Greg Mattson," Ric said.

"Here he comes now," the school-teacher said. "And he has Kid Hannigan with him."

Ric glanced upstreet toward Kitty's saloon. Onlookers stood on the saloon's long front porch and watched. Greg Mattson and Kid Hannigan were heading toward Ric's office.

"Somethin' wrong, Mr. Williams?" Smith Jones asked.

"We have a little problem," Ric confessed. "Just drop your lines and come into my office, please?"

"Me an' Finn'll watch their teams an' rigs," Sonny Horner said and added, "for a nickel apiece, of course."

Ric smiled. "Of course, Sonny."

The three farmers entered Ric's office, Smith Jones in the lead, Bob Winston holding down the rear.

"Sit down," Ric invited.

The farmers sat. They were tense and stiff. Ric's sudden change of attitude upon seeing Greg Mattson and Kid Hannigan come from the saloon puzzled them.

Ric stayed in the doorway, facing the street. Sheriff Ike Ratchford left the barber shop directly across the street and hurried toward Ric's office.

Ric glanced at the Merc. Malcolm Stewart was coming his way. Ric breathed easier now. He knew full well that neither Stewart or Ratchford favoured his cause more than the cause of Greg Mattson. Ratchford hurried this direction because keeping peace

206

was his elected job.

Stewart came because he loved peace and tranquillity. He was a great advocate of compromise, not force.

Ratchford stopped on the edge of the plank sidewalk. Stewart halted thirty feet upstreet.

Greg Mattson and Kid Hannigan passed Stewart. He looked at them and they looked at him and Mattson said, "You move fast for a man your age, school-teacher."

Stewart said, "I'm the type of man who ages slowly."

Martha stood beside Ric. Ric looked beyond Greg Mattson and Kid Hannigan. Kitty O'Neil had left her saloon and was walking rapidly in Ric's direction. Ric looked beyond the square-built saloon-keeper.

Melissa Wentworth also came this direction, but not at the rapid pace her boss assumed. Again Ric, despite the distance, saw and admired the blonde loveliness of the card dealer and her thin waist.

Martha Stewart saw Ric's admiring glance. Ric did not see her scowl because his eyes had moved to Greg Mattson and Kid Hannigan.

The pair stopped in front of Ric and Greg Mattson looked about and said, "Seems as if when me an' the Kid headed this way the whole damn' town came alive an' headed this way, too."

Ric looked at bearded Kid Hannigan. The Kid stood a pace behind his boss and three paces to Greg Mattson's left. He had both thumbs hooked idly in the front of his wide, cartridge-loaded gunbelt.

Greg Mattson looked at the sheriff. He said, "Howdy, Ike," and Ratchford said, "Howdy, Greg. An' you too, Kid Hannigan."

"I thank you, sheriff," Hannigan said.

Greg looked at Malcolm Stewart, then at Kitty

O'Neil, at Melissa Wentworth, hurrying to catch Kitty. An ironic smile touched his wind-cracked lips.

He turned his gray eyes back to Ric. "Three farmers — newcomers — inside, Ric?"

Ric nodded.

Greg Mattson said shortly, "Cat eat your tongue, Williams? Or are you afraid to open your mouth when among men?"

Greg Mattson's voice was heavy with sarcasm. Once again Ric Williams felt the old anger rise. Had this occurred on the grammar-school playground ten years ago he would have immediately tied into this arrogant young rancher.

He and Greg Mattson had not tangled in a fistfight since he'd come home from college. Greg might find him a different opponent now, one who definitely could handle his fist much better than before.

Ric had told nobody around here that at the university his junior and senior years he'd been lightheavyweight champ of the conference the university belonged to.

He'd taken a beating getting to the top of his weight class, but he'd finally made it.

"Cat ate my tongue," he said.

His eyes caught Ratchford's. The sheriff nodded slightly. That told Ric he was on the right track.

Nobody spoke for a long moment. Kid Hannigan stood stolid and silent, eyes darting here, then there, back again. Suddenly, without warning, Greg Mattson laughed softly — but anger lurked behind the laugh's seeming gentleness.

"I only come here for one purpose, Williams. Not to look over these farmers an' warn them, as you folks all expected."

Ric's brows rose, but he asked no questions.

"I understan' you hinted that the land my ranch

208

buildin's set on ain't homesteaded." Greg Mattson spoke to Ric Williams.

Ric said honestly, "I haven't the slightest idea. My father homesteaded Bar Diamond Bar's homesite right after building but I don't know about your father — he might have homesteaded Half Circle V land, or not. It's none of my business."

"I talked to Greg," Sheriff Ratchford told Ric.

Greg Mattson said, "I've searched all the old man's records. I can't find anythin' that points towards his homesteadin' thet land. I'm purty sure he never homesteaded it."

Ric said, "Sometimes that happens." His innate anger was falling in face of the fact that this cowman — and his hired gun — apparently constituted no danger . . . not at the present, at least.

"I'm goin' make sure it's under homestead," Greg Mattson told the onlookers. "Therefore I'm homesteadin' it myself, even if records do come up that my father also used his homestead rights on it."

Nobody spoke.

The big young cowman looked back at Ric Williams. "What do I do first to pertect my rights."

"Come back in about an hour," Ric said. "I'll be through with these newcomers then."

"What's the procedure?" Greg Mattson disregarded Ric's words.

"First you file a notice with me you wish to homestead. I then make sure you're eligible."

"I'm over twenty-one, a citizen, an' —"

"There'll be no reason you can't file," Ric said hurriedly. "An hour, then?"

"On the point," Greg Mattson said. "Come on, Hannigan."

The two headed back toward Kitty's saloon.

The townspeople drifted away, leaving only Malcolm Stewart, his daughter, and Sheriff Ratchford with Ric.

The sheriff mopped his wide forehead with his blue bandanna. "Sweat easy lately," he told the world. "Gettin' ol', I reckon."

He turned and crossed the street to the barber-shop.

Malcolm Stewart said, "Back to the Merc with me. Helping them clean out the back storeroom." He left.

Dark feminine eyes looked up at Ric. Martha Stewart said, "I was on my way to Grandma Hays' house. She's down with her bad leg again."

Ric said, "I thank you, Martha."

Martha sighed. "I wish someday men would finally get civilized."

She continued down the street. Ric admired her waist. Not quite as small as Melissa's, but indeed a pretty waist.

He grinned and turned and entered his office. His new clients still sat where he'd left them.

"I got a feelin' there's trouble here," bearded Smith Jones said.

Ric explained everything including young Jim Young's run-in the last week with Kid Hannigan. The farmers listened in silence. Ric finished and John Rogers said, "Jim's a man who can't handle his booze."

Ric looked at Rogers. "You talk as though you know Jim Young."

Rogers explained. He and Jones and Winston had worked on the Detroit police force with Jim Young. "His letters back home is what got us three out here," Rogers finished.

Ric was slightly surprised. Jim Young had told him nothing about writing home and recommending Black Butte range. He then explained the predicament Young was in by settling on grass and water claimed by Half Circle V. Freckle-faced Bob Winston then said, "On the way out we seen lots of native grass an' the cricks were runnin' bankful, Mister Williams."

Ric told about the long rainy season. "That doesn't happen often and at the right time," he told them.

"Jim tol' us about thet in his letters. He says Sage Crick can be dammed — jus' a small diversion dam — and it could irrigate hundreds of acres of head crops, the land on each side of the crick bein' that flat."

Jim Young was right. With the least rain Sage Creek Meadows became flooded by the creek which had very, very low banks. The flooding and washing in of new alluvial soil was what made the Meadows so worthy to Half Circle V ranch.

For after each spring or summer flooding bluejoint grass immediately grew high on the level land. Half Circle V mowers then went into action, mowing the grass for winter feed.

"Jim's surveyed that country," Smith Jones said.

Ric's brows rose. "Surveyed?"

"Yeah. Jim's an odd duck. Always readin' an' when he was back in Detroit he always went to night classes at some school to learn somethin' — book-keepin', surveyin', something about crops. Things like that."

All three were anxious to see Jim Young. There was nothing more that Ric could do. He warned them of the Half Circle V menace. Each said he was a good shot. Ric didn't doubt that a bit. Detroit had some tough sections, he'd heard.

Each had filed preliminary papers down at Mr. Maresh's office. All the papers lacked was legal descriptions of the homesteads each wanted.

Ric walked to the big wall map. He showed them the lay of the land. Black Butte town was here on the west side of Black Butte River and on the southeast flank of Black Butte peak.

His pointer pointed here, then there. He felt like a school-teacher teaching geography. He pointed where Sage Creek entered Black Butte River, a mere quarter-mile south of Black Butte town.

His pointer travelled the length of Sage Creek almost due west forty miles. Jim Young lived a mere two miles up the creek.

"You got other farmers settled?" Smith Jones asked.

"Three others. They came in last fall. They're excowpunchers, I'd say — anyway, they look like ex-cowpokes. They're north of Sage Creek —" His pointer travelled up the map. "— on Hell Creek."

The new farmers watched. John Rogers said, "Hell Crick comes into Sage jus' a few miles west of Jim Young's homestead, eh?"

"That it does," Ric said.

Bob Winston looked at the area east of Black Butte River, his eyes on Greasewood Creek which ran into Black Butte River a half-mile north of Black Butte town.

"Ain't go no farmers out thet way east?" Winston asked. "Can't see where you've blocked out homestead limits there, Mister Williams."

"No settlers out there yet," Ric informed, "but they'll come. That's sagebrush land and sagebrush land is good land. Land that grows greasewood has too much alkali in it to raise good crops — both white and black alkali."

The farmers got to their boots. They'd drive their loaded wagons out to Jim Young's homestead and spend the night there. "I'll meet you tomorrow morning there," Ric promised.

The new farmers trooped toward the door. Ric looked at his watch. An hour had passed. Greg Mattson stood in the doorway. He was big, hard-looking,

212

gun-hung, booted, spurred. Behind him stood his gunman, Kid Hannigan. And, as usual, the bearded Hannigan had both thumbs hooked in his gunbelt's front.

The farmers stopped. Greg Mattson and Hannigan blocked the doorway. Smith Jones headed the new farmers. Behind him was John Rogers, then Bob Winston.

Silence fell.

SIX

The farmers faced Greg Mattson and Kid Hannigan.

Greg Mattson and the gunman faced the new farmers. The farmers wore no guns. Half Circle V was gun-hung, dangerous.

Smith Jones broke the silence with, "With your pardon, gentlemen, we three would like to leave."

Greg Mattson didn't move an inch.

Smith Jones looked at Ric Williams. "I believe this is the Mr. Mattson you warned us about, Mr. Williams?"

Ric stepped forward. "It is, Mr. Jones." Then, to Greg Mattson, "These men want to leave. I'm sorry I kept them more than an hour. We had a lot to talk over —"

"Let 'em leave, then!" Greg Mattson moved to one side, just inside the door.

The farmers walked out. Kid Hannigan, out on the sidewalk, moved back a pace, eyes on the farmers. He spoke from the corner of his mouth to his boss inside Ric's office. "You need me any more, boss?"

"I don't need you, Kid," Greg Mattson said.

"Then I'll be headin' back to Miss Melissa's poker game," Kid Hannigan said. "Still got a bit of the rodeo winnin's burnin' holes in my pocket."

Ric said to Greg Mattson, "Sit down."

Smith Jones saw Ric in the window. He grinned and lifted his lash and sent it cracking over the heads of his horses. The team hit collars. Ric noticed the lash had not hit a horse.

The wagons went out of sight.

Ric spoke to Greg Mattson. "Your father might have homesteaded your ranch buildings. I could check with the big U.S. Land Office in Helena."

Mattson shook his head. "I homestead it today. Mebbeso the old man didn't file papers? Then if he didn't, some worthless farmer could come in, file on the property's site, and own the buildings."

"Your claim might prove false if there's an original homestead."

Greg Mattson's gray eyes looked at Ric Williams. "What the hell you tryin' to pull off, Williams? Another of your old shady deals, mebbeso?"

Ric's temper rose. His cheekbones reddened. He breathed deeply and said, "You come here for trouble, Mattson?"

"I came here to file a homestead. You seem to want to refuse to accept my filin'. But if it's trouble you want here I am, bucko!"

Ric caught his temper. "Okay, you make out filing papers. Here they are. You pay the filing fee, just like everybody else. And tomorrow morning I'll go out and find the township cornerstone and work back from it to your buildings and run out your one hundred and sixty acres of homestead."

"How much is the filin' fee?"

"Twenty bucks."

"Who gets it?"

"Uncle Sam gets half. I get the other half. What're you bellyachin' about? You've got lots of money."

215

"So have you, Williams."

"An' I didn't earn a bit of it. I inherited it all. My father's sweat and blood, not mine. And the same goes for you, Mattson."

"Don't you like it?"

"I'd feel a hell of a lot better if I'd made it myself instead of having it given to me."

For one moment Greg Mattson's handsome face showed something — but only for a brief clocktick. "You got a point there, Williams, much as I hate to admit it."

Ric sighed. "Fill out that form and if you have any questions ask me, Mattson."

"This question, here — the one askin' for boundaries."

"We don't know what they are yet. I'll know when I make my survey in the morning. I'll fill that in, then."

"Okay."

Greg Mattson wet the pencil's lead. Ric stalked to a window and looked out on Black Butte.

For the hundredth time he wondered if he'd done right by coming back to Black Butte after getting his law degree. He could have stayed in Missoula or gone to Butte or Great Falls and set up a law office. He'd graduated high in the small class and had had various offers of good jobs in all three of these biggest Montana towns. The junior U.S. senator had even asked him to go to Washington, D.C. as his secretary, hinting that soon his secretary would be reading Law for a supreme court judge.

Yet Ric had turned down all these offers and returned to the hate and strife of his old home town. He wondered why. His two relatives here — mother and father — slept in silent graves. He ran no more cattle. Weekends he rattled around the big Bar Diamond Bar ranch-house.

Weekdays a caretaker watched over the big buildings. Ric then realized the only time he felt really at peace with himself and the world was when he was at the ranch. Lately a number of thoughts had pestered him, thoughts he'd got from reading pamphlets on farming sent out by Uncle Sam's Department of Agriculture — most of them concerned with irrigation of the West's arid lands.

Uncle Sam's engineers advocated check dams. These were small dams with spillways you built at the mouths of ravines and coulees. When rains came the dams impounded the precious water.

If there was too much rain, it ran harmlessly over the concrete spillway — thus keeping the dam from being washed out.

Each dam had a headgate. A ditch could be built to this headgate and the stored water could be directed downhill onto fields.

Greg Mattson asked, "This question here, shyster."

The word *shyster* rankled Ric Williams. A shyster was a crooked lawyer. Ric knew Mattson deliberately had sandpapered him. Then common sense came in and established control. He overlooked the insulting word.

He walked over and looked at the question. It was simply a *yes* or *no* deal, very simple. Mattson had deliberately sought to pull him into a trap. Had he done so, Ric's office would have now been in a process of destruction.

Ric gave the answer. He returned to the window, mind on check-dams. Uncle Sam's boys knew their stuff. The state's U.S. Land office would send out engineers to do the surveying and scouting . . . and for free, he knew.

He remembered the low hills south of his ranch. They drained quite an area. Their coulees afford good areas in which to build dams. The land below sloped

217

gradually north. With check-dams, and a little rain, he had a hunch he could turn the acres south of the ranchhouse — and those surrounding it on the west, north and east — into a wonderful irrigated farm.

He had discovered these government pamphlets during his senior year in college. He'd learned all the information regarding such he could from proofs in civil engineering and forestry, for the forest service, he had learned, made much use of small check-dams.

Through ranch records he'd learned that his mother, Augusta Williams, had years ago filed on a homestead south of her husband's land. This gave her son control of the southern hills and their potential water.

Ric had then filed for his own homestead to abut his father's land on the north. This gave him three-quarters of a mile of land half a mile wide from the foothills north. He'd also learned he could file claim for four hundred and eighty more acres in his own name. This he'd promptly done. These papers were now being processed in the state's U.S. Land office.

When all was done and paid for he'd own a piece of land a mile wide and a mile and a half long, running north and south with the ranch-house in its approximate middle.

But time was dragging. To prove-up on a homestead certain improvements must be made for Uncle Sam to witness, and a fence was one of these. He decided that in the morning he'd look for a few workers who would go out and dig post holes and cut diamond-willow posts along the river to build a three-wire fence around the entire acreage.

Ric came back from prospective fields of sweet-blooming alfalfa when Greg Mattson pushed back his chair and said, "That should be it."

Ric studied the application. He had Mattson make a few changes here and there. "I'll be out in the morning at eight sharp."

"How about these new farmers? Where they settlin'?"

"On Sage Creek. Around Jim Young. They're ex-cops from Detroit, all friends of Young."

"Young got 'em out here, eh?"

"I don't ask my clients about their personal affairs," Ric said. "I only ask enough questions — and demand enough proof — of their eligibility to homestead, nothing more."

"An' collect filin' fee," Greg Mattson said.

"That's right. And you owe me twenty bucks."

Greg Mattson dug out his wallet. He threw a double-eagle on Ric's desk. "In the mornin'," he said.

"In the morning," Ric assured.

Mattson strode out, spurs jingling. Ric studied the application again. He noticed Greg Mattson was just a few days older than he. He thought of Sage Creek Meadows.

Sage Creek Meadows was actually on range once claimed by Bar Diamond Bar for Scott Mattson and Bill Williams had fixed an unmarked border between their two ranches directly after turning their Texas longhorns in on this Montana grass.

This boundary line cut straight east and west through the middle of Black Butte. Thus the town of Black Butte actually had been inside of land claimed by the Williams iron.

Thus also Sage Creek Meadows would be on land claimed through squatter's rights by Bill and Augusta Williams. So also would be Hell Creek three miles north of its junction with Sage. Nevertheless the Bar Diamond Bar had allowed Half Circle V to cut hay on Sage Creek for the Williams ranch had plenty of wild native hay on its southern flank on Doggone and Wild Willow and Cottonwood Creeks, streams entering Black Butte River some thirty odd miles below Black Butte town.

Thus his father had allowed Half Circle V to cut Sage Creek's hay. Ric smiled slightly. His thoughts were wasted. Uncle Sam owned Sage Creek except for the homestead taken up by Jim Young.

For a number of years ago some Musselshell Valley cowmen had taken the principle of 'squatter's rights' into the Montana courts. Their basis to claim on a particular piece of land was that they had occupied it first and grazed stock on it.

The state's highest court had upheld the lower courts. The land belonged to Uncle Sam. The cowmen had not homesteaded it. The verdict had been a big blow to the big cowman.

And a great one to the potential homesteader.

Ric glanced at the calendar. He had marked it, Church Social, for this day. Once a month the church gave a social, the money going to the school.

Who should he ask? Usually he went to the social with Jennie Queen. And if not with Jennie, then with Martha.

He knew that town-gossips waited anxiously to see which he would marry — Martha or Jennie. He'd ask Melissa Wentworth to go with him.

He'd seen too much of both Jennie and Martha since coming back from college. Jennie was her usual joking self but it seemed to him that Martha Stewart was becoming a little bossy, too much potential wife, lately.

But would Melissa go with him? She was, after all, a gambler, was she not?

To many Westerners gambling was not an honourable profession. A male gambler was not accepted in some measure. A female gambler was in many cases completely beyond acceptance.

He figured there were honest gamblers just as there were honest lawyers, bankers and other businessmen. Of course, there were dishonest professional and businessmen, too — but that was to be accepted. All classifications in this life held some weaklings.

The theory was that gamblers consorted with prostitutes and others of such nature. Kitty O'Neil had many chances to put in girls on the second storey of her saloon, a thing she never would allow. The upstairs was a respectable hotel usually occupied by drifting cowboys or salesmen.

Ric thought ahead to the social. Usually they were held at the schoolhouse or the church, usually the former.

Ric admitted to himself he went only because there was nothing more inviting to do that particular night. He enjoyed the company of bouncing Jennie Queen or Martha Stewart.

Were he not to go to the social he'd stay home and read some more pamphlets and he was pretty well filed up with Uncle Sam's words. Last night he'd read about building a reservoir below a check dam for storing even more run-off water.

Water that went over a dam's spillway would enter this big reservoir. Water from the reservoir would go into the head canal. If there was more rain than the dam and the reservoir could hold, this drained out the reservoir spillway.

The reservoir would be built a few feet above the surface of the earth. It would be long and not very deep. It could be built of concrete and rock.

He was on the saloon's porch-step when Greg Mattson and the Kid came out, heading for their saddle-horses. Neither spoke. They untied, swung up — guns blasting the air. They left town on the dead gallop.

Kitty O'Neil stood in her doorway. Her hands were on her hips and her lips a hard line. "Someday them two will run over some town child an' kill him," she said.

Ric nodded. "I'll bring it up at the social tonight. We're having a general election in August, you know. I'll talk about getting such a stipulation on the ballot then."

"Sheriff Ratchford is gettin' old. He should be retired."

Ric shook his head. "Being pushed to one side would kill him. The way to do it is to hire a deputy sheriff for him and gradually he'll see the light and retire of his own accord."

"That's a good idea, Ric. This town has no mayor. Why not put in a city government and elect a council and mayor. I know a young man who'd make a crackerjack of a mayor."

Ric smiled. "Introduce him to me sometime, will you?" Then, seriously, he explained that he wanted Miss Melissa Wentworth to accompany him to the social.

Kitty's sharp eyes studied him. "You're wantin' her to accompany you, not me. Jus' ask her yourself, and see what happens."

Ric grinned. "I'm not askin' you to talk to Melissa for me. I'm merely asking you if you think she'd go — or if she should go."

"You're blushin', Ric Williams!"

Ric's grin widened. "Okay, I'll ask her. Where is she?"

"At her table."

Ric stepped onto the long porch.

"Time this town needs to be waked up," Kitty said. "Some of 'em still look sidewise at me after thirty odd years of runnin' an honourable saloon and hotel."

Ric was lucky. Kitty had only two travelling sales-men at her table. They were playing a low-moneyed game just for amusement.

"This town needs rails," one said.

Ric bought a few dollars worth of chips. Melissa smiled at him and Ric liked her smile.

"There'll be rails when more farmers come in," Ric said. "I'm U.S. Land Agent here. The Great Northern has assured me that when there is enough farm and ranch produce to ship out to make it pay the G.N. will run up rails from Malta or a town along the steel."

"Farmers are coming in," one salesman said. "Milk River along the G.N. rails is crowded with families looking for homesteads."

"They'll come in," Ric assured.

Kitty came up. She spoke to both salesmen. "You boys are good at figures. I can't balance my books for yesterday. I'd sure be happy to set up a few for the house if you two'd take a look at my scribblin's."

"Certainly, Miss Kitty."

"A pleasure, Kitty."

Kitty winked at Ric. She and the two went into her office. Ric was alone with Melissa. Melissa looked at him.

Ric spilled out his invitation. Melissa listened and he detected merriment in her blue-green eyes.

Melissa said, "I'm a gambler. I was born into a gambling family. My father was Jack Wentworth, and he gambled over the world. My mother was Elizabeth Wentworth, and she ran a table next to my father's."

Ric nodded.

"I was toothed on a poker chip. I know what's bothering you. Will I be accepted at this social? That's your problem."

223

Ric opened his mouth to speak, but a gesture silenced him.

"You're a good man, Richard Williams. I know that you're not thinking of yourself — that if I accompany you you'll not be lowering your local social standing. You're thinking of me. You don't want me embarrassed."

Ric nodded.

"Well, I'm Melissa Wentworth. I'm twenty-two and never been married. If you want to know the truth, for what it is worth, I'm still a virgin — waiting for the right man." She blushed not a bit, Ric noticed. His estimation of her went upwards.

He wisely kept silent.

"Someday I'll find that man. I want a handful of children with him. I want to be a wife and mother. I'm telling you too much, maybe?"

"No, no. Definitely not. Go on, please."

"Before I came here I had a poker table across the river from El Paso, Texas — Juarez, Chihuahua, old Mexico, to be exact. Rich Texans came over to gamble because Texas has so many blue-sky laws."

Ric listened.

"One day I looked over the crowd and my stomach crawled. I cashed in my chips, walked across the International Bridge to El Paso, and got the first train north — and here I am."

"How do you like it here?"

Melissa Wentworth's eyes glowed. "I love it here. Every moment, every hour, every day — I'm a small-town girl at heart, I've discovered. I'm going to homestead here — so you save me a good homestead, eh?"

"That I sure will. How about tonight's social?"

"You and I, Richard Williams!"

SEVEN

Early next morning Ric Williams stood behind Greg Mattson's horse-barn talking to Mattson. Kid Hannigan was in the background, listening.

Ric explained. "Here is the section marker. It's forty feet from this barn's southeast corner and the section line. Now if you run your east homestead line straight north all your buildings will fall inside your homestead's limits except that stone building there."

Greg Mattson looked at the offending building. It was twenty feet by twenty, made of stone and concrete, and his father had had it built as a powderhouse, for Scott Mattson had dynamited stumps from the river bank to make a horse pasture, years and years ago.

"What if I run my east homestead boundary south?" Greg Mattson asked.

Ric grinned. "You'll have only one of your buildings inside your homestead, and that would be that little stone building."

"An' my other buildin's —? The house, barns, corrals, all thet — it would be on gover'ment land? Anybody could file on the lan' — an' own my buildin's, then?"

"That's right."

Greg Mattson frowned. "Couldn't you stretch the limits a bit south to take in this powder-house? I'll make it worth your while, Ric."

Ric said shortly, "You trying to bribe me, Mattson?" His voice had taken on hardness.

"Call it what you want, Williams. But I'll make it worth your while if you extend the limits far enough south to include this building."

Ric said, "I could report you to Uncle Sam. He'd bring up a charge of attempting to bribe a U.S. official."

"Who'd be your witness?"

Ric looked at Kid Hannigan.

The gunman laughed. "I'm like the three monkeys. I see nothin', hear nothin', say nothin'."

Ric spoke to Mattson. "There is a way to get control of the powder-house, though."

"Name it?"

"You could run your homestead south and hope your father homesteaded the area north, where your buildings are."

"No go on that. What if the ol' man never homesteaded? By doin' that I'd gain this shack an' lose all the rest."

Ric nodded.

Mattson had made up his mind. "Run your lines aroun' my main buildin's. An' if the ol' man has already homesteaded them, my entry would automatically be null an' void, wouldn't it?"

"It would," Ric assured. "No two can land on the same homestead. If this happens, the one filing first had priority."

"Thet college learned you a hell of a lot of big words," Greg Mattson said. "Maybeso in time you'll start talkin' so people can understan' you agin?"

Ric said, "My fee for running lines is fifty dollars and in advance, Mattson."

Mattson stopped, turned. "You don't trust me?"

"Uncle Sam's orders, not mine."

"You seem handy in turnin' the blame onto the federal gover'ment, not on yourself. What if I don't have fifty smackers on me?"

"Then your homestead entry is thrown out as null and void."

Greg Mattson took out his wallet. He threw gold pieces toward Ric. Sunlight glistened on the yellow metal. Ric saw two double eagles and an eagle land beside a sagebrush.

"You got a receipt coming," Ric pointed out.

"Give it to Hannigan."

Mattson went around the barn's corner. Ric picked up the money, anger burning. He spoke to Kid Hannigan. "I've already paced off the homestead's limits running north. We'll walk around them and I'll show you my stakes."

"One hundred and sixty acres?"

"That's right. A half-mile square."

"An' we walk that distance?" the gunman asked.

"Why not?"

"That's two miles, on the hoof."

Ric grinned. "I wanted you to walk it so you'd know exactly where the fence will go, but you can ride out and find the markers. I'll write you a receipt for the fifty bucks. You can ride the line or not. Makes no never-mind to me. I'm not anxious for your company, anyway."

Kid Hannigan had his hand on his holstered weapon. "Watch your tongue, lawyer!"

Ric laughed. "At least you called me lawyer and not shyster! My reputation must be picking up." He took a notebook from his shirt pocket and scrawled a receipt. "Here it is for your Nibs," he said, and swung up on his big bay gelding, Snorty.

Snorty carried quite a load beside his master for Ric had his tripod and measuring rod tied to the saddle, also. Wry disgust pulled at the land locator's innards. The day had not started out good. Then he remembered last night . . . and Melissa Wentworth.

To his surprise, Melissa had been quickly accepted. Her gracious manners and courtesy immediately registered with the men and while some older women grudgingly gave in the younger were soon in accord.

Neither Malcolm Stewart nor Martha gave the customary reading. Melissa was called upon. Ric discovered she'd been in some Shakespeare plays while in high school. She gave part of Macbeth. Ric watched the audience.

Men applauded heartily. Some of the older women — church-goers — gave what seemed grudging recommendation. The younger people — both male and female — also gave full applause.

During the lunch period Martha and Jennie Queen chatted with Melissa, who apparently had visited foreign countries. Others of the young people — both male and female — listened. Melissa became elated and happy. While walking home she held onto Ric's arm, and Ric liked that.

"I'm sure happy you invited me, Ric."

"You were great," Ric said. "Have a good time?"

"Wonderful."

They parted on the steps of the saloon. Except for a light or two upstairs, the saloon was dark — for Kitty O'Neil closed early most week nights for lack of customers. The night was calm. There was no moon but stars were dazzling bright in the cloudless Montana sky. She stood on the step above Ric and therefore was a bit taller than he.

She called gently upstairs, "Kitty, darling."

"Comin' down, Melissa."

Melissa spoke to Ric. "Miss Kitty is like a mother to me. My mama died three years ago — the same time papa died — cholera in Hong Kong. I was in college, in Texas."

"She's very nice," Ric said, and meant it. His mother and father had thought the world of Miss Kitty O'Neil.

Ric heard Kitty unlock the big front doors. Melissa said softly, "Thanks again, Ric," and she kissed him lightly on the cheek and ran to the door and disappeared inside.

Ric had walked home on clouds. He then remembered that both Jennie Queen and Martha Stewart had at times kissed him and his boots had gone down this lonesome dark street again on anything but solid soil.

Riding down on Hell Creek, he wished he'd had a talk with Greg — a serious conversation — about the fact that Greg said he was losing cattle to rustlers.

But the occasion had not arisen. All the time the sword's point came through, separating him and Greg Mattson. Ric Williams sighed. Why in the hell did two persons always have to hate each other?

He didn't like the word *hate*. He didn't hate Greg Mattson. He changed from *hate* to *dislike*.

Coming downhill, Ric looked over the farms — if such they could be called — of George Hess, Jake Mullins and Ward Griffin, his first three clients. All three had strung up three strands of barbwire around their quarter sections. Their farms were located on the meadowlands that Hell Creek — now tame and sluggish — inhabited.

Ric watered Snorty on Hell Creek. He looked

about. Cottonwoods and box elders were green and gave shade. Yonder had been a clump of diamond willows. An axe had cut out all the willows big enough to make posts. One of the farmers had done that cutting.

Snorty lifted his head, sniffed the air, then pricked his ears north, and Ric saw one of his farmers, George Hess, come out of the brush and head his direction, Winchester rifle in hand.

"Still hunting a buck?" Ric asked.

"Well, I'm shootin' to kill at a deer — buck only — if I happened to run acrost such, but us three after thet trouble Young had in town has been kinda keepin' up a guard, night an' day, Ric."

"Half Circle V?"

"That's right. We've seen a few riders in the distance. Couldn't tell who they was, but they might've been Mattson hands."

"And they could have been somebody else, too."

Slow-speaking Hess asked, "Like who, mebbe?"

"Cow thieves. Rustlers."

"You believe really that Mattson's lost cattle in the dead of winter to cow-thieves?"

"I have no reason to doubt his word."

Hess considered that for some moments. "You know him better'n I do. I've done heered you an' him has had dozens of fistfights, ever since in the first grade — so I reckon you know him better than me."

"I've always found Greg Mattson honest." Ric smiled. "And with hard fists, too." He touched a scar over his right eye significantly.

"They say he had cowboys take tallies on the dead cattle they found on roundup a few weeks back. A count like thet in my opinion couldn't be anyway correct, Ric."

"Why do you say that?"

"First, some would be killed by wolves an' c'yotes. Then when the snow melted the run-off water would be bound to wash some of the carcasses into the river and away they'd go — sink down or float off."

"You got a point there, but this spring the snow melted very, very slow — and there was very little run-off water."

"That's right. Lookin' back now I cain't remember Hell Crick gettin' but a few feet above normal when the snow melted. Now who in the name of hell would be rustlin' cows in the dead of cold winter?"

Ric tried being blunt. "He suspects you an' Mullins an' Griffin."

"Us — farmers?"

Hess's voice held a note of surprise. Ric wondered whether or not it was genuine or feigned. Hess was no fool. Neither were Mullins and Griffin. Surely they must have guessed they were under Half Circle V's suspicion?

"You sound as though that thought is new to you, Hess."

Hess gave this some consideration. "No, can't say it is. Me an' Mullins an' Griffin have talked it over, since hearin' Mattson made that statement — but we weren't sure although we figured so."

"Where are Griffin and Mullins now?"

"Mullin's seedin' corn. Griffin is seedin' wheat. I got most of my twenty acres in afore the rain. Got it in barley. Comin' up nice. Plowin' as much more as I can afore the dry comes again an' makes plowin' impossible."

Ric kicked a boot from left stirrups. "Swing up behind me, Hess."

"This horse carry double without buckin?"

"He carries double okay."

Hess put his brogan in the stirrup. Soon he was

231

mounted behind Ric's cantle. Snorty and his two riders came out of the brush. Here were the three farms of the three original farmers. Barbwire shimmered under the hot sun.

Each farmer had built a dug-out back into a hill. These had been warmer during the past hard winter than any frame or sod or log shack would have been. Each door-frame was covered by a thick canvas.

Ward Griffin's farm was first. Griffin was walking with a hand-seeder blowing out wheat kernels. He mopped his brow. "Glad you come along, Ric. Gave me a reason to stop workin' in this damn' hot sun."

Ric looked north. The next homestead belonged to Jake Mullins. Mullins had hoed up rows. He now walked along with a stick poking holes in the top of the ridges.

Into each hole, he dropped a kernel of corn. As he went to the next hole his big foot flattened the area he'd just planted.

Griffin cupped his hands to his mouth, his cry ringing across the prairie. Mullins stopped working. Griffin waved. Mullins started their direction.

"Howdy, men. Howdy, Mr. Williams. Ain't nothin' gone haywire now, has they?" Mullins asked.

"We four need to have a powwow," Ric said.

EIGHT

After conflabbing with the Hell Creek farmers Ric Williams reined Snorty south toward Sage Creek.

Six miles of bench-land lay between Hell Creek and the new farmers on Sage Creek. Sometimes the land was flat and then again it was marred by coulees and deep draws.

Rain had turned this region very green. Ric figured this land would never be farmed. Its contours were too rough and because of its elevation it could not be irrigated. Ric had read all he could find on dry-land farming. Dry-land farming meant you farmed without irrigation. Government reports showed that this area had about twelve inches of rain a year on the average.

Head crops such as wheat, corn, barley and oats needed one good soaking rain just after the seed had been planted. This sprouted the seed and brought up the plant.

Corn was completely eliminated here. It needed rain after rain, but the other head crops needed just one more rain after being sprouted. This rain should come when the plants were forming kernels. Then warm weather should occur, filling the heads and hardening the grain for the harvest.

Ric figured this bench-land was very valuable, though — at least, in his plans — for he intended to farm after settling other farmers. And on this bench-land he'd graze his full-blooded Shorthorn cattle, for he guessed this bench-land would never be taken up as homesteads.

He'd not raise cattle in the thousands as had his father and Scott Mattson. At the most, he'd never have over five hundred head, he figured.

And these would not be bony, longhorned, hard-beefed Longhorns. They'd be gentle, beef-to-the-hocks cattle. Each steer would have at least four times the beef a longhorn steer of the same age packed.

The steaks would be tender and juicy. And the Shorthorn beef would pull down the highest prices per hundredweight on the market.

Ric's prize cattle would be behind windbreaks or in barns when blizzards howled. They'd be dining on green alfalfa taken from one of the stacks his irrigated fields had raised. And spring and summer these cattle would graze on these bench-lands. Maybeso by that time Uncle Sam would charge a grazing fee per head but he felt sure that fee would not be high — if, indeed, such eventually would be fixed.

He was anxious to get on with this work. He'd put hands to work building check dams soon. Again he silently thanked his dead father for the money Bill Williams had left behind.

He'd build old Bar Diamond Bar into new Bar Diamond Bar. His pure-blooded stock would become well known across Montana. His young bulls would sell for a small fortune. . . . He was brought down to earth by Snorty stumbling. Looking back, Ric saw the exposed root of a big cottonwood tree.

Only one real dark cloud lay over this land — and

that was in the fact that Half Circle V was losing cattle.

Apparently cow-thieves were at work here on Black Butte range. He accepted Greg Mattson's words.

Before progress could be achieved the rustlers had to be ferreted out and eliminated, he knew. This basin could not prosper with thieves in the midst of its honest folk.

He'd pointed this out to his three Hell Creek farmers. He'd been blunt and to the point.

"All I know about you three is what I have seen and heard since I settled you on your homesteads. I don't know where you came from, what your past life has been — and frankly, gentlemen, I don't give a damn."

The three had listened in silence.

"I do know none of you has had a criminal record. Had you had such, it would have turned up on the final study made into your eligibility to homestead.

"But Mattson says he has been losing cattle. I can't say Greg Mattson and I are the world's closest friends but I've never found him or his father or mother to be anything but truthful."

"Don't look t'me," Hess said.

"Me, either," Mullins informed.

Griffin said, "I'm no cowthief."

Ric had held up his hand for silence. "I'm accusing nobody. But common sense and logic must tell you men that you're under suspicion."

Griffin asked, "What's the point, Williams?"

Irritation held the farmers. Ric chose his next words with deliberate care.

"I don't know how much cash each of you have. I don't care to know, either. But don't flash money around, please. By having a few bucks suspicion would grow stronger toward you."

The three knew full well what he meant. Cow-stealing was a capital offence in this primitive land. They hanged cow- and horse-thieves fast and without a trial.

"Black Butte's citizens look peaceful but when aroused they're a tough bunch. A few years ago a travelling salesman got a little fresh with one of the bigger girls. The town tarred and feathered him and rode him out of town on a rail to leave him on the prairie naked except for the tar and the feathers."

"I've heard about that," Griffin said.

"My father and our cowpunchers went out and picked the man up in a buggy and took him to our ranch where they cleaned him up and took him to Malta. He had a tough time in the hospital there but he lived through it."

"And he never harmed the girl, so I heard," Hess said.

"Never harmed her," Ric repeated. "Well, gentlemen, I guess that's all I've got to say."

"Thanks for the warnin'," Mullins said.

"We're still postin' a man on guard, night an' day," Hess said.

Ric nodded. "Your business, gentlemen."

He was surprised to meet Sheriff Ratchford two miles south on the bench-land. Ric had the feeling the sheriff had been watching him from concealment in the brush.

"Looking for me, sheriff?" Ric joked.

"Mebbe. Mebbeso not. You stole any Half Circle V cows lately?"

"Out scouting, sheriff?"

"Right, Ric."

Ric told of the lecture he'd just given his three Hell Creek farmers.

"How'd they take it?" Sheriff Ratchford asked.

Ric shrugged. "In their stride, a man might say. I

wonder if Greg Mattson's lost any head since calf-branding roundup?"

"He says he has. Had a marker over on Widsom Hill. Roan steer with a knocked-down off-side horn. Greg says the steer is gone. Scoured that range good, but no roan steer."

Ric nodded seriously.

"Lost another marker north of Black Butte about ten miles. Steer with a throw in his off front hoof. Born with the thing, Greg told me — somethin' like a baby born with a club foot, you might say."

"Cripple, eh? Could he travel fast enough to be run off, you figure?"

"Greg said he got along as good as a steer without the throw. He an' some of his hands worked that section for ten miles each way — and no club-footed steer."

"Where does Mattson think his range has less head than it should have, sheriff?"

Sheriff Ratchford rubbed his whiskery jaw. Snorty played with the cricket in his spade bit, making a musical sound — a habit Snorty had.

"From his complaint, I'd figger the north end has less than it should carry. The cattle runnin' south aroun' your father's ol' range hasn't been touched as much as the northern herds, Greg thinks."

Ric nodded thoughtfully.

"Since farmers has moved in all over eastern Montana the Stockman's Association has sure tightened its belt against cow-thieves. Got three special agents workin' with the Malta sheriff's office alone, checkin' meat sold along the railroad down south."

"Seems odd Greg hasn't called in a Stockman's detective," Ric said. "His father and mine were charter members of the Association. He's one of Montana's biggest cowmen."

"I asked him about this. He said this was his business an' not the Association's. I asked him what he meant by that. He jus' looked at me an' said for me to draw my own conclusions."

Ric nodded. "I've been wondering why he hasn't moved against my farmers, but that ruckus Young had with Hannigan is the only trouble he and my farmers have had — except a few fistfights between his men and my three Hell Creek farmers in Kitty's saloon."

"An' Greg wasn't involved in any of them fights. Only thing that caused them was that the farmers were drunk an' so were a couple of Half Circle V cowpunchers, too."

"How come he's holding back, sheriff?"

"I asked him that. He said he'd let the farmers raise their head-crops up high enough to amount to cow-feed an' then he'd move his hands in an' take over."

"That'd mean gun-play," Ric said.

"I mentioned that mebbeso there wouldn't be enough rain to raise crops. We jus' had a good rain but one rain don't make a wheat-field. He said he figured that the farmers couldn't stay — this was no farmin' land, he said. So he said he'd wait and see."

"Sensible thinking," Ric said.

"Main point of argument is them grass meadows on Sage an' Hell cricks. Half Circle V mowers has cut grass there for years. Enough farmers move in on them cricks an' take over Mattson hay then I think all hell might bust loose, Ric."

"I wrote Maresh in Malta. Asked him to send in no more farmers until this trouble is settled. Fact is, he might notify Uncle Sam and Uncle might send in the black troops from Fort Assiniboine to hold down peace."

"He might, at that."

"This is like sitting on a volcano," Ric said. "Man never knows at what moment it might erupt and hit him in the rump with red-hot lava."

"The whole country is on edge, Ric. The kids in town don't play Cowboy an' Injun no more. They play Half Circle V an' Sodbusters. Unless this is settled soon — an' danged soon — the whole range will be reachin' for guns."

"Rustled cattle," Ric said.

"Me, I figger them stolen cows is one of the big blocks holdin' up this thing. With that solved, Mattson will see things clearer, I'm sure — but this rustlin' has got to stop."

Ric said, "I figure Mattson thinks for sure those three farmers I moved in last fall are doing the stealing."

The lawman sighed. "Mind if I ride along with you to see how them new farmers are?"

"I'd welcome it, sheriff."

The three new farmers were okay. They were dead drunk along with their old buddy, Jim Young. The three loaded wagons stood before Young's crude habitation, horses out on Young's pasture. Rogers and Winston had drunk themselves into insensibility.

They slept in the shade next to Young's shack, snoring in drunken sleep. Smith Jones and Jim Young sat in the shade, backs to the shack's wall, and sipped from a bottle of Old Shoe, then took a drink of spring water as a chaser. Both were about ready to capsize, Ric judged.

Young tried to get to his boots as Ric and Sheriff Ratchford rode in. He couldn't quite make it. He sank down again saying, "Light an' rest your saddles, men. Have a cup or two with ol' friends."

Ric and the sheriff dismounted, gear creaking. Smith got to his feet with trouble and said, "I'll take your horses to the creek and water them," and Ric said, "Sit down, Smith. We watered our horses as we rode in."

Smith sank down again and reached for the bottle. He handed it to Ric who took a long swallow and handed the Old Shoe to Sheriff Ratchford, who raised it and merely wet his lips.

Ric's belly burned. He realized quite a few hours had passed since he'd cooked his early-morning breakfast. He killed the fire with spring water, and handed the water jug to the sheriff, who drank.

"How come you ride out all this way from town, Mr. Williams?" Smith Jones asked.

"Ain't but five, six miles into town," Jim Young told Smith Jones.

"Seemed longer when we druv out yesterday," the new farmer said. "Reckon it seemed long because we was in a hurry to join our old friend again."

"Thanks for the nice compliment," Jim Young said. "Have a drink on me, Smith."

Ric spoke to Young. "Haven't had any trouble, have you?"

"Trouble? With who?"

"Half Circle V."

"Coupla of Mattson's men rode by this morning early. They'd been sent out by their boss to see how long the bluejoint grass was on the Meadows, no more."

"Nothin' else?" Sheriff Ratchford asked.

Jim Young put blood-shot eyes on the lawman. "Should there have been anythin' else?" His voice held the belligerency of a drunk.

"Not a thing more," the sheriff hurriedly said. Without Young or Jones noticing, he inclined his head slightly — indicating to Ric they should go, and Ric turned Snorty east toward Black Butte.

"I rode out to establish section lines with you

boys," he said, "but that can wait, seeing you're all busy."

"I got their homesteads staked out," Jim Young said. "Did it in my spare time from thet map you gave me, Mr. Williams."

"I'll be back some other day," Ric said.

He and the sheriff loped toward Black Butte. The sun was hot and already bits of dust lifted behind hoofs, even after such a long and soaking rain.

Ric looked northeast. Between them and Black Butte was a long and low bench-land running east and west and ending on the west bank of Black Butte River.

This ridge was spiked with pine and buckbrush and occasional big sandstone boulders. When a boy he'd ridden his pony onto this rimrock and spent the afternoon hunting cottontail rabbits with his single-shot Marlin .22 rifle.

Quite by accident, he caught a flash reflection in one group of sandstones. He kept his eyes on the spot but didn't catch another. He told Sheriff Ratchford, "That big bunch of sandstones there. Straight north, almost."

"What about them?"

He told of the reflection. "Looked to me like the sun slanting off the glass of a pair of field-glasses, maybe. Anyway, somebody up there is watching us, sheriff."

"Kid Hannigan."

Ric looked at the sheriff. "Why the Kid?"

"My field glasses picked him up just afore I ran into you, Ric. Apparently he was trailin' you."

"Trailing me? I wonder why?"

"Reckon Greg Mattson wanted to know where you were going. Or mebbeso the Kid wanted to know, an' mebbeso he went of his own accord — not because his boss ordered him."

"I don't cotton to the Kid."

"Lotsa others don't, either. For one thing, they say he's a gunman, an' Greg hired him not to punch cows, but ride gun-guard over him. That's something completely new on this range."

Ric nodded.

"Then they remember he come in about the same time them three cowpuncher farmers of yours settled on Hell Crick. An' right after thet Greg Mattson complained to me he was losin' stock."

"Doesn't look good," Ric said.

"Not good at all," the sheriff said.

NINE

Ric Williams ate supper with Martha Stewart in the Longhorn Cafe. Usually he and Martha chatted and joked but this evening he was silent most of the time and Martha asked, "Something on the lawyer's mind?"

"For once, I'm thinking."

"About what?"

"Lots of things. You know, this town seems to be sitting on a powderkeg, with a slow fuse burning."

"Did you notice that, too? Daddy said the same at dinner this noon. It's all because of you and Greg Mattson."

"Thank you."

"No, that's the truth, Ric. You're moving in farmers. They're squatting on hayland Greg claims. And then Greg says that since you moved those three farmers on Hell Creek he's lost cattle."

"I wonder if he really has."

"Why would he say different?"

"To promote trouble — more trouble — between him and my farmers. And with me, of course. Push things to a climax faster."

Martha thoughtfully cut her steak. "Well, I know

243

Greg — we both went to grammar school together. Frankly, I don't think he has such a devious mind — a mind that could conceive such a situation — or am I wrong?"

"You're not wrong. I think he's more straight-forward, as you say — and he'd have a hard time thinking up such a situation."

"Let's talk about something else, eh?"

"Such as what?"

Ric shrugged. "You got me."

Ric sensed an unspoken barrier between himself and this pretty brown-haired teacher. This was something new. It had not been there until he'd escorted Melissa Wentworth to the social.

Later on that evening he visited the Queen home. Jennie was talkative and her usual self, but Ric also sensed a wall between him and this lovely young woman. Now he knew how a husband felt when his wife caught him kissing her sister.

Ric felt full of cake and coffee and a nice long kiss from Jennie who had stood on the porch floor with Ric on the step below and had repeated what Martha had done just a couple of hours before.

Ric didn't understand why he'd made these two social calls. He had the impression he was saying good-bye to the two girls. It was a loco sensation and was groundless.

He started for home, then looked upstreet toward Kitty O'Neil's saloon. Two lights were upstairs. That meant two customers for her hotel. The saloon was lit, too — but it looked as though not all the kerosene lamps were lighted. Kitty lit all the lamps only when she had many customers.

Ric decided to investigate. Sheriff Ratchford and another old-timer stood at the bar drinking beer, the bar's only two customers. A drunken cowboy slept on the pool table. Somebody had pulled off his boots and spurs so he'd not make holes in the pool table's expensive cloth.

Kitty had many times told him spurs and pool-tables didn't mix. He glanced at Melissa's table. None of the three poker tables was occupied. His heart fell. Melissa evidently was upstairs in her room. For some reason he wouldn't admit to himself he wanted to see the blonde woman again.

Sheriff Ratchford called, "Have a beer with me an' Slim, Ric boy."

The bartender dozed on his high chair. Ric reached over the bar, speared a bottle of Great Falls Brew, uncorked it with the corkscrew on his jack-knife, and lifted the bottle, eyes on the stairway.

His heart jumped. Melissa was coming down the stairs. She wore a long black dress with a white jabot and her hair was done in a nice blonde bun behind her pretty neck.

She came to his elbow. "I heard you men talking upstairs and I heard your name called, Ric." She smiled prettily. "No trade tonight — and I was sitting alone, tired of reading —"

She did not drink, even beer. Black Butte town had learned that — to its surprise — in a short time. A woman who worked in a saloon — a gambling woman — and she didn't drink. . . . Was it possible?

"Let's sit down and talk," Ric said.

"Let's go outside on the porch. How are the mosquitoes tonight?"

"Enough wind to drive them off."

Ric killed his beer and then followed her delightfully small waist out onto the porch, where they sat on the top step.

Melissa said, "I haven't seen you all day."

Ric gave an account of his day. To his surprise she

told him she'd rented a small building and was starting a saddle and harness shop.

Ric scowled. "You know anything about saddles? Or harnesses?"

Melissa laughed. "Only that they're made out of leather. But a salesman who spent a day here — Mr. Hans Christenson — said he knew a young man who is an apprentice to Koke down in Malta and this young man wants to start a saddle-shop — leather shop, that is — and I got some money to spare."

Ric knew Koke. Koke built some of Montana's strongest and best saddles. The last time in Malta he'd bought a new latigo strap and he'd talked to Koke, who said he was very busy repairing harnesses for the new settlers.

"When you get in lots of farmers, my shop will be very busy, I'm sure. What do you think of my plan, Ric?"

Ric caught her two hands. He held them. She made no effort to free them. "I think it's wonderful. I know that apprentice, too. His name is Sam Hoffard."

"That's the name. I should have him — or a letter from him — on tomorrow's stage."

"He'll come. I know him well. He went to school here a couple of years. I was in the seventh and eighth grades and he was in the second or third."

"Oh, that's nice."

"I talked to him the last time I was in Malta. He asked me if this town had a saddle and harness shop."

"So far the Merc has been selling saddles and things saddles need, I understand."

"Yes, but to repair a saddle, they send it out. And I daresay the Merc hasn't a harness in stock."

"I asked. They haven't."

Ric grudgingly released her hands. "Congratulations, Melissa."

"I'm so happy. I know I'll make a success."

"Were you a drinking woman, I'd drink to you on that."

"Your bottle is empty. Don't hesitate about drinking another because I don't drink."

"You don't even drink a beer now and then?"

She shook her blonde head. "I'm not a prude. Others can drink if they want to. That's their business. But I've seen what alcohol can do . . . if carried to a great degree."

"Nobody could make a drunk out of me," Ric said. "Only beer, and then not much of that — it makes me sick."

They talked for another hour, then Ric went to his bachelor quarters. He slept little. He was up and dressed before dawn and he rode out of Black Butte town when it was still dark . . . and he fell out of circulation for around two weeks.

Sheriff Ike Ratchford noticed that Ric's land-office was closed the next day. He picked up Ric's mail when the northbound stage finally rocked in. The stage carried one salesman and a tall young man whom the sheriff vaguely recognized.

"Could I ask you your name, young man? I'm Sheriff Ike Ratchford."

"I'm Sam Hoffard."

"Son of Minnie an' Ralph Hoffard?"

"That's right."

"Oh, I remember now. You went to school here some years gone an' then your folks moved to Malta. How's your father and your good mother?"

"Both fine, sir. Thank you, sir."

Sheriff Ike Ratchford tried Ric's door. It was locked. He shoved the letters under the door.

He'd noticed one was from Mr. Clarence Maresh, U.S. Land agent, from Malta. He remembered Ric saying he'd written his boss asking him to send in no more farmers until this damn' trouble was over . . . if it ever would be.

Maresh had evidently received Ric's letter. This letter was Ric's reply. No more farmers had driven in. Maresh evidently was holding them back. So far, so good, the sheriff thought.

The lawman figured Ric had ridden out early, evidently checking on the whereabouts of the three Hell Creek farmers.

He came back on Main Street. Miss Melissa Wentworth and Sam Hoffard came out of the saloon. They came downstreet half a block and then Miss Wentworth unlocked the door of the small building the other side of the Gunther drugstore and both entered.

Sheriff Ike Ratchford scowled. That little building had been vacant for some years.

The building belonged to the Widder Matthews who had long tried to rent it out but couldn't because nothing happened in town that would require a store or any establishment.

Sheriff Ratchford had a long nose. He had learned over the years that it paid him to be inquisitive.

Accordingly, he made it a point to pass the old building. Both of its windows were wide open. He figured they were open because somebody wanted to ventilate the building's insides.

The door was open, too. He looked in. Melissa and young Hoffard both had brooms and were sweeping cobwebs from corners and the ceiling.

"Cleanin' the joint out, eh?" the sheriff said.

Melissa stopped sweeping. "I'm opening a saddle and harness shop here," she said. "Mr. Hoffard here is working for me. He'll be the man who does the sewing and riveting."

"Sheriff Ratchford remembers me from the days I lived here," Sam Hoffard told Melissa.

"Harnesses, too? Along with saddles?" the sheriff asked.

"With farmers coming in, there'll be a lot of harness work," Melissa said. "Mr. Hoffard is renting a horse and riding back to Malta with a check on my account there. He'll buy the sewing machines —"

"More than one machine?" the sheriff asked.

"A machine for me, too," Melissa said. "I can learn to sew leather, I'm sure."

"I'll teach you," young Hoffard said.

"By golly," the sheriff said. "I'll wager inside a month you'll be buildin' saddles, Miss Wentworth. You're a woman who when she makes up her mind can do whatever she wants."

Melissa Wentworth leaned on her broom and looked about. "Guess we got them all out, Mr. Hoffard — the spiders and cobwebs, I mean. I wonder if Ric has another horse beside Snorty — one I could hire to have Mr. Hoffard ride back to Malta?"

"Ric ain't in town," the sheriff said.

"Oh. . . . We had a nice talk last night on the porch steps and he never mentioned leaving town today."

"Snorty's gone," the sheriff explained. "An' he don't have no other cayuse. Kitty's got some horses eatin' their fool heads off in the town livery, or didn't you know that, Miss Wentworth?"

"I know that, sir. But I dislike asking her to lend us one, she's been so good to me —"

"Sure, she'll be offended if you don't ask. Could I spread the word aroun' about your new establishment?"

"You sure can. We'll be in business in about a week. Is that right, Mr. Hoffard?"

"Keerect, Miss Wentworth."

"I've already told the *Bulletin* about my new business," Melissa said, "but word of mouth is better advertising, I am sure — so I'd thank you, Sheriff Ratchford."

"You're welcome, Miss Wentworth."

The sheriff left. He kept an eye open but Ric Williams didn't ride into town that day.

He checked Ric's office next morning at daybreak. The door was still locked. The back door also was locked and Snorty wasn't in the barn.

He had a key to every establishment in town, so he unlocked the front door and entered.

Ric's bed was made. The sheet held no body heat. Ric's saddle and riding gear were gone. So was his canteen and grub-bag.

Fear entered him. Had Ric been ambushed — and killed — out on the range? He put Greg Mattson beyond suspicion. Greg was like his father, good old Scott Mattson — he fought openly.

But those three cowpuncher-farmers. . . . On Hell Crick. . . . Mebbeso Ric had tipped his hand the other day by telling them they were suspected of being cow-thieves.

Mebbeso they'd ambushed Ric, done away with him?

You're imaginin' things, Ike Ratchford. . . . This trouble has been piling up, piling up — it's got you on the raw edge, like it's got a lot of other people here. . . .

He saddled a buckskin and rode the ten miles south to the old Bar Diamond Bar spread. The world was growing green, he noticed — the rain had washed the dust from the cottonwoods and pines and they glistened in the rising sun.

Ric's old caretaker was feeding his chickens when

the sheriff rode in. "Aim to talk a little to your boss," the lawman said.

"Ric isn't here, sher'ff."

The lawman scowled. "When last was he here?"

"Doggone me, sher'ff, I can't recollect to a day, but I think it was about a week ago —"

"Close enough, an' thanks."

The lawman then cut across country heading northwest. The sun was acquiring heat rapidly. He rode at a walk or a long trot. The earth was becoming powder-dry.

He saw tracks of deer, elk, and cattle. Yes, and occasionally tracks of horses. This had been Bar Diamond Bar graze before Ric had sold all of his cattle.

Now Mattson Half Circle V stock grazed on this grass. When Bar Diamond Bar had sold out Half Circle V had doubled its acreage but wisely Greg Mattson had added no more head.

The lawman figured Half Circle V ran over a range at least forty miles deep and the same distance in length. He had once figured out how many square miles Half Circle V stock grazed over. Forty times forty made sixteen hundred square miles. Each square mile held six hundred and forty acres. This Greg Mattson ran cattle on slightly over a million acres of Montana prairie.

And he paid not a cent in taxes or any other form for the use of the land. He paid his cowpunchers thirty dollars a month and found and a pair of good cowboy boots sold for fifty bucks and up.

The big cowmen had had their heyday, Sheriff Ratchford realized. Now they were through on government tax-free graze. Barbwire and windmills were moving in. These two would have to pay taxes. With taxes schools could be built, expenses paid, and the country would progress instead of stand still, as Black Butte town had done since built.

He hoped and prayed Greg Mattson would give in without causing gunsmoke and death. Ric had a good idea when he'd said that if Mattson caused trouble he'd see if soldiers couldn't be called in from Fort Assiniboine down southwest a hundred miles or so.

He searched for tracks left by a herd of cattle. He found none.

When rustlers stole they stole in big numbers. That was only common sense. And a big number made a lot of tracks.

He figured it about fourteen miles to the Sage Creek Meadow farmers. By that time his horse would have covered twenty-four miles, at the least. Finally Sage Creek was below him.

He drew rein and briefly rested his horse. Slouched in saddle, he gave himself over to the beauty of the land below, now green and growing from the recent long rain.

He lifted his eyes to the land beyond Sage Creek. Hills rose, tumbled, became dim in the heated distance, then again rose from their mirage. And all the while high and black-crowned Black Butte to the northeast held its century-old silent guard of this mighty land.

Only then did he put the horse down the incline. When he came to the farm-settlement he found the four of the new farmers out stringing wire around a homestead site.

The new farmers were now sober. The sheriff noticed each had a rifle close at hand, weapon usually leaning against the wagon or a nearby shrub. He asked if Ric had been out.

"Ain't seen him since the day you an' him visited," Jim Young said.

Jim Young said, "He's gone to Malty. He mentioned to me mebbeso he'd go there on some kind of business."

"That's undoubtedly where he went," the sheriff said. He went to turn his horse and Young grabbed the bridle-reins at the bit and said, "Sheriff, you ain't thinkin' nothin' bad's happened to Ric?"

"What could it be?"

"Ambush, mebbe?"

"Mattson is too big for that. Or, anyway, I think so."

"But thet damn' Kid Hannigan. He's a killer. You can see it in his eyes, the way he packs that big pistol — how he kin shoot with it."

Sheriff Ratchford had been thinking the same.

"Or them other three farmers north of here on Hell Crick," Bob Winston said. "I ain't never met 'em but Jim here says they look like hard-cases, all three of them."

"Don't draw verdicts on people you don't know," the sheriff said. "No, wherever Ric is, Ric's all right."

He debated about heading north and talking to the three cowpuncher-farmers. He did some mental arithmetic.

His buckskin had already carried him twenty-four miles. He figured some six miles, if not a mile or two more, to Hell Creek. From Hell Creek east to home would be another fourteen miles.

He totalled forty-four miles. He crossed Sage Creek and rode toward the northern foothills a half-mile away.

He figured mowers could cut the bluejoint inside of two weeks. Ric's Sage Creek farmers occupied some of the highest grass areas. That would not sit good with Greg Mattson. For Mattson needed every spear of hay he could get for winter-feeding. Last winter he'd even run out of hay. His cattle had had to drift with blizzards to eventually die of hunger.

When he rode down on Hell Creek Jake Mullins came out of the brush, Winchester rifle in hand.

"Got a guard out, eh?"

"Thought it best."

The sheriff looked ahead. George Hess was hoeing in his garden. Jake Mullins planted corn. Head crops were up and green.

Sheriff Ratchford asked if any of them had seen Ric. None had seen him since he'd delivered his warning.

"He missin'?" George Hess demanded.

"Anybody even think about doin' wrong to thet man an' he has me to deal with," Jake Mullins said.

"Repeat that for me, too," Hess put in.

Griffin said, "Same goes for me."

"This ain't nothin' serious," the sheriff hurriedly said. "Don't go off half-cocked, boys. Ric might've jus' decided to ride south to do some business in Malta."

Griffin said, "I'll ride into town tomorrow, Sheriff. We need a bit of supplies, anyway, an' I'll check with you then."

The buckskin was leg-tired when at last the sheriff rode into town. He racked the horse in his barn before a manger of hay and went to Ric's office. He unlocked the door. Wind rattled the windows despite the wood being swollen from the rain. Wind came in under the door, too.

The wind stirred papers on Ric's desk. For the first time, the sheriff noticed a note-size piece of paper on the floor.

Evidently the breeze had blown it from the desk. The sheriff picked it up and read it. It was addressed to him and dated two nights back.

He grimaced as he read. Then, he re-read. Then he said to the four walls, "I'm gettin' ol' an' I overlook points. Time was when I'd have looked for jus' such a piece of paper like this."

He put the note in his pocket.

"An' I put myself an' Buck over forty miles of ridin'. Useless ridin', jus' because I didn't use my eyes."

He stood there — a bluff man, a blunt man, a hard man who could, when occasion demanded, be soft and yielding, a man who loved humanity and hated the evil and the evil doings of those he loved.

He said to the walls, "I wish there was some way a stupid ol' fool like me could kick himself in the ass."

The walls, of course, did not answer.

TEN

This was the morning of the day Sheriff Ike Ratchford made his long ride. Greg Mattson awakened at five that morning. He had a hell of a headache. He'd sat alone in his office the night before killing a pint of Saddlemaker.

He'd sat with his boots on his desk and a pail of ice beside his swivel chair and a glass and the whiskey on the desk. In a way he had enjoyed the misery his thoughts had plunged him into.

He had a slough of money and property but he wasn't happy. Maybe it was because he was unmarried and had no wife or get?

He then remembered boyhood friends who now were married and had families. They were unhappy, too — or so it seemed to him.

He dropped his boots and picked the Bowie knife off the desk and hacked at the ice pail. The bucket was half-full of water for the ice had melted in the heat and the hunk of ice kept rolling away with each hack.

He cursed hotly. "One of these days where everythin' goes wrong," he told the walls. "Now all I need

256

is that damn' Hannigan's face to look at — an' the night would be completely ruined."

He corralled the ice.

Just then a knock came to the door. "Boss, you in?"

Damn it, anyway — Hannigan's voice.

"What'd you want?"

"That pinto horse — Patches."

"What's wrong with that piebald, pie-eyed bastardly geldin'?"

"He's down in his stall. Bloated big as a young elephant."

"Shoot the bastard!"

"Shoot him?"

"Yeah, shoot the —" Big Greg Mattson caught himself. I'm gettin' drunk, he silently told himself. This fool might take me word for word. "Where's he been grazin'?"

"Out on the south horse pasture."

"There's lupine grows there. He's et some of that. Get ol' Wad an' his long syringe and give the pinto the works from behind."

"Okay, boss. I'll report back."

"Not until mornin'. I'm tired. I'm goin' hit the hay soon."

"All right, boss."

Greg Mattson carried the ice corralled between his hands to his desk. He laid it with a book on each side. Then he hit with his Bowie's handle. Finally it cracked into two pieces.

A smile broke across his grim face. He tried the smaller piece for size. It slid into the glass.

He poured whiskey over it. Then he put in a dash of ice-water. He over-filled the glass.

Glass in hand, he settled back into his swivel-chair. And, at that moment, boots again stopped outside.

The young rancher tensed in his chair, fingers clutching the damp glass.

"Boss, you inside?"

Greg Mattson's muscles relaxed. The voice belonged to a cowpuncher he'd posted in town to watch Ric Williams's movements and also to see if any more farmers freighted themselves in.

"What is it, Lon?"

"Jus' rode in from town."

"More farmers?"

"No more farmers but Ric Williams is gone, boss."

"What'd you mean by gone?"

"He ain't in town. Wasn't in town all day, to the best of my eyesight. Me, I think he was gone yesterday, too."

"You *think*? You don't *know*?"

"Not fer sure, boss. Sometimes he goes out the back door an' gets his hoss an' rides off through the brush an' a man lookin' from the front don't know whether he's gone or not."

"Where'd he go?"

"Nobody seems to know. The sher'ff — he was gone all day, too. I talked to him an' tried to fin' out where he was but I got only a grunt or two outa him, no more."

"Ratchford always has been a talkative cuss," Greg Mattson said. "Mebbeso Williams is out at his ranch?"

"Not there. Loren an' Elmer are out there, keepin' an eye open. Loren sent Elmer into town to tell me the ranch has only the caretaker an' that the sheriff was there early this mornin'."

Greg Mattson considered that. Plainly Sheriff Ratchford had gone to old Bar Diamond Bar to see if Ric Williams was there.

"Ride back to town an' keep both eyes open, Lon."

258

The boots left. Greg Mattson had lifted his glass again. He had scouts out watching both sets of farmers — those on Sage Creek, those on Hell Creek. He'd ride out and check with them come morning. He fell on his bunk completely dressed except for his boots and hat and immediately fell into a drunken, snoring sleep. He automatically awakened at five, his usual rising-hour. He'd had but five hours of sleep, if that much — but he didn't feel sleepy. He shaved, ate a big breakfast and then went to the horse pasture, two lumps of sugar in hand.

"Croppy, boy. Croppy, boy."

Croppy was a bay gelding, eight years old. He grazed with the other horses in the night-pasture. Greg Mattson noticed the grass had grown a lot in the last few days. That rain had been a looloo.

Croppy lifted his head. He had ears about an inch long — therefore the name Croppy, from crop-eared.

"Come on, you bay bastard — sugar, Croppy, sugar."

Croppy came at a fast trot, tail up. Greg Mattson, ever the cowpuncher, noticed idly that the bay's tail was rather long, and he made a secret memo to some-day soon trim it shorter.

Mattson held the sugar in one hand and the other was hidden behind his back holding fifteen feet of light maguey rope, the loop already formed. Croppy was a wise one.

He'd come up for the sugar but have one eye roving around, and if you made the slightest move-ment toward him with your free hand — off he was on the dead gallop, escaping capture. He wouldn't allow a man even to scratch his neck. For the man might suddenly grab him by the mane right behind the ears.

And ahead would be a long and laborious and

sweat-hot day under a heavy Navajo saddle-blanket with a heavy saddle over that and an even heavier burden — a rider — in the saddle.

As he nibbled sugar, his whiskery nose rubbing Mattson's palm, Mattson slowly drew in his hand, gently moving Croppy's head closer — and Croppy's roving eyes roved even more, watching the left shoulder for if it moved the hand behind the back would suddenly appear — and he figured that hand held a noose.

The time came. Greg Mattson whipped the maguey noose free. Croppy immediately turned to bolt. The loop shot out. The maguey catch-rope was too short. The noose fell on Croppy's mane halfway down.

And Croppy, tail up, heels kicking, was gone.

Cursing under his breath, Greg Mattson pulled back the soap-weed rope. This day wasn't starting out too good, either.

Shorty Fillmore rode up on a blue roan gelding. "Open the gate an' I'll rope 'im for you, boss."

Mattson opened the wire gate. Shorty rode into the pasture.

Shorty galloped toward the horse, catch-rope down. A few days before a cowpuncher had roped one of the ranch's top saddle-horses. He'd caught the horse on the dead run.

Instead of riding in close and taking up the slack in his rope the cowboy had put his roping-horse solidly and quickly on his rump, the slack immediately running out of the rope.

The cowpuncher had been tied hand-and-fast to his saddle's horn. The top horse had hit the end of the twine. He'd gone tail over head, landing hard on his back.

He didn't get up.

He'd broken his neck.

Mattson had seen it clearly. He knew the horse was dead. He had started for the cowpuncher, rage in his heart, his face bleak and all-killer.

The cowpuncher had read his boss's savage intentions. Fear had torn through him. There was just one thing to do — cut himself loose from the dead horse. His catch-rope was tied fast to the horn. He'd not have time to untie it. He whipped out his jackknife.

He slashed at the rope, cut it.

Then, low in saddle, he galloped away, bullets singing over him. And Greg Mattson had stood there, covered by dust, six-shooter yammering, not shooting to kill but just to scare.

Now big Greg Mattson watched his cowpuncher lay the twine on Croppy. Croppy knew what was ahead. Croppy was smart. He ran in the centre of the bunch of horses in the pasture; so that he'd be harder to rope among the sea of heads. The cowpuncher missed two throws but snagged the crop-eared bay on the third.

The cowpuncher dallied. He brought Croppy to a slow halt, the other horses still running. He pulled Croppy in at halter-rope length and trotted back to Mattson, Croppy following.

"He's a smart little bastard, boss."

Greg Mattson almost said, "Wish some of the hands had the brains this bronc's got," but kept his mouth closed. "Thanks, friend."

Soon he had the horse saddled and ready. He stopped at the cook shack and the grumbling Chinese made him two sandwiches.

First, Mattson rode to town, ten miles south along Black Butte River. The sheriff was home but nobody knew where the land-locator had gone. Mattson bought a pint of Old Rose at Kitty's, admired Melissa Wentworth's thin waist and beauty, wondered if he

could make any time with the lady-gambler — and
then decided he'd try that, after this trouble was
settled.

He rode west along Sage Creek.

Croppy followed a wagon-road through the grass.
The sight of the wagon tracks angered Mattson.

A few months back, this road wasn't here. Farmers
had made it. Ruts were cut deep.

The tracks ran through Sage Creek's best meadow-
land. Here Half Circle V always cut its best hay. He
found himself thinking of this land as his personal
property.

It was not his. It belonged to Uncle Sam. Now
farmers were filing homestead-entries on this land.
They were putting the land to private use. They now
owned the land. Greg Mattson's anger rose.

But with anger was logic. The Stockman's Journal
last month had devoted its entire issue to the question
of homesteaders moving in on a cow-outfit's graze. It
used as an example the cowman-nester trouble some
years before down in Wyoming when Wyoming cattlemen had tried to gun-out homesteader Nate Champion
and his fellow sodbusters.

Cattlemen had killed Champion and his partner.
They'd shipped in two trainloads of hired guns. These
guns never were put to use. Public opinion and the
law had stepped in first.

The cowmen had been defeated. The gunmen
who'd gunned down Champion had been forced to
flee for their lives ahead of the law, outlaws and
fugitives. The homesteaders had won. They now lived
in peace.

The Journal warned Montana cowmen. *Don't
fight the homesteaders!* The cowman would lose.
Public opinion and the Law were against him. The
cowman who had run on open range could now do

but two things.

He could up-breed this stock. Buy pure-bred bulls and his cows would throw good calves. Longhorns had had their day. They were just bone and hide. Markets demanded good beef now.

Shorthorn, Angus, Herefords. . . . One good steer could tote three times the beef a longhorn carried. Better beef, too — marble-grained, tender. And one pure-bred ate no more — probably not as much — grass than a longhorn.

Thus the cowman could cut down on his range. He could grow more and better beef on one-third the range he'd used for longhorns. This cut down his expenses. Where he'd hired three men before he could now hire only one.

How would he get his land?

Through his cowpunchers. Almost all had homestead rights. Almost all swore never would they follow a walking plough.

Settle these cowpunchers on homestead where there was tall grass and high water — the best spots on the range. Pay them while fulfilling homestead obligations to Uncle, and then transfer the property to your name.

A homestead didn't need much improvements. Uncle only called for a fence, a few acres ploughed, a shack. And with a few years the cowpuncher would have a clear patent to his homestead. He'd own it, lock, stock, and barrel.

But all the time he'd been on the ranch's payroll. The ranch had paid him to homestead and the agreement was that for a few hundred more dollars he'd sign over his homestead to the ranch.

Cowpunchers never had much money. Two hundred bucks to one of them would probably be the biggest sum of money he'd ever have. Cowpunchers were fools. They worked for slave wages. They slept in bunkhouses that reeked of human stink and with dirty bedding crawling with bedbugs and other vermin.

Yes, this entire setup was changing. Yes, and changing fast. The cowpuncher's day was almost over. He would disappear with the longhorn. No more trail-drives of thousands of miles. No more riding for days and not opening a gate or seeing a fence.

Big roundups were over. Done with, finished. Now a man would call himself a cowpuncher as he rode along on an old plough-horse driving home the milk-cows. Or riding along a fence that was a few miles long seeing if the barbwire and posts needed repair.

Greg Mattson grinned. He'd make a big pretence of planning to run out these sodmen. But first, he'd try buying them. Hell, none of them had any money.

For Greg Mattson knew this was marginal land — close to desert land. It lacked enough rain for successful farming. And what little rain came, came at any time of the summer.

He'd try these Sage Creek farmers out. See if they'd sell after proving-up, and Half Circle V paying them a few bucks a month for squatting, the agreement reading that after they'd got their final papers they'd sell to Half Circle V. Oh, for a hundred bucks, mebbe-so — no, he'd go to two hundred. But it would all have to be in writing.

The day of the verbal promise and the handshake was over. It had died with his father and with Bill Williams. Now all was paper, and signatures — and recordings, down at the county court-house. The day when a man's word was a man's bond was gone. Too many foreigners coming.

Nevertheless, wariness rode in the saddle with him. You could never tell about these newcomers. For all a man knew each and every one might be a wanted man in another state for everything ranging from molesting a woman to murder.

He neckreined Croppy across a quarter-mile of grass to ford Sage Creek and disappear in the hills.

Soon the grouped wagons of the three farmers came into view in the southwest.

The wagons were bunched on Young's homestead. He remembered Young and Kid Hannigan close to blows during the last day of the Black Butte Stampede. Young had been pretty drunk and plainly he'd wanted trouble, bumping so deliberately into the Kid.

He dismounted with Croppy hidden. He took his field-glasses from their case and went ahead to squat in the protection of a bunch of big sandstone boulders.

The farmers were cooking dinner. Greg Mattson scowled. Noontime, already? He glanced at the sun. Yep, chuck time.

He suddenly realized he was hungry. Breakfast was a long time and many miles back. He felt okay now that he'd been in the open air on a good horse.

He'd not eat with the farmers, though. Half Circle V had a linecamp two miles across Sage Creek Meadows at Dead Coyote Springs.

The linecamp had grub. He kept linecamps always stocked. When the Springs got low on water a cow might wade out in the blue ooze and bog down so he sometimes stationed a cowpuncher there.

He'd head for Dead Coyote and cook something.

But first, he'd parley with the damned farmers.

ELEVEN

Jim Young saw Mattson ride downhill across Sage Creek. He handed the skillet to Smith Jones.

"Rider headed this way."

He put his field-glasses on Mattson. Finally he lowered his glasses. "Greg Mattson."

Bob Winston reached for his rifle leaning on a wagon wheel.

"Don't get too ambitious," Young told the ex-policeman. "Unless he's got some weapons hid back of him on the hill, Mattson's alone."

Winston pulled back his hand.

Young again had the skillet. The big frying pan was heaped high with deer liver. John Rogers had killed a five-pronged buck this morning in the diamond willows along Sage Creek.

When Mattson rode in he held his right hand high, palm out, in the redskin sign of peace.

The four exchanged wary greetings.

Mattson sniffed. "Deer liver?"

Young said, "Deer liver it is."

"Care for a bite?" Rogers asked.

Mattson shook his head. "Et jus' before I left

266

town," he fabricated. He pulled a small smile to his lips. "You boys got some stakes out, I see — an' some bob-wire. You're squattin' on my best bluejoint hay land."

The four farmers didn't smile. Mattson noticed the one called Winston glanced at his rifle close at hand resting on its stock against a wagon-wheel.

Mattson said, "Think you'll homestead it to the finish?"

Again, he'd said the wrong thing. Actually, they might even think that sentence contained a threat, so he hurriedly said, "If you do get final papers — or drive that way — an' need a little money —"

He stopped. He was stumbling like a bronc in hobbles. Jim Young came to his assistance with, "I think I see yore point, Mr. Mattson. You might buy our homestead entries? Am I right on thet point?"

Mattson nodded. "We might work out something." Then he added, "Unless I kin run you off, first."

That was all bluff. Pure bluff. But it might have some effect. Behind him were some twenty odd cow-punchers. And the political power of huge and well-known Half Circle V.

And the gun of Kid Hannigan, too. Naturally word had got around how Kid Hannigan had outshot both himself and Ric Williams. Hell, these people thought he had hired Kid Hannigan as a gunslinger to turn against the farmers.

"Maybe we won't run?" Smith Jones's voice was hard.

Mattson shrugged. He saw no further use in talking to these men. His tongue had got him off on the wrong boot.

He looked at Jim Young. Grim face. He looked at Smith Jones and John Rogers and Bob Winston. And for a long moment hard and hot rage struggled inside the young rancher.

These damned eastern ex-cops were squatting on land he'd long considered belonging kit and parcel to Half Circle V. They were helping break to smithereens one of Montana's pioneer cow-outfits, carved out of this wilderness by the guns of his father and his father's cowpunchers against the Sioux, the Cheyenne, the Blackfoot — not to mention the deadly Crows.

Now that other men had died and bled and fought to build up this wilderness these bastards were coming in — and legally, too — to profit by the sweat and blood of men such as Bill Williams and Scott Mattson.

He turned Croppy. "Take it easy, hands." He rode straight west toward the foothills. He was straight-backed. He knew that one of these could raise a rifle.

They could bury him out here on this wilderness. And if the four kept their big mouths shut nobody would ever know what had become of him.

He thought of Ric Williams.

Nobody seemed to know where Ric was. Had somebody killed him and buried him out here on the range? He'd planned to ask the farmers if they'd seen Ric. He decided to scout the other farmers. They were the ones he suspected of cow-thievery. They'd been here since last fall. The four he'd just talked to had just arrived.

Later on they might steal his stock but not right now. They hadn't been here long enough. He then remembered the liver in the skillet. Maybe that wasn't deer liver?

Might be liver from a calf. A freshly-butchered calf, one of his spring calves. . . .

This problem was getting complicated. It had a hell of a lot of tough angles. What would his father — Scott Mattson — have done in a similar situation?

Scott Mattson would have sold every head of longhorns he owned. He'd have homesteaded for himself — if he'd not already homesteaded Half Circle V's buildings — and hired cowpunchers to homestead.

He'd go beyond Ric Williams. He'd have bought pure-blooded cattle — Angus, Shorthorns, Herefords — and started over again. And undoubtedly within a short time he'd have been producing as much — if not more — tonnage in beef on a hell of a lot less steers and with a much greater profit.

Mattson fried eggs and bacon after baking biscuits in the linecamp.

The day was blistering hot. Croppy chewed blue-joint in the lean-to barn in the shade. Greg Mattson dozed off for an hour. A terrible dream awakened him. He sat up and looked about and then remembered where he was. He held his head in his hands. He was sweating but not from the nightmare. Nightmare sweat is cold. This sweat was hot.

Outside the sun hit with such heat you'd swear it was trying to pick up every drop of rain that had fallen during the rain-spell.

Nevertheless, a man and horse had to move through it.

He searched for cow-tracks. He found some but not those of a herd of any size. As he rode north, the tracks fell back. Almost every head he missed had been run off his northern range.

North was Canada and Indian reservations. He'd ridden north as far as Timber Mountain, Saskatchewan. Timber Mountain had had a mild gold rush. He'd figured his beef had gone there to feed itinerant gold-seekers.

He'd discovered different. Royal Canadian Mounted Police had the situation there well under control, as usual. No Half Circle V beef was being smuggled into Canada. Timber Mountain miners ate Canadian beef and Canadian beef only, the Mounties said. They'd doubled their guard along the Montana-Saskatchewan border.

He'd also checked at Indian Reservations. There was at that time a political struggle between the Army and the Department of Interior for control of the Indians and their reservaions.

For the Indian was a healthy plum. Forced onto reservations, it took millions of dollars to feed and clothe and house him and his during the year — and the two governmental departments each sought control for the money involved.

Reservation agents were caught in the middle. Their well-paid jobs were at stake, not to mention side-graft in purchasing supplies for the redskins. Thus for some time — until their fate was decided — they were forced to play the game honestly.

No bribes, no side-money from dishonest sutlers, nothing out of ordinary — who wanted to lose a very high-paying job for a few bucks coming in from stolen cattle? After this question of management was settled, yes — definitely yes, but until then, play it cool and honest, friend.

But cows couldn't fly. Cows left tracks behind. This was a riddle. Most cattle had disappeared from the north end of his huge range. And yet there was no market for them up north.

Miles and miles of worthless badlands lay to the west. Without water and with only occasional salt grass, they were uninhabitable, their only occupants a few bobcats, some coyotes and the animal both the cats and coyotes lived off of — the lowly cottontail rabbit.

No cows would wander into that worthless area. If so, hunger and thirst would soon drive them east onto water and grass again.

East lay Hungerford's Pitchfork outfit that ran all the way east to the Dakota line. And the wealthy Hungerford family surely wasn't stealing cattle. That eliminated Pitchfork.

And the Hungerfords made sure no stolen cattle crossed their graze. Rustlers had tried before and had been gunned down.

The cattle had to be going south.

He'd checked with Sheriff Ratchford. Ratchford had then checked along the Great Northern rails where the new population — the farmers — were settling rapidly.

He'd checked as far west as Pacific Junction and as far east as the Dakota line. He'd come back with the report that the state's Stockman's Association had detectives out watching the area for stolen beef. Every beef delivered to a butcher shop there had to be stamped as passed by the Association. And the Association did not tolerate thieves, Greg Mattson well knew.

Dusk was heavy when he halted a tired horse on the south rim of Hell Creek valley, the shacks of the three farmers below him — the farmers that had been cowpunchers and now hung onto the handles of a walking-plough.

It was time to light the old Rochester kerosene lamp but none of the *jacals* had lights, he quickly noticed. Evidently none of the farmers was home? Or maybe they sat in the gathering dark without lights for lamps attracted mosquitoes?

Mosquitoes were a terror here on this northern range. Only the howling of the wind made any kind of living permissible during mosquito season, which lasted from spring to winter.

Here the wind stopped blowing only two times a day — at dawn and at sunset. Without a strong wind, mosquitoes swarmed in by the millions. Range horses took it on the run. They gathered in groves of cotton-woods or box elders. Mosquitoes will not stay in an area smelling of manure.

Mosquitoes do not bother cattle like they do horses. Thus cows fared better but still got well bitten. When night came, the mosquitoes departed. Sitting there slouch-saddle on the rimrock, big Greg Mattson waited for lights to come into life in the cabins below — but none came.

Finally he decided the cabins were without occu-pants. Nevertheless, wariness was in him. He came in from behind, hidden by the creek's trees. He left his horse and went ahead on foot, rifle in hand.

Perhaps these three were out stealing cattle. He approached the house of George Hess. A dog came out barking but, as he barked, he wagged his tail. Greg Mattson hunkered and quietly said, "Come on, mutt, come on."

He had a small piece of jerky beef he'd had in his saddle-bag. The dog came closer, sniffing. The two dogs at the other cabins had taken up a raucous yap-ping. The dog gulped the meat. He moved in and Greg Mattson played with the dog's long ears. The dog liked that.

Had any cabin been occupied surely the dogs would have brought that occupant out into the open to investigate, but no doors opened. Soon the Half Circle V owner was behind Hess' cabin.

Hess's barn was empty.

Neither of the other two barns held a horse but both held a couple of cows. He knew what property — real or moving — each homesteader had. He'd made that his business early.

Each had but one saddle horse. Each had four head of work horses. Greg Mattson looked out into their pasture.

The work horses were on pasture. He could see their legs. He then squatted and idly rubbed a collie behind the ears. Where were these cowpunchers who had turned hoeman? Out rustling his cattle, maybe? Anger and rebellion struck the big young rancher. His jaw hardened. He frowned. He felt powerless. The night made him a prisoner. Were it daylight he possibly could have traced the three and determined which way they had ridden, at least.

There was nothing he could do here. He went openly to his horse and mounted, one dog following him. He pointed Croppy southeast toward Black Butte town. His ranch was directly east. It was closer than the cowtown but he wanted a drink in Kitty's and a hot meal at the Longhorn. He was halfway to town when he heard hoffs ahead coming toward him.

He pulled off into a coulee, the dog following. The night now was dark. He could not see the riders. They were heading toward Hell Creek. One sang in a voice soaked by booze.

Greg Mattson did not recognize the voice. Suddenly, the dog darted away, heading for the riders, some hundred yards south.

The booze-singing stopped. The hoofs stopped. Mattson heard a man say, "My God, that's my dog Shep. Now what the hell is he doin' out here this far from my cabin?"

"Must've been headin' for town lookin' for you, Hess."

Mattson then knew the horsemen were the three farmers heading for their homesteads. Evidently they'd merely ridden into town. His theory of their being on his range rustling his cattle evaporated. This definitely hadn't been a good day.

"Come on home, you ol' sonofabitchin' dog," Hess

said and then added, "We're ridin' like our broncs are wind-busted. Let's put a few miles ahin' us in a hurry, eh?"

The horses broke into a hard lope. Soon their hoofsounds had run out against distance.

Black Butte town held but a few lights when the Half Circle V owner rode in, Croppy feeling the many miles he'd put behind him since sunup. The Longhorn was closed but a few lights showed in the saloon and he swung down there and twisted reins and stalked inside.

Three men were at the bar. Nobody was at the tables. He wished Melissa Wentworth had been at a table. He would have liked to see her loveliness again.

One of the men at the bar was Sheriff Ike Ratchford and the other two were Malcolm Stewart and a man Mattson did not know.

The sheriff introduced the stranger. "Mr. Clarence Maresh, Uncle Sam's top land agent, comin' up from Malta. Clarence, Mr. Greg Mattson, owner of Half Circle V."

A stiffness entered Malcolm Stewart. Mattson and Maresh shook hands, Mattson knowing full well that this well-dressed tall man knew he and his ranch were against the farmers on this range — and those yet to come.

Kitty broke the tension by coming downstairs at that moment, long dressing gown making her square shape even more unfeminine.

"Heard your voice from upstairs," she told Mattson. "Are you hungry, Greg?"

Mattson smiled. It was good to have somebody thinking of you. "I could eat the —" He stopped, grinned. "Anythin' you cook, Kitty."

Kitty spoke to the bartender. "I'll take over here, Jake. See that his mount's stabled, has oats and plenty of hay."

The bartender went out the back. Kitty O'Neil moved her bulk into the kitchen.

Greg Mattson reached over the bar and snagged a bottle of Musselshell Beer from the ice box. He opened it with his jackknife and drank, the cold brew sweet against his dust-filled throat.

Sheriff Ratchford said, "Well, my nightcap is down, so I'll head for home, gentlemen. You comin' with me, Malcolm?"

"For my bed, too," the ex-school-teacher said.

Clarence Maresh said, "And this man for his bed upstairs. I'm sorry I didn't get to see Mr. Williams. I hope he's in his office tomorrow."

Mattson spoke to the sheriff. "Ric ain't in town?"

"Hasn't been for some days."

Mattson scowled. "Where do you suppose he is?"

"I don't know. He said nothin' to me about leaving."

"Think somethin' happened to him?" Mattson asked.

Malcolm Stewart listened. Clarence Maresh listened.

"I don't know," the sheriff said. "I've looked around an' foun' nothing. Well, goodnight folks."

The sheriff and Stewart left. Maresh said, "Glad to have met you, Mister Mattson," and started climbing the stairs.

Mattson's mind went to Ric Williams. Where in the hell had Ric gone? A touch of fear hit him. Had Ric discovered who'd been stealing Half Circle V cows?

He then thought, None of my damn' business. . . .
Or was it?

TWELVE

Ric Williams knew there would be no peace on Black Butte range until this cow-stealing business was stopped — if indeed there'd be peace then. He knew he could never settle farmers on Black Butte grass as long as the farmers were suspected of rustling.

He was sure his first group of farmers on Hell Creek were not cow-thieves. He'd watched these three all winter.

Still, a man could not be sure. . . . Anyway, this rustling would have to be stopped.

He'd made one error, though — he later discovered. He should have told Sheriff Ratchford that he was leaving and would try to solve this stealing. But he'd not done this, so that was that.

Within a few days he'd covered the northern route of investigation that Greg Mattson had earlier covered. He discovered the same facts as his long-time school-opponent had learned.

No stolen cattle went into Canada. The Indian reservations were using none, either. None was being driven across Pitchford range to the east. There were but two directions the stolen cattle could go.

One was west, into the naked, ugly badlands. They could not be held there without hay being hauled in and water also being delivered. The other direction was south.

The end of the fifth day he sat in a saloon in Malta and used his eyes and ears. He'd picked out one of the lowest dives in the skidrow section.

He was unshaven and his clothes were dirty but he'd bathed in Milk River before riding into this red-light district. He soon discovered something new to him. Miles south in the Little Rocky Mountains there was a gold boon.

Placer gold had recently been discovered. Two gold-towns had sprung up overnight. He'd heard that at least ten thousand miners and families and mine-owners were congregated in the two towns.

Gold had been discovered late last fall. Greg Mattson had started losing cattle about that time, Ric remembered. Ten thousand mouths needed a lot of meat.

Two hours later, he was riding south. He figured it about sixty miles from Malta to the first gold-town. The country consisted of rolling land. Two big cow-outfits ran cattle in this region.

They were the Turkey Track and the Mill Iron. Both were tough, hard-boiled Texas outfits who'd driven thousands of worthless longhorns up the Montana Trail some twenty years back.

Both outfits had a tough record in regard to cow-thieves. Each hanged a man even if only suspected of rustling. Thus cow-thieves stayed away from Turkey Track and Mill Iron brands.

Ric felt sure neither Turkey Track or Mill Iron lost beef to rustlers. For one thing, a rustler usually never stole from an outfit close at hand. To do so would bring suspicion down on him . . . and the hangman's noose. Therefore he stole from distant outfits.

Ric spent three days in the first mining town and two in the second. Both were in the Little Rocky Mountains. Both were mad, gold-crazy towns with many saloons, whorehouses and no schools or churches. And both had many mouths to feed.

He made the rounds of the mine commissaries and butcher shops posing as a rancher with beef to sell. His ranch, he said, was south across the Missouri in the Musselshell basin. He sold not an ounce of beef.

Each commisary and butcher-shop bought beef from an outside source, he learned — but he was not told where that source originated. This he had to discover on his own hook.

He'd never been in the Little Rocky Mountains before. Once when a child he and his father had had a reason to ride to the Mill Iron. He'd then seen the mountains in the southwest distance.

He'd never forgotten them. His father had told him that they were the last extension of the Big Rocky Mountains in Montana. Bill Williams had said that the last chain was the Black Hills of Dakota.

He was sure nobody he knew was in this area. Word of the gold rush might have reached secluded Black Butte town but if so he couldn't remember hearing about it. While in the nearest town, he saw but one man he knew — and why this man was in this gold-crazy town, he then did not understand.

He'd decided to secretly watch the biggest commissary in town. Sooner or later, somebody would deliver beef to it. He'd then trail this somebody and see, if possible, where the beef came from.

He made camp on the mountain beside the commissary. Night and day, the town and its stamp-mills clanged and screeched and hollered. Others camped on the hill — miners looking for work, women,

278

children.

The second day of watching he saw a man below talking to the butcher and head-cook of the commissary. Ric put his field-glasses on the newcomer.

He watched, heart beating strongly. His glasses clearly showed the man. Finally the man walked away out of sight. Ric Williams lowered his glasses, still doubting his eyes. For the man had been chunky, wore range-clothing, and a black beard covered his square face. The man had been none other than Kid Hannigan.

What was Kid Hannigan doing here? Had Greg Mattson canned him and had the gunman come here looking for work?

Or was he here to sell stolen Half Circle V beef?

Ric never saw Kid Hannigan again but that evening four wagons drove in behind the commissary, their loads covered by dirty tarpaulins. Each wagon had a double-box which meant they each carried quite a load.

Ric was squatting under a pine tree playing a listless game of whist with a miner off shift. "What's that?"

The miner looked. "Them's beef wagons. They come in about every three, four days. Deliverin' beef to the commissary."

"Wonder where they come from?"

"Damn' if'n I'd know. Your play, friend."

Ric laid down his cards. "Jus' remembered I got to meet the boss of the Circle Circle bar. He promised to meet me at this time. Yesterday. Said he might have a table open for me."

Ric posed as an itinerant gambler.

Within a few minutes, he was behind the commissary, hidden in a shed, watching the wagons being unloaded not more than forty feet away.

He learned nothing about the beef. The meat packed no hides; therefore, no brands. The beef had been dressed out and cut into quarters. But he did later learn who had hauled in the meat.

"Them beef haulers," a man said. "Them's the Cullen gang, mister. Tough bunch. Got a camp down below on the mountain. Clyde Cullen jus' a week or so kilt Tike Qualey."

"I'm new here," Ric said. "Tike Qualey?"

"Was our town marshal," the gambler said. "Tough bastard from Texas. Town-tamer there, I heard. Fast gun, but Clyde Cullen was faster."

"What'd they fight about?"

"Damn' if I know. Cards or no cards?"

Later Ric heard that the marshal had accused Clyde Cullen of rustling beef because how in the hell could a man raise so much beef on a mere quarter-section of land with only one old milk cow in evidence?

Ric also learned about the Cullen farm, two miles south of town on the level country.

A farmer had owned the homestead. One day he'd mysteriously disappeared. The Cullen clan had then moved in.

Ric camped in the pines from which he overlooked the Cullen farm. He did not have to wait long.

Three days later seven wagons left the farm, heading north. Each spring wagon-seat held a driver. Ric had seen the drivers around town.

Each had packed a pistol on his hip. All had the looks of cowpunchers, not mule-skinners or farmers. Swaggering men, who usually travelled in twos or threes. . . .

Each wagon sported a very high box. That meant each could carry double the ordinary load. Each wagon was pulled by four horses abreast.

The three Cullens rode ahead. Each led an unsaddled

horse. That horse told Ric they'd ride hard and fast to wherever they were going, changing from one horse to the other.

Ric followed, hiding to the pine and spruce footing the Little Rocky foothills. Twenty miles north he ran out of such protection. He then followed coulees and draws far to the west of the wagons.

The three Cullen brothers had long ago ridden out of sight in the blue haze of distance. Ric had seen them close in the mining town. He had judged them to be in their twenties.

Each packed a great family resemblance. Ric figured that until you got to know each well only then could you tell Clyde from Ed and Ed from Lon and Lon from Clyde.

All were short, stocky men. All wore old range-garb — runover boots, clanging spurs, blue jeans, faded shirts — and each packed a gun on his hip, and two, he'd noticed, had their guns tied down.

Plainly the three expected trouble . . . and were prepared for it. They hung together; where one was, his two brothers were.

Ric figured the man who was foolish enough to challenge one had the other two on his hands, whether he liked it or not.

He also noticed all wagons carried a load, tarps covering this. He wondered what the loads consisted of.

The wagons followed the Malta road until they reached the northern end of the mountains. Here they departed from that road and continued on northwest on what appeared to be a new road.

It held deep ruts. Wagons had gone over it during the last rain-spell.

If the wagons continued in this direction they'd cross the Milk some twenty miles west of Malta, Ric figured. They'd then head into the rough badlands constituting Half Circle V's western border.

Things were beginning to add up, Ric figured. These thieves apparently drove stolen cattle west into the badlands. This could be easily accomplished. They were smart bastards.

Ric deduced that the three Cullen brothers had ridden ahead to shove Mattson steers into the badlands; an easy task.

Cattle grazed to the edge of the rough country. All a rider had to do was circle a few head and haze them into the badlands. Other riders could pick them up, chase them west, and soon the badlands would have them completely hidden.

He moved at night. After the wagons made night-circle he'd come down in the dark and ride ahead some twenty miles or so, finally picking out the spot where undoubtedly the wagons would reach the next day.

This was easy to determine. Wagons leave tracks. Points where men camp are sure to have debris left behind to mark their locations.

Ric then picked out a high butte to hide on. He'd bought grub in the Little Rocky Mountains and he supplemented this by cottontail rabbits he caught with horse-hair snares.

Three nights later, the wagons came to the Milk River. They were further west of Malta than he'd reckoned. If they continued on this angle they'd be in the badlands about thirty miles west of Black Butte town.

He kept close watch on the land below and on his back-trail. For hours he squatted looking south-east toward the mountains, now hidden by distance, but he discovered no riders. The cow-thieves had picked their trail well, for each night's stop was close to a spring or a small creek heading north, a tributary of the Milk River.

That night the wagons made camp in Milk River's cottonwoods. Ric was surprised next morning to see two big water-wagons move north with the others. These water-wagons had evidently been stationed along the river awaiting the other wagons. He still did not know what was under the tarpaulins. The wagons began moving northwest toward a canyon leading out of the badlands some few miles away.

Ric rode down-river into Malta. His father had been a friend of the Malta sheriff who had once sheriffed the Black Butte area until his father and Scott Mattson had split the county to make Black Butte town a county-seat and Sheriff Ike Ratchford its lawman.

"You're Richard Williams, ain't you?" the sheriff asked.

"I am."

He learned that Sheriff Ratchford had a bulletin out for him.

"Seems like you suddenly disappeared, Mr. Williams, an' Ike Ratchford's worried about you."

Ric said, "I'll square things with him." He then told the sheriff about the wagons and the Cullen brothers. "Where'd the wagons cross the Milk?" the lawman asked.

"Squaw Crossing."

"That's west of my line of jurisdiction, Mr. Williams. My line is two miles east of Squaw Crossin' at Willow Point. That's in Sheriff Ratchford's territory." His seamed eyes narrowed. "This is a kinda wil' tale, young man."

"I know that, but it's true."

"So far them wagons ain't done nothin' unlawful. You got no concrete evidence they're cut to haul back stolen beef."

"You ever hear of the Cullen brothers?"

"Sure have. I'll tell you about 'em."

The Cullens were Canadians. They were wanted up north for train- and bank-robberies. They'd fled into the United States about five years before.

"Some claim they work with the Cassidy bunch now an' then, holdin' up banks, but nobody can prove that. Far as I know, there are no charges against any of the three in Montana."

"Why don't the law take them into custody and notify the Mounties?"

The sheriff grinned. "I don't work for the Royal Canadian Mounted Police," he pointed out.

Ric went downtown. By sheer accident he met young Sam Hoffard coming out of Koke Saddlery.

"All the country's lookin' for you, Mr. Williams. Some even claim somebody's shot you down on open range an' killed you."

Ric noticed a wagon and team tied to the Saddlery hitching-rack. The wagon contained two upright stitching machines.

"You driving out to Black Butte?" Ric asked.

"I sure am. Leavin' right now. Them's the sewin' machines for Miss Melissa's new business there. Goin' drive all night. Cooler then an' easier on my horses an' a man an' team makes better time."

"Can you wait a minute or two?"

"Sure can. Why?"

"I want you to take a letter out to Sheriff Ratchford."

"Deliver it to him first thing on reachin' Black Butte."

Ric wrote rapidly but to the point. He then addressed the envelope and sealed it. Hoffard put the envelope in his shirt's breast-pocket and buttoned his vest over it.

"Sure can't lose it now," he said.

"You deliver that in the morning and I'll buy the first saddle you make in Black Butte, and I give my word on that."

"Your word's good with me, Mr. Williams."

THIRTEEN

Sheriff Ike Ratchford was frying his ham and eggs the next dawn when he saw young Sam Hoffard unlatching the front gate. "Now what the hell is wrong?" the sheriff asked himself.

He was in a surly, unhappy mood. He'd been searching the range for any signs of young Richard Williams. He'd climbed buttes and scouted with his field glasses and he'd seen riders crossing this wilderness but always they turned out to be one of the three in classification.

The first group were drifters. With spring-roundup finished ranches had laid off riders until fall beef-gather was started some months away. Thus there was a surplus of jobless cowpokes riding here and there either riding the grubline or looking for riding jobs which weren't.

The second group was the seven head of farmers Ric had moved in. The third and most abundant group were Greg Mattson's Half Circle V riders.

He even found himself wishing that Montana had buzzards. Were there buzzards a man could tell where every dead thing lay on this wide range — be this cow or horse or man or what have you.

"You're the young man who's gonna work for Miss Melissa in her saddle-shop, ain't you?"

"I am. I got a letter for you."

"Letter? When'd you start workin' for the postal service?"

Sam Hoffard smiled. This sheriff was a crusty old character, no two ways about that. "Mr. Williams gave it to me to give to you last evenin' when I left Malta."

"You mean — Ric Williams?"

"Yeah, the land agent."

"You saw him in Malta? Last night? How was he? In good shape? He's been gone — hell, lotsa days."

"He tol' me this letter'll explain all that."

Sheriff Ratchford elatedly dug in his pocket. "Ric pay you?"

Hoffard backed away. "Ric offered to pay but I said no dice. He then tol' me he'd buy the first saddle made — that I made, too — in Black Butte."

"I'll buy your first bridle. Headstall, reins and — not a ear-split headstall, but one that buckles under the jaw. An' a plain curb-bit."

"I thank you, sir."

Young Sam Hoffard left. Sheriff Ratchford slit open the envelope. First he read rapidly, then he read the second time more slowly, and the third time he read very, very slowly, lips moving.

The letter digested, he stood and stared out the window at his garden, his mind darting here, then there.

Should he call in Greg Mattson on this? He debated this but for a moment. Naturally Mattson would be called in. They were stealing Mattson's cattle, weren't they? And Mattson had a crew of tough cowpunchers. Men like that Kid Hannigan. Suddenly the sheriff's

287

eyes pulled narrow. Hell, he'd not seen Hannigan for some days — about as many days as Ric Williams had been gone.

Greg Mattson didn't know where Hannigan had gone, either.

But now he knew where that gun-throwing bearded bastard had gone. Ric's letter told him.

Three days ago Greg Mattson had been in town and asking if anybody had seen Kid Hannigan.

"How come you hire a gunman?" Sheriff Ratchford had asked.

"Gunman?" Greg Mattson's gray eyes had stabbed holes through the lawman. "Who t'hell says Hannigan was a hired gun?"

The sheriff had shrugged. "Everybody aroun' here. Hell, he's liquid fire with his cutter, Greg. He showed that when he outshot both you an' Ric Williams when the stampede was on a few weeks ago."

"Jus' 'cause a man's good with a weapon is no sign he's a gunman," the young Half Circle V owner said shortly. "I hired him to punch cows, not sling a gun."

Sheriff Ratchford wisely had kept silent.

"I ain't ready to sling guns with Ric Williams an' his farmers," Greg Mattson continued. "From what I've heard, Ric's done sent orders down to Malta to send in no more farmers. For all I know, he might have given up his big idea of becomin' a gentleman land locator."

"Some one of these days one of you'll kill t'other," the sheriff said. "An' all because of nothin'."

"Nothin', you say?" Greg Mattson had sobered. "You said it, sheriff. Over nothin', absolutely nothin', damn it to hell!"

"Then how come you hired Hannigan?"

"Because he came recommended to me as an all-aroun' cow-hand, which he sure as hell is."

"Mind if I ask who recommended him?"

"Not a bit. Frien' of mine. Big wheel for the Stockman's Association down in Helena."

"How come he recommended Hannigan?"

"God damn, sheriff, but you're full of questions today. Here I jus' asked if you'd seen Kid Hannigan an' you want a life history of him from me. Friend said Hannigan was his brother-in-law an' Hannigan needed a job. Thet answer your questions?"

"Don't get rough with me, Greg!"

Greg Mattson had studied the old sheriff. "If it was my day to laugh, I'd sure as hell laugh, Ratchford. But I laugh only on Fridays an' this is Wednesday."

Breakfast finished, Ratchford went to his barn, led his sorrel gelding out and pumped a bucket of water for the horse, then saddled and bridled and swung up. He looked down at his empty rifle-scabbard. Then he dismounted and went to the house and returned carrying his Winchester .30-30. He put the rifle in the boot and led the horse to the gate and once outside swung up and rode north toward Half Circle V.

The effects of the long rain were almost gone. Already grass was turning brown. He looked at the western sky. Far off on the horizon were a few dark clouds. Rain here invariably came from the west or northwest.

Greg Mattson was breaking a blue roan gelding to saddle, for he rode the ranch's rough-string. He claimed that you had to teach a horse how to buck. He said a bronc bucked because he'd been trained to buck or because he was afraid.

And once a horse got into the bad habit of bucking he wanted to buck every time a man swung up on him. Sheriff Ratchford agreed with this. He'd broken every head of his personal saddle-horses himself.

But not a one had a chance to buck. He first tied one in a stall. He fed him hay and oats. He made friends with the horse. Then he saddled and unsaddled, getting the bronc used to a saddleblanket and saddle and hackamore.

Finally, he swung gently into leather, time after time, the horse tied to the stall. Thus he got the horse used to his weight. Finally, after a month or so of this, he got the horse in the open, and gently eased into saddle.

If the bronc threatened to buck, the sheriff pulled his head up with the hackamore's rope — for long ago he'd learned a horse cannot buck if he can't get his head down between his legs.

He turned the bronc in a circle, this way, then that, until all desire to pitch had left the green horse. He didn't ride far the first week. Just a few miles a day, no more.

He rode with a hackamore rope for about a month before he used a bridle and bit, and then the bit was a plain snaffle, nothing more, for he didn't want to bit-gall the bronc's tender mouth.

And in short time, he had a horse — a real tough cow-horse, one that knew him, and one he knew. This was the way Greg Mattson broke Half Circle V's rough-string, also.

Greg Mattson saw the sheriff riding in. As he pulled in the rancher said, "I ain't as bitin' as the other day in town. This time I'm worse."

"You need a spring dose of sulphur an' molasses," the sheriff said. "I mind your good mama givin' you such each spring."

Mattson smiled. "You remember right, sheriff. Anybody seen hide or hair of that damned fool of a Ric Williams?"

"I got a letter from him today."

"Letter?" Mattson scowled. "The idiot done got so scared of me he done fled the country?"

"Here it is, Greg."

Mattson handed back the letter. "Don't concern me in the least," he said.

The sheriff studied him. "He's trackin' down whoever mebbeso is stealin' your Half Circle V cattle."

He had emphasized the word *your*.

"I never asked him to," Mattson pointed out.

Sheriff Ike Ratchford kept a straight face but inside he was surprised and mystified. He'd expected this tough young man to want to immediately saddle and ride out for the cow-thieves.

"You're losin' money," the sheriff said.

"I got a lot of money. Too damn' much, in fact. There are three danged beautiful young women down in town. Martha, Jennie an' Miss Wentworth. An' you know what?"

"What?"

"My money's made me so damn' suspicious of thinkin' a woman would marry me only because she wanted my money that my life is becomin' cramped aroun' any of them three, an' it hurts me. I mean that."

Now it was Sheriff Ratchford's turn to be cynical. "My heart bleeds for you," he said. "You ever hear of the Cullen gang?"

"I have. An' I have no desire to tangle guns with 'em. I'm a young man an' I look forward to a middle age of work and an old age of jus' sittin' an' rememberin'."

"He saw Kid Hannigan in the Little Rocky Mountains."

"So the letter says. I reckon the Kid went there to try to get some of thet gold, which of course he won't get."

"Mebbeso Hannigan's workin' in cahoots with the Cullens, stealin' stock he was hired to pertect?"

"That's happened afore, I've heard an' read."

"You don't suspect him, then?"

"I don't."

The sheriff sighed. "Mebbeso you're right, Greg. I kinda liked the overbearin' bastard, myself. What'd you think of Ric's plan of action? Sounds mighty sensible to me, it does."

"Not to me, sheriff."

"Why not?"

"Sounds kinda childish. Him on a butte back in the badlands spyin' on them Cullen sonsofbitches. You on Flat Top Butte, gettin' instructions he flashes by a hand mirror he packs. Then me or one of my hands on Black Butte watchin' both you an' him an' you —"

"You won't be able to see either him or me," the sheriff said. "The distance is too far for naked eyework."

"I know. Credit me with a nickle's worth of brains, at least. He'll flash a signal to you — then you flash one toward Black Butte —"

Sheriff Ike Ratchford scowled. This young man didn't seem to take this seriously. He was up against something he didn't understand and in such cases he became angry — and anger now was rising.

Greg sure t'hell wasn't the fightin' bastard his ol' father had been. Ol' Scott would have headed right out fast after them cow-thieves with a six-shooter tied onto his hip an' a loaded rifle in his hands, waddies streakin' behin' on plough horses, all of them also loaded down with killer-hardware!

An' on the way to the gunfight ol' Scott might have picked up his ol' trail buddy, Bill Williams, and a handful of Bar Diamond Bar cowpokes and ol'

Bill an' his rifles would have ridden with Scott . . . .

In them days, cowpokes were loyal to their irons. They'd die for their brands. But nowadays —

Sheriff Ike Ratchford spat hugely.

He opened his mouth to shoot out a hot bunch of words, but Greg Mattson spoke too soon. "Now let's say it's a cloudy day an' no sun — Or dark night an' impossible to reflect light from a mirror —"

"Yeah?"

"Then what do we use for a signal?"

"You read Ric's letter, didn't you?"

"Yeah, he said somethin' about buildin' a small fire back of where them rustlers is. You'd see this fire on Flat Top Butte an' you'd signal by fire whoever was on Black Butte an' get the word through that way."

"Small fire, hold a blanket in front of it — three times blottin' it out, was the rule."

"What's to keep them Cullens from seein' the fire?"

"Ric'll be behin' the rustlers — west of 'em — with hills atween him an' them so's they kint see the fire. Hell, that's easy to arrange."

"Okay, I'll post a man on Black Butte. You know, I've done a lot of ridin' — an' thinkin' — the last few days, 'specially since Ric done hauled ass out."

"Ridin'? An' thinkin'?"

"Yeah, both. Never knew I was capable of thinkin', did you now?"

The lawman grinned. He liked this young guy and at the same time he didn't like him. Life was just a hell of a mess of stupid contradictions.

"We'll let that ride," the sheriff said. "What you been thinkin' about?"

"Well, first I talked to each an' every one of them seven farmers Ric hauled in. I talked civilly an' as a frien', although it was hard to do."

"What'd you talk about?"

"Well, I led up to it, gradually. Each could homestead an' I'd pay each twenty bucks a month an' when they had deeds to their homesteads they'd sell each an' every deed to me for a coupla hundred bucks — an' Half Circle V would own their land, then."

"What'd they say?"

"Each an' every manjack of 'em turned me down. I even went to forty bucks per month — with them doin' nothin' but settin' — an' five hundred each deed, an' they still turned me down."

"They must wanta stay, eh?"

"They sure do. So then an' there I come to one conclusion, sher'ff."

"An' thet?"

"No use fightin' them. That'd land some of us dead an' the rest in Uncle Sam's federal pen. Work with them. Buy their hay for stock feed. An' get my cowpokes on homesteads jus' as fas' as Ric can lay them homesteads out!"

Sheriff Ike Ratchford suddenly felt at least eighty years younger. He took out his red bandanna and mopped his sweaty forehead. "You showed logic, Greg — real deep logic, man. An' I congratulate you."

"I took you off the fish-hook, eh?"

"Me an' lotsa others, Greg."

"Now let's talk about cows. No, not them rustled cows of mine — jes' cows, plain cows."

"Okay. Shoot."

"These damn', worthless longhorns, for instance. Ric was wise. He got rid of all of his'n. Shipped 'em out to the last horn. I'm goin' do the same."

"An' then what?"

"Stock the ranch with good cattle. Angus, Shorthorns, Herefords. Ain't made up my min' jus' what breed, yet. I'll run on open range till it's all gone. Then my cowpunchers'll deed grass-homesteads to me. An' the way I figure, some parts of this country — the hills an' rough sections — will never be homestead. No farmin' land there."

"I agree."

"Okay, we got thet settled. Now, let's talk about them rustlers — an' them cows of mine they been stealin'. Them original wagons, now. I think they carry butcherin' equipment — tripods folded down, things like thet."

"So Ric's letter said."

"Them water wagons, now. They'll furnish water in the badlands. I only got one big question."

"An' it, son?"

"Let's say the Cullens kill an' butcher back in the badlands. Won't the meat spoil in this heat goin' all the way acrost country to the Little Rockies?"

"I've considered that. Them wagons might have salt sacks."

"I see. They'd salt the meat down good afore movin' it, eh?"

"Thet's my opinion," Sheriff Ratchford said.

Mattson rubbed a whiskery jaw. "I agree. But what say we get a signal from Ric sayin' them rustlers are leavin' the badlands?"

"Keep on."

"Ric flashes to Flat Top. Your man there flashes to my man on Black Butte. We head out acrost country for thet canyon those wagons entered. An' by the time we get there them wagons'll be acrost the Milk an' headin' south."

"Best place we could catch them is in thet narrow canyon."

"You station somebody on Flat Top. I put a hand on Black Butte. But you an' me ain't in this locality.

We're down on the Milk watchin' thet canyon. Along with as many men as I kin raise to help us, which I think is damn' few. These new cowpunchers — them new breed — they ain't got much loyalty to the iron that pays their wages."

"I reckon they don't, Greg. I was thinkin' of the same plan. Come mornin' we head out, headin' for thet canyon."

"I'll meet you in town, sheriff." Mattson patted his horse's shoulders. "Damn thet Ric. A stupid son, thet fool. Ridin' all thet way alone — into thet gunsmoke territory —"

Sheriff Ratchford said nothing.

"Ridin' to see who butchers my cows — an' me not askin' him to. The stupid bastard might've got hisself kilt!"

"Only way peace can come, Greg."

"I meet him, an' you know what I'm goin' do — jus' because he's so damn' bull-headed?"

"What're you goin' do?"

"Beat the crap outa him!"

FOURTEEN

But the Cullens did not butcher in the badlands this time. They apparently aimed to butcher somewhere closer to the mountain towns. The reason was simple: terrible summer heat set in. Even though salted down, meat would soon spoil in the torrid climate. They had a stolen herd of around two hundred Half Circle V cattle waiting, mostly bony steers who were just beginning to put on a little meat, for the grass had grown since the long rain.

From his high vantage point on a tall butte a mile west of the holding-grounds Ric Williams squatted and watched through his field-glasses, his horse hidden behind him in the brush.

It was the best look-out he could find in this eroded, colour-slashed worthless badlands. The butte's flat top held a little soapweed and buckbrush, which was very little for a horse to graze on. Actually, the bronc wouldn't eat the grey soapweed that clung to the barren earth. Were he to eat this his tail would be up and he'd be physiced until his belly rumbled.

And Ric depended on a fast and tough horse in good physical shape. He figured the water in his canteen — if used sparingly — would keep him and the horse for two full days, maybe three.

The closest water lay straight east out of the badlands at Carson's Well, a natural always-flowing spring on what had been the boundary between his father's Bar Diamond Bar and Scott Mattson's Half Circle V.

From where he hunkered he could see Flat Top Butte some ten miles to the east, an upthrust heaved by nature millions of years ago into the blue Montana sky. He could not see Black Butte. Distance hid the black-topped dome.

He tried out the little hand-mirror he always carried in his saddle-bag the morning of the second day. The sun was rising and he was sure the reflection could be seen on tall Flat Top.

He pointed the mirror toward the sun. He moved it in short, jerky motions. He then waited. He got no returning flash. He tried again, again, he drew a blank. It then occurred to him that the sun was behind whoever was on Flat Top — if, indeed, anybody were there. Thus the person there could not flash a signal toward the west but only to the east and partways north and south.

He tried again when the sun was at noon. He again got no reply. Another try, then another — still, no answer. Doubt struck him. Had young Hoffard delivered his message to Sheriff Ike Hatchford?

His spirits suddenly lifted. For far to the east, from the rocky summit of Flat Top, came a series of flashes, plainly the reflections of a mirror.

Four flashes would indicate that the cattle were being moved. On the last flash he would twist his mirror as much as possible to show the direction the stolen steers were headed.

If he signalled by fire, three interruptions would mean the cattle were being butchered on the spot,

298

four that they were being moved south.

Elation touched him. His message had got through to the lawman. He felt sure Sheriff Ratchford would notify Greg Mattson.

Those steers — those stolen steers — below bore Mattson's brand, so surely Mattson would be concerned? Ric Williams a few times had mentally kicked himself in the rump for trailing down these rustlers. These cows were not his. And he faced the simple truth: this might end in a gun-battle.

And a bullet didn't give a hoot who it killed.

Still, this rustling had to be halted, for once and for all. Without peace and lawfulness, there could be no progress.

And progress, to Ric Williams, meant nice farm homes, schools, churches, and happy families.

He was sure Greg Mattson and Sheriff Ratchford would have others helping them. He'd asked the sheriff to intercept the wagons when they came out of the badlands ten or so miles south, just north of Milk River.

He soon saw how the cow-thieves operated. Moonlight was bright and they gathered from the cattle wandering close to the east edge of the worthless country. These were chased into the labyrinthine area some five miles and at this point they were held in a rather large natural clearing the floor of which was alkali soil and soapweeds.

Here the cattle had been butchered. Ric's field-glasses showed wooden tripods dismantled and lying on the side of a hill. He saw newly-disturbed earth at the base of the north hill.

He guessed hides and guts and heads and hoofs were buried there. Thus no stink could waft eastward for miles and hit the nostrils of cowpunchers riding the edge of the rough country.

The thieves had even hauled in a wooden water tank. This they filled with water from the water wagons. Bales of hay were pulled out of the tarp-covered wagons and distributed around to the hungry cattle.

Ric was not surprised when he saw no cattle being butchered. He'd half-expected the gang to drive the stock out and butcher somewhere closer to the mountains because of the terrible heat.

He felt sure these rustlers had operated some time back in this god-forsaken area of salt grass and alkali. No cowpuncher would ride this deep into the badlands. Even the most stupid would know no cow would wander this far into this hell. He counted the cow-thieves. First, the three Cullens, killers all. Then seven skinners on the wagons; two on the water-wagons. That made twelve. Then three cowpunchers had been here when the wagons had rolled in.

These three had been slyly hazing Half Circle V cattle into the edges of the badlands. Now that the wagons had arrived they began shoving these cattle toward the Cullen camping-area.

Ric had lots of time to think. And, most of the time, his thoughts went toward women, centering on dark-haired Martha Stewart, then on light-haired Jennie Queen — but mostly they settled on thin-waisted Melissa Wentworth.

Yes, and he thought of Kid Hannigan, too.

What had called Kid Hannigan into the Little Rocky Mountains? What earthly reason had the Kid to be in that gold-mad town? Had he quit Greg Mattson? And had he ridden south?

Where was Hannigan now?

At that moment Kid Hannigan was in Sheriff Ike Ratchford's office in Black Butte. Greg Mattson was also there, slouched in a chair.

300

"Never learned a damn' thing in them mountains," Hannigan was saying. "There's a lot of meat comin' in there from somewhere but damn' if I could fin' out where it's comin' from." He looked at Greg Mattson. "Might jus' as well come out with it, Matt-son. The Association sent me here to stop this rustlin' — but I ain't got off home-plate in my investigation."

"Kinda figured thet," Greg Mattson said.

"Why didn't you tell us?" the sheriff asked.

"My orders was to work without nobody knowin' my real chore. I've worked for the Association for four years now on a number of jobs but this is the first one that's stumped me."

"It didn't stump Ric Williams," Mattson pointed out.

Hannigan looked at the lawman. "What'd he mean by that, Sheriff?"

Sheriff Ratchford told him. Hannigan's brows rose at the mention of Ric spotting him in the mountain gold-camp.

"Hell, I never seen him," the detective said.

"He saw you," the sheriff said.

"You ridin' out with us?" Greg Mattson asked.

Hannigan spread his hands significantly. "I'm a stock detective. My orders are to see that every job I'm on is brought to a successful conclusion."

Sheriff Ratchford shifted in his swivel chair. "Here's our deal, detective. Greg an' me has looked it over from all angles an' come to this conclusion."

Kid Hannigan nodded.

"Ric's flashed out there are eleven cow-thieves. They'll head out south on the road they entered the badlands on — north of the Milk at Squaw Crossin', a few miles out of Willow Point." The sheriff explained. "Willow Point is the west limit of the sheriff down in Malta. My county dips down to the Milk there so Squaw Crossin' is under my jurisdiction — and my sworn duty says I'm to enforce the Law impartially an' completely throughout my entire county."

"Well said," Hannigan assured. "What'd we do, then?"

Greg Mattson spoke. "We get our hands down on the Milk in the timber where their trail comes out. An' we stop them then an' there, Hannigan."

"How many hands we got, boss?"

Greg lit his cigarette. "There's the sheriff, an' me, an' you — an' only three others; old hands thet came up with my father and mother an' the longhorns years ago from Texas. I asked my other hands if they'd fight for the ranch agin rustlers if the rustlers could be found."

"What'd they say?"

"Under no circumstances."

Kid Hannigan scowled. "The new-fangled breed of cowpokes," he told the world. "What'd you then do, boss?"

"I fired the whole goddamned bunch. I'm hirin' new hands after this is settled and —" He told of the oncoming roundup to clean his range of longhorns.

Hannigan rubbed his whiskers. "We'll be outnumbered by a few guns. How we gonna fight them?"

Greg Mattson spoke to Sheriff Ratchford. "You tell him, sheriff. You thought of the idea."

Sheriff Ike Ratchford carefully and fully explained.

FIFTEEN

The day was terribly hot with a cloudless sky until five in the afternoon when dark clouds came up out of the northwest.

Ric had doled out his last spoonful of water to his saddle-horse at noon that day. He and his horse had to go out for water or perish.

He could not go east to water at Carson's Well. To reach the Well he'd have to pass through enemy lines. And if seen, the odds were too great for one man alone. . . .

The rustlers had done no butchering. Plainly they intended to drive the herd out and butcher somewhere else. Both water-tanks were empty. He'd seen the last of the water pulled out of each that afternoon.

The rustlers were without hay, too. Cattle bawled weakly against thirst and hunger. Common sense told Ric the cattle would have to soon be moved to water.

Darkness finally came. The sun tipped down into the west. Overhead the clouds were darker.

Ric figured the clouds were filled with rain. When darkness was complete he built a small fire back on the butte where it could not be seen from below.

He took off his shirt. He made three deliberate passes with the shirt in front of the fire, the agreed signal saying the herd was being moved. He got no answering flashes from Flat Top.

He tried two more times. Still, no answering signals. There was nothing he could do but leave.

The dry taste of defeat was sour in his mouth. Nobody had been on Flat Top. He put his mind to work and in this thinking received new hope.

Sheriff Ike Ratchford was an old and experienced hand at this law-enforcement business. He'd not be in Black Butte town or on Black Butte. He'd be with his posse south along Milk River waiting either for a herd of stolen cattle or wagons of butchered but stolen beef to come out of the rough country, heading south toward the Little Rocky Mountains.

But still, it seemed logical he should have somebody stationed on Flat Top Butte to give a return signal, didn't it? Or did it?

Ric's plan was to water himself and his horse in Milk River. Then if the sheriff and Greg Mattson were not in the cottonwoods there he'd bird-dog the rustled cattle to their butchering spot, and thus know where they'd been slaughtered, at least.

Rain hit him on the back a few miles from his hiding-place. It came in with a strong wind.

The cloudburst whipped in with driving rains. Within a few minutes water careened off the side-hills, dirty and fast-flowing. The water question was rapidly solved.

The cloudburst stopped as suddenly as it had begun. The badlands were soaked. The wagon-road was slippery slime. The moon wheeled upright, round and big and yellow. Moonlight glistened off pools of water.

There now was no wind. The world was clean and

golden, the rough hills standing out in clear relief. He rode out of the badlands onto the level land leading south to Milk River.

Small coulees carried run-off water into the river. Ric rode through the darkness of the cottonwood trees. He'd cross the river and ride across the south prairie to hide in the southern hills until the herd and the wagons and the rustlers emerged.

He came to the river. Here was a rocky crossing with a hard bottom and about hub-deep on a farm wagon. His horse demanded more water.

He looked about, a feeling of tension running across his belly. Moonlight glistened on the rushing water, now muddy from the rain. Finally, the horse had drunk his fill. He raised his head.

Then it was that a harsh voice behind him said, "Up with them han's, fella! Move quick, damn' it!"

Ric raised his hands, immediately recognizing the stern voice.

"Ike Ratchford," he said.

There was a moment's pause. Then the voice said, "By golly, if it ain't Ric Williams!"

Ric lowered his hands. "Figured you might be here, sheriff. Who you got with you?"

"Boys are back in the bresh, waitin'. This way, Ric boy. Good to see you again, son."

"Glad to be here," Ric said, grinning crookedly.

That was the understatement of his short lifetime. Behind him came a herd of rustled cattle — now about three hundred head, he guessed — and behind that came the wagons. And all represented one thing — red, roaring, flaming guns.

For more than stolen cattle were at stake. The very lives of the three Cullen brothers — Clyde, Ed and Lon — were in danger. If captured alive, there was only one thing ahead for each and every one of these thieves — and that was the hangman's noose. . . .

If captured these men would never see the inside of a court-room. They would be hanged immediately and on this spot.

Each of the Cullens — and the men with them — knew their fate if captured, and Ric Williams was damned sure they'd fight until death.

He followed Sheriff Ike Ratchford into the brush, the sheriff explaining he'd left a man on Flat Top Butte, but the bastard must have gone to sleep. They came to a clearing. Here were saddled-horses. Ric counted eight. He remembered there were fifteen rustlers.

Odds always favoured the bunch with the most guns. Thus the odds favoured the fighting Cullen brothers and their twelve gunhands.

The posse hunkered back in the darkness. One voice said, "Good to see you again, Ric."

"Same to you, Kid Hannigan."

"They say you saw me in the mountains. I'm an Association detective, an' I travelled under cover. You found the rustlers, though, an' not me — so how about me recommendin' you to the Association as a detective?"

Ric grinned. "We'll discuss that later, Hannigan."

Lee Porter, Stan Musket and Gus Welton also greeted Ric — they were long-time Half Circle V hands who'd trailed up from the Lone Star state with Scott Mattson and Bill Williams. To them the only home they'd ever had was the roof provided by the Mattson family.

All were well into their sixties, Ric knew — possibly Lee was in his early seventies. His heart fell. He had a weak fighting force on his side. He then realized one man had not greeted him.

This man stood well back in the shadows. Ric saw

306

he was big and tall and he guessed he was Gregory Mattson but he wasn't sure until he heard Greg say, "Well, here we are, Williams."

His voice still held its old cynicism. Once again it grated on Ric Williams, raising his blood a degree or two. Wasn't the man even going to thank him for risking his neck in finding these rustlers?

"How are you, Greg?"

"Waitin'," Greg Mattson said.

The tension was so thick you could cut it with a dull Bowie knife. Ric was glad when the sheriff said, "All right, Ric, tell us what you know."

Ric talked rapidly, explained, then said, "What's your plan of action, Sheriff?"

Sheriff Ratchford told him. Ric listened carefully, all the time smelling kerosene — and why kerosene out in this wilderness?

He soon discovered the answer.

SIXTEEN

Gun-hung and all killer, Clyde Cullen rode point, Winchester .44-40 crossed in front of his Amarille saddle.

His roan's flanks were full. He'd watered from run-off water back in the hills. He was fresh and wanted the trail, pulling on the reins.

Behind Clyde Cullen came three hundred and twenty-four head of stolen Half Circle V longhorns, spooky and edgy, swinging their razor-tipped racks, ready to fight man or beast.

Cloven hoofs ground Montana mud. Where but a few moments before had been liquid dust was now sloppy mud. Steers slipped, fell. Others walked over them, horns down, looking for trouble.

Behind the herd rode five riders, including the two other Cullen outlaws — morose Lon and grim-faced Ed. These riders hazed the cattle forward. They were soaked to the bone and wet and angry but each had been sure to cover his pouched pistol with a bandanna or such when the cloudburst had hit.

Behind the hazers came the nine wagons, the empty water-wagons taking up the rear, the seven farm wagons directly behind the hazers. Broad rimmed wheels slipped in mud. Shod work-horses had rough walking on the white alkali spots. These were very slippery. Water had penetrated the white alkali but a few inches making it sloppy as soup.

The cattle had drunk their fill from mudholes along the way. They now wanted to get on grass; still, few did any bawling. They moved south — a sea of glistening horns, an ocean of broad wet backs — headed for Milk River and the grass of the open prairie.

They moved in almost silence. The whole thing had a ghostly air about it. The tall, bony man riding point, Winchester at the ready, a killer and highway robber wanted in many states throughout the West.

And behind him the stolen cattle, moving silently forward, compact and powerful — ready to explode into violent, murderous action for the slightest reason.

And overhead the cloudless night sky of old Montana. The blue, endless sky that now held a full moon which threw brilliant light over the badlands, the wagons, the hazers, the herd and the stern killer who rode gun-guard in the front, Clyde Allen Cullen.

Clyde Cullen rode a hundred feet ahead of the horns behind him. When he came out of the badlands he was clearly seen under the moonlight. He drew rein for a long moment, Winchester half raised, and he rose slightly on stirrups, eyes moving here, then there, searching and probing — a wolf in saddle, a lobo sniffing the air, searching out trouble before trouble searched him out.

The slight wind was from the southwest. It brought him a strange scent, an odour which definitely should not be present in this wilderness air. Was it the faint smell of kerosene?

Eyes missing nothing, hard fingers curled around the rifle's stock just behind the trigger, he considered this point — and sniffed again, deeper this time. He held the air in his lungs, examining it; finally, he exhaled, deciding his nose had played false.

He looked at the dark rim of timber almost a quarter mile away that rimmed Milk River. He swept his eyes along it. He saw nothing alien and the moonlight was bright and clear.

He settled back in saddle. His fingers lost some of their firmness on the rifle's stock. All was well. This herd would soon be across the river and threading its way south through the hills toward the butchering-spot. All was okay.

He twisted on oxbow stirrups. He looked behind him. The cattle were leaving the ravine. They rolled south in dark silence. He glimpsed his brother Ed, riding right flank. Lon would haze left flank. And behind would lumber the nine wagons.

He raised his right arm. The signal meant all was well and to push cows ahead. Then he straightened in saddle and gigged his roan ahead — into the raw flames of a roaring hell!

For suddenly a hundred feet ahead flame lanced upward into the moonlight. He pulled in savagely, horse rearing, his rifle at the ready, wondering first if an errant lightning bolt had not hit the prairie ahead, driving even the wet earth into snarling redness.

He then quickly noticed that three fires had been started and then each had whipped both directions. He remembered the acrid smell of kerosene. His quick mind rapidly drew conclusions.

Somebody had spread something dry — like old hay — in a half-circle ahead, had soaked this with kerosene — and had just now lit it afire. One match had started the fire in the middle, directly ahead. Two other matches had ignited this kerosene-barrier on each corner where the hills came down and formed a natural funnel.

The terrible truth hit him, driving red across his brain. He and his brothers had ridden into a gun-trap!

For one blinding red second, the world stood still. Here was this outlaw, risen on stirrups, frozen in saddle, rifle half raised, stern eyes trying to pierce this rising rim of fire — and seeing nothing through the flames.

And the longhorns behind. . . . They too, were a solid, ugly mass, eyes wide and reflecting fire, horns down and ready to charge to kill — but yet knowing they, like all bovines, would never, never rush through fire.

And behind them the hazers, also high on stirrups, trying to stare over the backs of the cattle.

And behind the hazers the nine strung-out wagons in the narrow badland defile, halted now with rearing, plunging horses smashing against collars, horses that wanted to run ahead into what they figured was freedom — hazers and drivers and wagons and teams penned behind thousands of pounds of longhorn power that might, at any moment, bolt backwards.

Lon Cullen spurred ahead, smashing his big sorrel stud through the cattle, fighting to reach his brother's side up there ahead, just inside this ring of roaring fire.

Back of him rode Ed Cullen, spurs working, catch-rope smashing cattle left and right, short-gun tied to his hip, rifle still in boot but loaded.

Then, the cattle wheeled, and stampeded.

There was a grand mixup of mad cattle and mad men on horseback. Two rustlers went down, hoofs grinding over them and their fallen horses. Somehow Ed and Lon Cullen made it through, a steer's ripping the entrails from Lon's horse, sending the horse lunging forward, guts trailing, to collapse and die, kicking angrily and without gain against death.

"Kill the sonsofbitches!" roared Clyde Cullen.

Lon Cullen screamed, "I'm on foot, brother."

Clyde Cullen reined his roan close. "Swing on behin' me!"

Their only hope was to drive horses through the flames. All knew that a horse is scared to death of fire but if driven hard by spur and whip a horse will, if forced, dash through fire.

For there was no retreat. The canyon behind was a grinding, deadly melée of struggling, striving cattle, of cowboys dehorsed and being ground down, of wagons with teams gutted by horns.

Never before had Ric Williams seen such a scene. Gus Welton had torched the centre of the dry hay that had come from an old haystack a rancher had built of hay cut on the river's north side.

Stan Musket had lit fire to the west end, Lee Porter firing the east. The three old-timers had all lit their sulphurs at the correct moment. They'd then run into cover back along the river in the brush.

For Ric had said stoutly that none of the old-timers would face the rifles and short-guns of the Cullen gang. This left Sheriff Ratchford, Kid Hannigan, Greg Mattson and Ric against the three Cullens.

Kid Hannigan was put out of business within a few seconds. A Cullen bullet dropped the detective's horse. The horse fell imprisoning Hannigan's leg under him.

Hannigan's rifle slid from his grasp. It landed out of reach. He reached for his pistol. It, too, had fallen. It also could not be reached by the pinned-down, angry man.

"Take the bastard the nearest to you!" Sheriff Ratchford spurred toward Clyde Cullen, six-shooter pounding lead into the moonlight.

From the corner of his eye, Ric saw Clyde fall from saddle, with Sheriff Ratchford plunging on, riding hard with six-shooter upraised.

Greg Mattson screamed, "The one over west for me." He meant Ed Cullen, and his six-gun also flamed.

The two — Mattson and Cullen — rode toward each other. Then, Ed Cullen slid from saddle, horse loping on, and Mattson pulled in, bronc rearing.

That left Lon Cullen for Ric. Cullen left saddle, landed on one knee, rifle raised — and he shot once and missed.

Ric roared past the kneeling outlaw. And, as he went by Cullen, he leaned low in stirrup, using his .45 as a club — and he smashed steel across the outlaw's skull as Cullen fought feverishly to jack a fresh cartridge into his rifle's barrel.

Lon Cullen went down on his face in the mud, knocked cold. Ric wheeled his horse and stared about, six-shooter ready — but this part of the fighting was over.

The three old-timers ran from the timber. Back in the canyon cattle bawled as they smashed over horses and wagons. Within a few minutes, the only living member of the Cullen gang, one Lon Cullen, joined his brothers in death.

When Kid Hannigan had been freed from under his dead horse he'd grinned and said, "Hell of a detective I make. Even my hoss has got it in for me, him pinnin' me down like thet."

A stray bullet had caught Greg Mattson high on the left arm. He held a bloody bandanna over the wound. "No, don't need your help, Williams," he said shortly. "I'll get along without your sidin' me."

Ric bit off a hot reply.

"Ain't got no bones broken," Mattson said. "Jus' a

bullet through the meat, no more — thank God fer thet.''

The sheriff spoke to Gus Welton. "You an' Greg head down river to Malta an' the doctor.''

"Jus' as you say, sher'ff.''

Mattson's horse was fidgety. Mattson got his left boot in stirrup, grabbed for the horn with his good hand, missed. Ric stepped forward, plainly aiming to help.

"I don't need your help, Williams. God damn it, can't you understan' the King's English!''

Ric stepped back. He glanced at the sheriff. Ratchford didn't meet Ric's gaze.

Ric then knew he and Greg Mattson would be enemies until one of them died. It wasn't a good thought, but it was reality. And it had no reason for being, but it was there — apparently always would be there.

Mattson got into leather. He and Gus Welton rode south and out of sight.

Sheriff Ratchford said, "We'll have to bury this man. Damned if I'd know where a shovel is. Guess we'll have to get one outa Malta.''

"I'll ride in with Greg an' Gus an' bring one out,'' old-timer Stan Musket said.

Ric said, "I reckon we'd best go up the canyon an' see if anybody's livin' after them dogies got done with those wagons an' teams an' drivers.''

He still felt heavy at heart because of Greg Mattson's rebuffs.

The four of them walked into the canyon's black mouth with rifles at the ready, a needless precaution, for everywhere was bleak and bloody destruction.

Cattle were down, some dead, some living. Two gutted broncs lay still harnessed to destroyed wagons. Rifles and six-guns soon put the injured animals out

314

of business.

Twelve men had been behind the herd. Five lay dead, hoof-hammered into the mud. The other seven apparently had escaped by somehow climbing the canyon's steep and slippery walls.

"They'll never return to rustle another cow," Kid Hannigan said. "Bet wherever they are they're still runnin'."

"No use tryin' to trail 'em," the sheriff said. "Man might ride into an ambush an' be kilt We've been damn' lucky so far in this. Lots more luck than I figured on."

They tied the dead men together at the ankles and pulled them out through the mud to where lay the three dead Cullens, using a catchrope Lee Porter came back with after taking it from the saddle of dead Lon Cullen.

"I'm leavin' in the mornin'," Kid Hannigan told them. "If I went back to Black Butte, thet farmer Jim Young'd sure as heck pick trouble with me. He bumped me thet day of the stampede on purpose. He seems to hate the very sight of me an' don't ask me why. Some men jus' seem born to hate the other man, I reckon."

"There's truth in thet," Sheriff Ratchford said.

REAL WEST

The true life adventures of America's greatest frontiersmen.

THE LIFE OF KIT CARSON by John S.C. Abbott. Christopher "Kit" Carson could shoot a man at twenty paces, trap and hunt better than the most skilled Indian, and follow any trail — even in the dead of winter. His courage and strength as an Indian fighter earned him the rank of brigadier general of the U.S. Army. This is the true story of his remarkable life.

__2968-5 $2.95

THE LIFE OF BUFFALO BILL by William Cody. Strong, proud and courageous, Buffalo Bill Cody helped shape the history of the United States. Told in his own words, the real story of his life and adventures on the untamed frontier is as wild and unforgettable as any tall tale ever written about him.

__2981-2 $2.95

ROMER ZANE GREY

Classic Tales of action and adventure set in the Old West! Characters created by Zane Grey live again in exciting books written by his son, Romer.

THE OTHER SIDE OF THE CANYON. Laramie Nelson was a seasoned Indian fighter, cowhand, and shootist, and above all a loner. Although he was one of the most feared gunmen in the Old West, his word of honor was as good as his sharpshooting.

__2886-7 $2.95

THE LAWLESS LAND. Back on the trail, Laramie Nelson confronted an outlaw chief, performed a top-secret mission for President Grant, and tangled with a gang of blockaders aiming to start a range war.

__2945-6 $2.95

KING OF THE RANGE. The Texas Rangers needed somebody who could ride all night through a blizzard, who could track like an Indian, and who could administer justice from the barrel of a Colt .44 — they needed Buck Duane.

__2530-2 $3.50

SPEND YOUR LEISURE MOMENTS WITH US.

Hundreds of exciting titles to choose from—something for everyone's taste in fine books: breathtaking historical romance, chilling horror, spine-tingling suspense, taut medical thrillers, involving mysteries, action-packed men's adventure and wild Westerns.

SEND FOR A FREE CATALOGUE TODAY!

Leisure Books
Attn: Customer Service Department
276 5th Avenue. New York. NY 10001